AVERY THORN
Into The Seas Embrace

THE NAMELESS SYREN SERIES

THE NAMELESS SYREN SERIES BOOK 1

This is a work of fiction. Names, characters, businesses, places, events, and incidents are either the products of the author's imagination or used in a fictitious manner. Any resemblance to actual persons, living or dead, or actual events is purely coincidental— or used with permission.

Into The Seas Embrace volume 1© 2018 by Jennifer Natoli.

All rights reserved.

ISBN: 978-0-578-43724-8

Edited By Jennifer Natoli, Amber Jamrock, And Emilee Robins

Cover Design by Jay Aheer

INTO THE SEAS EMBRACE

This book is dedicated to my long time best friend Amber. For without her this book would have never been created.

I would also like to thank my other best friend Emilee. If she and Amber hadn't worked together my dream of seeing this book published on time would have never happened.

THE NAMELESS SYREN SERIES BOOK 1

CHAPTER ONE 6
CHAPTER TWO 18
CHAPTER THREE 32
CHAPTER FOUR 35
CHAPTER FIVE 47
CHAPTER SIX 68
CHAPTER SEVEN 88
CHAPTER EIGHT..93
CHAPTER NINE 109
CHAPTER TEN 118
CHAPTER ELEVEN 125
CHAPTER TWELVE 149
CHAPTER THIRTEEN 171
CHAPTER GOURTEEN...178
CHAPTER FIFTEEN..195
CHAPTER SIXTEEN 216
CHAPTER SEVENTEEN 228
CHAPTER EIGHTEEN...258
CHAPTER NINETEEN 267
CHAPTER TWENTY..283
CHAPTER TWENTY-ONE...295
CHAPTER TWENTY-TWO...305
CHAPTER TWENTY-THREE...315
CHAPTER TWENTY-FOUR...318
CHAPTER TWENTY-GIVE 327
CHAPTER TWENTY-SIX...332

INTO THE SEAS EMBRACE

CHAPTER TWENTY-SEVEN 342
CHAPTER TWENTY-EIGHT 350
EPILOGUE..364
ACKNOWLEDGMENTS 367
ABOUT THE AUTHOR 368

Chapter One

Atalanta

"I know I've said it before, but I believe this is it. This is the one!" my father exclaimed as he, my sister, and I stood outside of our new home.

It was hard to believe that sentiment when he had said the same about our last house not five months before. And then, lo and behold, two days ago, Dad came home and told us to start packing.

In a record four hours, the three of us had packed up the few boxes we had even bothered to unpack, loaded up the rusty Ford pickup, and left our home/not home of Forks, Washington to move less than an hour south, to the small town of Argos. After spending a day hiding out in the nearby inn, Dad had secured us a new house and drove us out of the tiny town, up into the mountains.

I scrunched up my nose. "Dad, it looks like a murder shack."

The small house had definitely seen better days. The wood was wearing away from the constant beat of the ocean's salty breeze. What was probably once a nice wood cabin looked like something dragged from the ocean, dark and damp with areas covered in moss. The window panes were no better, as they were cracked, murky, murky and cracked, or just plain missing.

"It's far bigger than a shack, Pumpkin. And what murder shack ever had such a nice view?" He gestured over to the left of the shack, out to the cliff drop-off.

I had to begrudgingly agree that the ocean view was to-die-for as we admired a glimpse of the setting sun, with purple, gray, and blue layers of clouds dancing with the sun's yellow and orange flames. It was a rare sight at the moment, as it was late January in northern Washington state, which was known for its constant rainy days.

I crossed my arms and tried not to smile. "Fine! It looks like a murder cottage. But, have you ever read *A Series of Unfortunate Events*? That's also on a cliff and nothing ever goes right with having a house this close to a cliff."

"That house was actually hanging off the cliff, Atalanta. This one is not. So don't exaggerate," he said matter-of-factly.

I gave him a bit of cool father credit there. I didn't know he ever read the series.

"Well, I think the view is nice," my sister interposed.

He looked over and beamed at my sister. "Thank you, Cal."

"But she is right," Cal sighed and tilted her head to study the house. "it is a murder shack. I'm expecting Michael Myers to come walking through the door any moment."

"Aw, come on! Stop your whining! It's much nicer on the inside, I promise. You big babies."

Apprehensively, my sister and I each heaved a box out of the back of the truck and carried them through the heavy wooden door that our father held open for us.

He wasn't totally wrong. The inside didn't look like the set of a classic horror film but it did look like it hadn't seen human life in a while. On the scary movie checklist there were cobwebs, leaves on the ground, rat droppings scattered in every corner, the air so thick with dust an asthmatic person would die instantaneously, and last but not least a bat who had been sleeping up in the rafters till our entrance had spooked him into exiting.

"Seriously, Dad?"

"Yep," he said, popping heavily on the P.

I rolled my eyes and stepped further into what seemed to be the living room.

The walls were probably in the best condition, with only slight water damage and made of modern drywall instead of wood. They were painted an ugly sea-foam green, though. Ugh.

The laminate wood floor was coming up in spots and had definitely seen some rodents if the chew marks were any indication. There wasn't any furniture, but there was a really nice brick fire place, and when I cautiously stepped further into the room I could see into the kitchen, which was rather big, and did have relatively new equipment.

My ever-optimistic sister put down her box and looked around. "With lots of paint-"

"A bulldozer," I chimed in.

"And a lot of hard work, I bet this place would look just as nice as the other ones."

With our constant moving, we really couldn't afford a lot of nice places, so our father would scoop up rundown properties that the bank had foreclosed on and we would fix them up. Since picking up forgotten places had the additional benefit of being inconspicuous, we really didn't mind too much.

My father pulled my sister and I close into a hug as he looked around our new home. "I know it hasn't been easy…but thank you for hanging in there."

I stared at my father. He looked much older than his actual age of 38. Dark midnight skin, haggard by the stress of raising me and my sister so young, and being the bread winner of the family for years. His close-cropped hair was far more salt than pepper but at least his eyes, while heavily bagged, sparkled with humor.

I smiled. "I'll get the broom."

If there was one thing my sister and I had learned early, it was to clean before unpacking—otherwise there would be twice as much to clean. So, after pulling the boxes out of the truck, we stuffed them on the porch and got to work while Dad ran to find the nearest grocery store to wrangle up dinner.

Sweeping out all the cobwebs, dust, and rat shit we could find, we moved on to the washing. If given the option, I would have hosed the whole inside down with soap and water, but the next best thing was the good old mop, bucket, and Fabuloso.

"So, which room do you want?" Cal asked as we finally finished up the front of the cabin.

I only stared at her, unsure of how to answer. As the older sibling, she normally just claimed whichever room she wanted and let me take what was left.

"Oh, don't give me that look. Yes, I'm going to actually let you pick this time," she said, her hands at her waist.

Squinting at her suspiciously, I slowly opened the door to bedroom number one. This one was the master and looked rather nice, with an actual carpet and very few cobwebs, but this one was for Dad so I shut the door until it was time for Cal and I to clean it later. Behind the second door was a much smaller room, also carpeted, but with large bay windows that looked out into the forest back down the hill the cottage was propped on. Finally, behind the third door was an identical room to the second, except it partially faced the ocean and partially the forest.

I gave a small smile. "I'll take this one."

"I thought you might."

I looked back over my shoulder at my sister. Like me, her skin was a warm espresso brown, but unlike me, she was very feminine looking with gorgeous forest green eyes and long, soft curls that I had never been able to achieve. My hair was uncooperative and would sooner form into a giant rat's nest than behave.

So I opted to keep it as short as Cal would let me rather than deal with it.

I also tried not to be envious of her curves that the guys loved to stare at everywhere we went. I looked like a little boy next to her with my stick figure and B cups. I say *tried* not to be envious, because I knew the green monster reared its ugly head when I saw how easily she could pull off booty shorts and a tank when I only looked good in frumpy hoodies.

"Thank you," I said to her and shut the door to my new room. "Have you seen the bathroom yet?"

"No, I haven't. I think it's this one," She pointed to a door we had yet to open down the hallway, which ended in a window.

Shuffling towards it, the two of us cautiously opened the door and saw something that made both of us scream, slam the wooden door shut, and run for our lives.

Outside, we both bounced back and forth on the balls of our feet, rubbing our arms as we had practically jumped out of our skins.

"THAT WAS THE BIGGEST SPIDER I HAVE EVER SEEN!" Cal screamed.

"WE HAVE TO BURN THIS HOUSE DOWN! We have to call Dad! Maybe he can get the deposit back!" I shouted.

She grabbed my shoulders and forced me to look into her eyes. "No, we can do this. We will go back in there and face this ourselves."

"You're insane, did you see its legs? They were fat and hairy! It's gonna kill us!"

She took a deep breath in. "It may very well kill us, but I won't let it take our bathroom privileges!"

With that, she stormed back into the house, grabbing the broom as she went.

"Calilope, you're a braver girl than I," I muttered and inched inside after her.

Later that night after Dad had returned, Cal and I told him our brave tale of defeating the spider, as we settled down on the porch huddled next to a space heater, eating the champion's dinner of Kraft mac and cheese. None of us were fantastic cooks but we managed to get by. There was still a lot of work to do, but we had moved all of the boxes into their correct rooms for us to more than likely only half unpack again. The real bummer was the lack of furniture. A girl could only love blow up mattresses and sleeping bags for so long.

"While I was in town, I saw that they had a library," Dad said around a bite of cheesy goodness.

I raised an eyebrow at him. "And?"

"...And I was hoping you would finally consider donating a few of your books," he said carefully.

"No."

He sighed. "Pumpkin, half of your boxes are books and the collection is only getting bigger."

"How could you ask me to part with my babies?"

"I almost broke my back carrying in that last one."

"You did not! Dad, I need my books."

I couldn't get rid of my books. They were my life blood. The stories inside of them were beautiful escapes from the reality that I lived. I had to do something. So I did the only thing I could think of.

I gave him the puppy dog eyes.

Thats right. Full pout and everything.

He looked like he was about to crack. I could see it in his face, but in the end he groaned and said, "I know. And I wouldn't ask you otherwise. Please honey, you know that we can't…"

I bit my lip to hold back the tears. I understood. The fewer belongings we had, the quicker it would be to pack up and leave. If we wanted, we would live out of our backpacks, but years ago we had learned how much living like that destroyed us.

He ran his hands through his hair and let out a long breath. "How about this? You donate your books, and I'll get you a Kindle. That way, you can have all the books you want."

It wouldn't be the same as holding a real book in my hand, smelling that redolence, feeling the sensation of the paper against my fingers, but he was right.

I felt Cal take my hand beside me. Looking up at her, I saw understanding in her eyes but I also saw encouragement. She wanted this too.

I nodded. "Okay, I'll head over there tomorrow."

He leaned over and kissed my forehead, murmuring his apologies. I wanted to be angry but I couldn't blame him. We ate the rest of our dinner in silence.

"Before I forget, these are your new IDs"

Dad held out the brand new Washington State ID cards to me and Cal. I stared at the reflective surface and gave a little sigh of relief that at least our first names were staying the same this time. I hated when we had to change it, as it was a lot more trouble to memorize new names on a short notice. I was a Tiffany once. Not that anything was wrong with the name, but it just...didn't feel like mine.

My eyebrows rose as I looked at the birthdate. "This says that I'm nearly eighteen. Does that mean I'll be attending school here?"

My father nodded. "It does, you start in a couple of days. Hopefully, you'll finally be able to finish out your senior year."

"You're darn determined that I get that diploma. You know that I could just get a GED, right?"

"Yes, but I'm determined to have both my daughters get the full high school experience. That includes me chasing away boys—or girls, no judgement—you going to prom, and me seeing you walk across that stage in a cap and gown."

Considering I had actually just turned twenty, this was a weird sentiment. I had missed getting a diploma and going to prom nearly three times so far, with us having to randomly get up and leave in the middle of the night. Cal had gotten lucky during her senior year, as we had lived there for more than a year before we had to skip town.

"Well then, let's hope you get your wish, because I'm not going to stay the same age forever," I said with a chuckle.

Cal gasped. "Do you think we have enough time to find you a date and get you a dress to prom?"

"Its January..." I said, tilting my head at her, my tone skeptical.

"The perfect dress and date take time, little sister."

I rolled my eyes. "Because John Hobes was such a great date to your prom? He slept with every girl at that school and was a major creep."

"Yes, but he still paid for the limo, dinner, and the hotel he didn't sleep in. And since he was such a man slut, taming the beast into taking a single girl to prom made me the hot commodity. I never said I slept in that hotel room alone, just not with John."

"This is not a conversation a father should be hearing." With that, our Dad picked up his bowl and headed inside.

I looked back at my sister. "But those guys, they were just trying to get into your pants because of who you took to prom?"

"In their eyes, a girl with the power to bring a guy like John to his knees is a girl worth chasing after. Like I always try to tell you, a little confidence is all you need," She said, pride in her tone.

I bent my head down and fumbled with the sleeves of my jacket, tugging them lower. "Easy for you to say."

"Hey, we've all got our baggage, Atalanta. And you may not believe it, but your spark is coming back."

With that, my sister gave me a quick side hug and joined Dad inside. I didn't want to go in just yet. It was nice out. If I had to guess, it had snowed the night before, as the blankets of white looked rather fresh. I loved snow, especially fresh snow. It was so fluffy, and looked beautiful when light hit it just right.

I shivered and scooted closer to the space heater.

I still didn't know how I felt about the cold, though. For most of my life we had spent it down south in much warmer climates.

While I sat there, basking in the warmth of the space heater, the whipping wind that had been blowing for some time finally settled and the soft sound of the crashing waves finally drew my attention. From my point on the porch, I could just see where the sand turned to sea and beyond. The inky blackness of the water churned through the barely visible darkness.

It was a full moon tonight, but as it always was during this time of year, the cloud cover was heavy. Only letting small glimpses of light sparkle against the waves here and there.

I sprung up and squinted.

"What..." I hissed through my teeth staring off at a point in the water, hoping to see it again.

INTO THE SEAS EMBRACE

There! There it was again. Breaking through the inky black waves was something. A shadow. A light. I would have said it was some sort of fish but did fish glow like that?

It was too far.

Quickly, I sprinted off the porch and towards the cliffside, breaking through the undisturbed snow. Coming closer to the drop-off, I skidded to a halt and crouched low as if that would help me see it better.

I scanned the water near where I had seen the odd glowing shadow but there was nothing, only inky blackness calmly swaying with the currents. Until I saw the weird luminance out of the corner of my eye and flicked my site in that direction. I watched as a massive tail surfaced through the water, the webbed spine along its back lined with light. Before it went back under, I caught a glimpse of its backend. A tail fin positioned horizontal with the body, and like the spine, it was bioluminescent.

No sea creature I knew had a tail like that one.

I sat back, my mouth agape. "Holy Nessy. There are sea monsters in Argos."

Chapter Two

Atalanta

"I'm telling you Cal, I saw it!"

"You probably saw a whale, Atty."

I shook my head. "Too small to be a whale, and have you ever heard of a whale that glowed?"

She shrugged. "Mutation. With all the crap they dump in our oceans nowadays?"

"Maybe, but I'm gonna stick with sea monster till I'm proven wrong. It's more fun that way," I chirped and leaned back into the seat.

The town of Argos was a sea shanty of a town. It was small, everything consisting of faded paint and cracked wood, with only one, *maybe* two of everything: one bar, one diner, two *whole* clothing stores. Though, for some odd reason, there were four different tourist shops sporting mermaids out front. I didn't even know small towns like this had tourists.

"Do you actually know where we're going?" I asked looking over at Cal, who was squinting at the street sign.

"No idea," She said slowly. "but only one way to find out."

Cal slowed the truck to a stop in front of a shop that displayed the logo of a needle and thread on its window. Outside, two older women were sitting on a bench, bundled up together in what looked to be a handmade quilt, sipping something out of mugs.

Cal rolled down my window and leaned over the bench seat of the truck across me to stick her head out of it. "Excuse me! Do you happen to know the way to the library?"

The two women shot their heads up from their conversation and looked at us wide eyed for a moment before smiling.

"Why hello, new to town?" one of the women asked.

"Just moved here." Cal said with a friendly smile.

"Well, welcome! My name is Charlotte, and this is Mona," She said gesturing to herself and the woman next to her.

"Hi, I'm Cal and this is my sister Atty."

And so there I sat, uncomfortably, for several minutes as the woman chatted with Cal before finally telling us how to get to the library. Down the road, make a left at Doogle's and up the hill. It's the building on the right, you can't miss it.

We followed the directions and eventually came upon two buildings. They were right, we couldn't miss it. It was bigger than I expected, a solid two stories, and looked much newer than the rest of the town. A modern building made of concrete instead of the rest of the town's wood and brick, painted a deep blue. There were multiple murals running along the side of the building. The biggest one at the front was a quill scrolling itself across a piece of parchment, and on that parchment were the beginning lines to a poem.

It was many and many a year ago,
  In a kingdom by the sea,
That a maiden there lived whom you may know
  By the name of Annabel Lee;
And this maiden she lived with no other thought
  Than to love and be loved by me - Poe

I read them aloud as we walked up to the doors of the library, each carrying a box of books.

"That's a poem by Edgar Allen Poe, right?" Cal asked as she bumped her butt against the handicap button, automatically opening the doors for us to walk through.

"Yeah," I said following behind her. "It's about jealousy and lost love."

"Weird poem to put on the side of the library."

I nodded. "Maybe. But Poe is also a famous poet. So that could be why."

The inside wasn't as brightly lit as expected. It wasn't dark per se, but much more of a soft warm light than most libraries I had been to in the past. I could see that it was a very spacious library though, with an open second floor lined with bookshelves. The air was crisp with only hints of that musty book smell wafting towards us as the fan blades hanging from the high vaulted ceilings turned. I spied plenty of little nooks and comfy chairs that would be perfect for huddling into for a good read.

"Whoa," I breathed.

Cal chuckled next to me. "I think I see a little drool there, Sis."

"This library is nice for a town like this," I murmured.

"I'll take that as a compliment then."

Looking to our left, I saw there was a large wooden counter behind which was a man too attractive for his own good. He had dark curly hair which was partially pulled back into a ponytail, as some of it fell forward to frame a clean shaven sharp jaw. Flawless lips, straight nose, and dark brown eyes were framed by the thick black glasses he wore.

He wasn't staring at me but at the computer screen in front of him as he typed away. Though, seeing as he was the only person around besides me and Cal, I had to assume he was the one who had spoken.

Heaving the box of books up to a better position, I stepped closer to the counter. "Do you work here? Well, I mean, of course you work here. What I meant to say was...um...hi."

He glanced up from his computer for a total of three seconds, his gaze cold and assessing before going back to the glow of the screen.

I bit the bottom of my lip and shot a pleading look to Cal, begging for her to take it from here, but she just gave me that stern sister look. The one that said to suck it up and put on my big girl pants or else she would purposefully embarrass me to make me regret it.

Taking a deep breath, I rigidly inched closer to the counter only to be shoved from behind by Cal's boot on my ass, causing me to slam the box of books down a lot more forcefully than intended to catch myself.

I scrambled to apologize only to notice the guy hadn't even flinched. He was looking at me now though, one thin dark eyebrow raised.

Not knowing what to do, I decided to roll with it. "My sister and I have come to donate some books to your library."

I watched as a small cocky smile tugged at the corner of his lips before he said, "Our Young Adult romance section *is* pretty slim."

"Why would you assume that they would be YA Romance?" I asked, unable to help myself.

He stared at me for a moment before answering, like he was thinking deeply on his answer, which was somewhat annoying.

"Because you're a teenage girl. Don't all teenage girls read that garbage?"

I scoffed and put my hands on my hips. "First off, not all of it is garbage. Second, I'm slightly offended you would assume that's what's actually in that box."

I waved at the box, encouraging Mr. Judgmental to open it and see for himself. He looked from me to the box, then gracefully stood up from his chair to open it. He was rather tall. While I wasn't a skyscraper at my five foot nothing, he definitely had a good foot on me. I also noticed he was far too nicely dressed for a desk job at a small town library: black slacks with a crisp navy button-down with a perfectly tied black tie behind a form fitting vest. I also spied a jacket draped across the back of his chair that probably completed his suit.

He gingerly opened the box to reveal what I knew, without even looking, was a text book of World Mythology, A Collection of Sherlock Holmes, and an Anthology of American Literature before and after 1865. And that was only what was stacked on the top.

Mr. Judgmental picked up one of the books and studied it. "I stand corrected."

I couldn't help the triumphant smile that pushed to the surface. Of course, he had no idea that it just so happened that the box in front of him contained all the fancy literature and textbooks. The other two boxes we had brought with us contained plenty of the Young Adult books he had so readily turned his nose up towards. I enjoyed myself some good literature, but nothing beat curling up with a good fantasy or trashy romance.

"I'm Cal, this is Atalanta." Cal finally piped up, placing down her box next to me and holding out her hand for him to shake.

He took her hand. "Percy. I'm the librarian."

My eyebrows raised. He didn't look much older than me, perhaps in his early to mid twenties at most. Yet he was claiming he actually ran this library?

"Hey, Atty, I'm gonna go get the other box, okay?" Cal said, mischief twinkling in her eyes.

I nodded, continuing to observe the stranger before me as he rifled through the box of books.

"So are you *The* Librarian? Like Flynn Carson?" I asked, curious to see if he would get my reference.

"If you are asking if I am the person who runs around the world collecting magical artifacts for the library, then no. But I do in fact run this library."

I smiled, glad that he got the reference.

"But you look so young. Aren't librarians supposed to be old women?"

"Aren't teenage girls supposed to read cheesy romance novels?" He asked, holding up my copy of Bram Stoker's Dracula.

"Touché."

We were silent for a couple of minutes. I stood there awkwardly, fiddling with the sleeves of my jacket while he pulled the books out of the box one by one and inspected them. Where was Cal?

"What's your problem with Young Adult romance anyway? They aren't all bad, you know," I blurted when the silence became too uncomfortable for me to bear.

He glanced at me before going back to sorting through the books.

"They aren't realistic." He responded, clipped.

"Well," I said, putting my finger to my lip in thought. "Most fiction novels are fantasy or Sci-Fi, so that's not a very good argument."

"Then," he paused in his rummaging of books. "The guys are often too perfect, the girls are always whiny Mary Sues, and more often than not, the girl breaks it off with the guy about three quarters through because of some stupid misunderstanding only to fix it by the end."

I pursed my lips and tilted my head, thinking about his reasoning, only to sigh and nod when I realized they were pretty well-founded.

"You're right, a lot of them are like that, but not all. You just have to find the good ones."

At his skeptical look, I huffed and bent down to open the box that was at my feet. Rummaging through its contents I asked, "Are you a fantasy type or can you read contemporaries and not be bored to death?"

"What do you think?" It may have been my imagination but I could have sworn I heard him chuckle when he said that.

It made me want to hear him laugh for real.

"I think you could go either way, but contemporary is your go-to because you like the human experience more than the world-building of fantasy."

Finding the book I was looking for, I stood up straight to see him staring at me, his eyes wide.

"What?" I giggled nervously. "Was I right?"

He narrowed his eyes at me and I realized that I did indeed guess what his preferred type would be. But I had seen the way he looked at the literature books so it was an educated guess.

Seeing as how I wasn't going to be rewarded with a response, I moved on.

Hugging the book in my hands closer to my chest, I said, "Now this is one of my all-time favorite Young Adult romances. And before you say it, yes, you caught me. I am actually a teenage girl who reads books that are targeted to teenaged girls. But as you saw, I read other things too so cool down that judgmental look I already see forming on your face."

He at least had the decency to attempt to look bashful when he broke eye contact and scratched the back of his head. The move pulled his shirt taut against his stomach and I could see the outline of a very well toned, very drool-worthy body. Making sure my jaw wasn't hanging open, I continued.

I held out the book for him. "It's a humble romance. The girl, while cute, isn't perfect and neither is the guy…well, maybe a little, but you got to give it somewhere. The most important part is that it doesn't have any of that annoying drama that a lot of other books like it do. And it isn't like this huge lust at first sight thing either, they start out as friends."

Taking the book gingerly from my outstretched hands, he examined the front cover. "A western?"

I shook my head. "No, not really. Just read it and tell me what you think."

He looked back up at me. "Isn't telling a stranger what to read a little presumptuous?"

"Perhaps. However, as the town's only librarian, I would think it might be your job to help the girls in this town when they are asking for book recommendations. If you don't know anything about the books in your YA romance section, how will you be able to help them? Look at this as expanding your horizons. Helping the good people of Argos," I said with a wide smile, confident in my selling tactic.

The scrutiny of his gaze should have made me run for the hills. Hell, I almost did, but I had come too far to stop now. Besides, Cal had still not returned with that other damn box of books and it had to be at least a six mile walk back to the house through woods.

Finally, he sighed and carefully placed the book down next to his computer, separate from the others.

I beamed, taking that as confirmation that he would read the book.

"You're an interesting young woman."

I stiffened, realizing my mistake. Rule number one, don't draw too much attention to yourself. You are a simple girl. Nothing more, nothing less.

I broke eye contact with him and began to fiddle with the zipper on my jacket. I had never noticed before how worn my clothes had become. Only a year or two old, the Walmart clearance rack muddy-brown jacket was missing a button on the right cuff and the stitching was coming undone at the sleeves from my constant fidgeting with them. I knew there were several holes in different parts of the jacket as well.

In that moment, I wondered what I probably looked like to this man. With his fancy suit and neatly combed, long flowing hair, next to me with my rat's nest of a head, bargain bin jacket, dirty jeans and boots. I mean, I knew I wasn't bad looking. I could be downright attractive if I put my mind to it, but I doubted raggedy clothes helped.

Thats when it popped into my head. *Rule number five, get a job to help you assimilate and blend in.* The extra money didn't hurt either. I could use that to get some new clothes.

"Do you happen to know of any places I might be able to work part-time while I'm not at school?" I asked.

He thought for a moment before answering, "Unfortunately, our part-time position is filled, otherwise I would ask you to work here so that you could be the one to watch over the teen section. However, I believe there's a position open for aftercare counselors at the community center next door."

I smirked. "No getting out of reading for you, Mr. Librarian."

Kids. I could do kids. God, I hoped they weren't super young. I did not want to be responsible for someone's three year old.

Cal chose that moment to finally return with the other box of books. It was obvious by the smug smile on her face that she had taken her sweet time on purpose.

"Here we go!" She huffed as she placed the box next to the other at my feet. "We better get going. There's still lots of unpacking to do."

No, there wasn't.

"Wait," the librarian said holding up his hand. "Would you like for me to write you a receipt for all of these? Every penny counts during tax returns."

Cal waved him off. "That's okay. It wouldn't be a donation if we got something out of it, now would it? It was nice meeting you."

Cal began to pull me away when I was swamped with a wave of sadness as leaving the boxes became all too real for me. I knew the books wouldn't technically be going anywhere beyond the library and back, but that didn't mean I would likely see them again. Some of the books in those boxes got me through the worst time of my life and leaving them behind...it was like leaving behind a part of myself.

Feeling the burn of tears forming in my eyes, I quickly shot a glance between my books and the man that would now be their keeper.

"Take care of them for me," I said, my voice cracking a bit.

I didn't see judgement or confusion in his eyes, only a genuine understanding in those deep brown eyes that stared right through to my soul.

Without a word, he nodded and I turned away from him and the boxes. I took a deep breath, reminding myself to keep it together. By the time we had gotten in the truck I was able to bury my sorrow deep into its own special little hole and my mood was almost passible as content.

On the way out of the parking lot, I flinched when our engine backfired. "Time for Dad to give Old Yeller a tune-up, it seems."

"Don't you try to change the subject, girl. I want deets. I did not stand out in the cold to give you two some alone time to hear about this rusty old bucket," Cal chided, her grin wide.

I gaped at her for a moment before slapping her leg. "I knew it! You left me alone on purpose! How could you do that?!"

"He was cute," She shrugged. "and I saw the way you looked at him. Besides Atty, I haven't seen that side of you in months, at least around anyone but me and Dad. How you stood up to him, all 'I'm about to prove you wrong, biatch!'. I wasn't about to just get in the middle of that spark."

I couldn't help the blush that burned its way up my neck and across my cheeks. Curling myself up onto the bench seat, I clutched my knees closer to my chest.

"That was pretty great, wasn't it?" I said, my voice a little breathless.

"Hell yes!"

INTO THE SEAS EMBRACE

My small smile grew wider as I stared at her. I loved my sister. With her only being a year and a half older than me, we had always been close. She was the one who had kept our family together these past few years. The one who had slowly picked up the pieces of me and Dad, gluing them back together until we resembled people again.

She turned to me. "Hey, let's go give you a makeover, celebrate your re-found badassery!"

I blanched, hardly daring to imagine what she might have in mind.

"Oh, nothing too drastic! Unfortunately, we don't have enough money at the moment for that. Maybe some box dye, and I can get you some new earrings. I know the holes have mostly closed but it should't be too bad. What do you say?"

I absentmindedly ran my fingers over the small holes in my right ear. In one of our last locations, I had been attending a prep school and it was a lot easier to blend in when I wasn't all pierced up. So, I took most of them out, only keeping the small barb in my left brow. It would be nice to have at least that little bit of myself back after having to give up my books today.

I nodded enthusiastically. "Okay! Just not green. I do not think green would look good with my hair."

"I was thinking purple."

Chapter Three

Percy

I watched as the two girls drove away in a beat up blue pickup truck, the engine backfiring like a gunshot. I turned and headed back towards my desk, which was now covered in books and blocked off by the two boxes the girls had left on the floor.

It had certainly not been an encounter I had expected today. The town of Argos did have its share of tourists during the warm seasons, thanks in part to the mayor's efforts, but on a Tuesday morning in the middle of winter? I could not decide if it was pleasant to see fresh faces enter my perpetually empty domain or a nuisance as I picked up one of the boxes they had left and brought it into my office.

The room, like the rest of the library — if not darker — was sparsely lit and probably would have been a pain for a normal human to navigate without bumping into the piles of books. They were stacked up in just about every corner and free surface besides my personal desk, which was free of books, although piled high with paperwork. Looking around, I opted to just place the box on top of the papers, smooshing the pile down.

Sighing, I looked around. "I'll clean next week."

It wasn't necessarily dirty per se, but it was dusty and perhaps a bit unorganized. My library assistant, Jason, would beg to differ as he was a bit of a perfectionist, but that is why I kept him around: to organize the rest of the library. Not my office.

Opening the box, I peered inside only to shake my head and break out into a grin. It was full of fantasy and romance books, the exact kind I would have expected a girl like her to have. Though, she played me well with that first box.

My cheeks began to ache as the muscles for smiling were so rarely used as I continued to stare at the books. I picked them up out of the box and slowly examined them one by one; they were clearly well-loved and cared for. I had to wonder why she was getting rid of them. It had been obvious by the look on her face as she had been leaving that these books meant a great deal to her.

Picking up a particularly worn one, I opened it to the title page and was shocked to see that it was signed by the author.

"To The Girl With No Name,

I hope this book brings you the inspiration to keep moving forward.

- Jamie Addams"

"The girl with no name," I muttered as I ran my fingers along the words transcribed by the author.

Carefully, I placed the book down and picked up another one. This one was not signed, neither was the next one I pulled from the box. Going on a hunch, I pulled out one that looked more worn than the others, and I was correct, as the inside was signed by the author, again addressed to: The Girl With No Name.

Intrigued, I walked out of my office and brought in the next box. An hour later, I still had a question with no answer. Fifty-three books she and her sister had brought in, and of these fifty-three, sixteen of them were signed to 'The Girl With No Name'.

I thought back to the girl. Her sister had said her name was Atalanta. Perhaps it was one of those poetic things? She felt she did not have a sense of identity, so that was how she saw herself? Teenagers in this day and age certainly fancied themselves to be the next John Locke.

But no, perhaps that wasn't it. That girl had gone through something. It was clear by the way she fidgeted and refused to meet my eyes unless we were discussing these books and her guard was down. The way she stiffened when I called her interesting. Her clothes were in terrible disarray as well.

And then there was the other thing.

Pulling up a mental map of the coast line in my head, I thought back to the night before when I had gone for a swim and had seen lights on one of the cliff sides. Thinking on it, I was certain it was the old Winchester Cabin.

That cabin had been abandoned for years and was sure to be worse for wear. Then, lo and behold, the girl I had spotted on the cliff walks right into my library the next morning, full of mysteries and mischievous little smiles.

INTO THE SEAS EMBRACE

Curiosity to know more about this girl burned in my center as I stared down at the book she had given me to read, this one too also transcribed to 'The Girl With No Name.'

One way or another, I would have my answers.

Chapter Four

Jason

The smell of brine and the sound of a seagulls call. Deep ocean currents and shimmering scales. That was the world I grew up in. But here I sat, at this desk, watching a seventy-year-old who could not care less about my education, halfheartedly teach math.

Why did I need math?

Beyond the basics, why would I need to know something like imaginary numbers? It wasn't real! Unlike me. I was considered an imaginary creature and I was certainly real. So what did that make these numbers? Were they imaginary or not?

"Mr. Clark, would you care to look up from your book and start paying attention to my lesson?"

I looked over to the kid sitting next to me with his head stuck firmly in a Dungeons and Dragons monster manual. I couldn't blame him. About ninety percent of the class, including me, had checked out well over twenty minutes ago, but at least we were being discreet about it. When the teacher called his name again, I gently bumped his leg and jerked him out of his reading haze.

He looked over to me in irritation. What had I done? I tilted my head towards the front of the classroom where Mr. Stevens stood glaring at him.

"This is math, not English. Put the book away," Mr. Stevens scolded.

Disheartened, the kid shoved his book into his backpack and slumped forward, his hands propped up on the desk together to hold his chin.

Unfortunately, that was about the most eventful thing to happen the entire class and probably all day. When the bell rang, I stood, not having to bother with the book bag grab-and-shuffle due to my habit of keeping my messenger bag I had used since freshman year always slung on my shoulder, even during class. Now that I was a senior, the poor thing had seen better days. What was once a dark canvas green was now a sun bleached, faded brown with patches of duct tape in places. It only had a semester left of school, and I had high hopes that it could make it.

Making my way out of the classroom door, I met up with Davie, who had the class across the hall. He was standing with his girlfriend Margo, bickering about something as usual.

"Jason, you can help us with this." Margo turned to me, not even bothering with a hello.

I rolled my eyes and smiled. "Of course, you know I just love being your arbiter."

Repositioning my bag as I put on my coat, I turned and made my way with the two of them out of the hall and into the schoolyard. It was really just a fenced-in, crumbling black top with scattered trees and patches of grass now covered and dying in the winter snow. Our school, like our town, wasn't all that big or well kept.

With a population no bigger than the nearby town of Forks, Argos, Washington sported a proud 2,563 people. Most of which were fisherman.

"Davie thinks that the school mascot should be changed to a chipmunk, but I think thats dumb. It should be a dragon!"

"Why a dragon?" I ask, moving to sit at one of the few lunch benches available before it was snatched up.

"Because dragons are cool?" Margo replied, her freckled nose scrunched up, eyes squinted. As if dragons being cool were the obvious answer.

Davie's own nose scrunched right back at her causing his glasses to ride up. "Dragons being cool can't be the only reason to make one the mascot. If we went on those qualifications alone, then lots of things could be the next mascot. Like Superman, or an albino tree!"

"Both of which would be way better than a chipmunk," Margo shot back.

The both of them joined me on the opposite side of the table, rifling through their bags to pull out their lunches. Strike that, they pulled out their lunches for each other. Once out of the backpacks, the boxes did their daily swap of owners. Despite their constant bickering, Davie and Margo had the sickly adorable habit of making lunch for each other.

"But at least chipmunks are real, and vicious," Davie said.

I pulled out my own tuna sandwich and commented, "The fact that you think chipmunks are vicious doesn't help your case, Davie."

"But seriously Jason, as class president," Margo began, shoving a big bite of what looked like charred salmon in her mouth and then continuing as if she wasn't eating coal. "It's up to you to help decide the next mascot. So what's it going to be? A wimpy chipmunk?"

"Or an imaginary dragon?" Davie retorted, taking bites of perfectly normal looking food.

I had to hand it to Margo, watching her eat Davie's meals that were overcooked, undercooked—and sometimes both—every day was almost inspiring.

"How about neither?" I chuckled.

Feeling the thirst begin to creep up my throat, I reached back into my bag for my lifeline. I learned from a very young age to never leave home without at least a good liter of water for when the thirst hit. But this bottle was still empty from when I drained it earlier.

"Ah, hold on guys. I have to go fill my water bottle." I said, standing and shaking the nearly empty bottle.

"Okay, fish," Davie mocked, with the very uncreative nickname he used to point out how much water I drank.

He wasn't far off. But if he ever noticed I wasn't the only one in school, heck in the town, to be practically strapped to a water fountain, he never voiced it.

Taking my bottle and bag, I quickly made my way to the bathrooms inside to fill up before the scorching thirst in my throat became unbearable. Argos' middle and high school were held in the same large T-shaped building, only separated by floors. The middle schoolers were still in their second floor classrooms while the high schoolers were on their lunch period, so the first floor hallway was deserted as always.

Briskly, I made my way over to the water fountain and began to take large gulps from the pathetic stream of water. Sated, if only for a moment, I filled up the bottle only to feel the need to down it a few moments later. Sighing, I began the slow process of filling the bottle again.

It had been a few days since I had been able to make it down to the beach, what with studying for exams, student council president duty, and training the new freshmen for the swim team. I begrudgingly told myself that I would need to make the trip out tonight before the cravings got worse.

Bottle filled again, I rummaged through my bag to pull out a little blue tin labeled SEA SALT, and surreptitiously tilted the contents into my bottle.

After giving it a good shake, I took a swig from the briny liquid, the salt water much more refreshing as it made its way through my blood stream.

I smacked my lips, satisfied, and turned to go back to my friends when I came face to face with a small picture of a girl.

She stared up at me, her eyes wide. "Did you just drink salt water?"

Oh, shit.

"Uh, no? Just water," I scoffed, as I tried to keep my voice from jumping up an octave.

Oh, shit. Oh, shit.

She pointed to my water bottle. "But I just watched you dump salt into the bottle and then drink it."

Shit. Shit. Shit.

"It wasn't salt. It was vitamins," I said quickly.

She shifted, her small hips jutting out to one side, hands resting on them in that full power mode that all women seemed to possess, an eyebrow cocking upward.

"The bottle of salt is still in your hand."

Fuck.

I studied the girl. She was tiny, much shorter than my own 6'2", in dark worn clothes way too baggy for her slim frame, and her hair looked like it had been attacked with a lawn mower holding a paintbrush...but despite that, she was cute. I didn't know exactly what it was, perhaps it was her creamy brown skin. A color you really didn't see in this rural northern town. Then her eyes, brown with hints of green, brimming with this confidence that just pulled me in, or maybe...just maybe it was her adorable button nose that reminded me of a bunny.

She had several piercings in her right ear and one in her left eyebrow that screamed 'I'm a rebel'. Yet, she was wearing pink lip gloss and her long sleeved hoodie read "TEAM QUIN".

Soft Punk would be the words to describe this girl.

But the big problem was that I didn't know her. She certainly wasn't part of my Pod and definitely new to the school, so...

I gave a wide smile and simply tossed the bottle over my shoulder and into the trashcan I knew was there. "I have no idea what you're talking about. See you around."

With a wink, I walked off, quickly leaving her behind and back to my friends. When I got outside, I was relieved to see that she hadn't followed me. She was so small, not really young looking but I hoped that she was a middle schooler who was transferring in. It would make it easier to avoid her until the year was over.

The rest of lunch went by quickly. Davie and Margo pitched me ideas on different possible mascots for the school. It was tradition that every eleven years, the school would change the mascot. This past eleven we were The Wombats, and before that, The Cougars. Two weeks ago, the principal called me into her office to tell me that as the student council president, it would be up to me to decide. I had until the end of the term.

I honestly had way more important things to worry about.

"Did you and the rest of the council pick a theme for Prom yet?"

Like that.

I groaned and scratched the back of my head. "Honestly Margo, you would have an easier time getting those three to go skinny dipping in the bay with sharks than you would getting them to actually decide on something."

My fellow council members, the triplets, Dina, Enya, and Pema, never got along and I was pretty convinced they only joined the council because I became president, as they spent most of their time making goo-goo eyes at me.

We all packed up our lunches as Margo and I separated from Davie, who had his next class on the other side of the building while Margo and I shared English together. As the class was literally right next to the exit, we didn't have to go very far.

Finding our usual seats next to each other, we sat down and Margo continued.

"Well, I say you should go with the theme *A Midsummer Night's Dream.*" she suggested as she slid her coat off her back and onto her chair.

I tilted my head as I took off my own coat. "You want us to be running around the forest in the middle of the night, high on love?"

"No, you dingbat. Picture this: we go set up a bunch of fairy lights in the Doncreek clearing. We could easily get tables and a basic platform out there, and it would be pretty with some purple and white tulle."

I squinted my eyes and propped my chin on my hand, trying to envision what she was selling. "It's not a bad idea, honestly a lot better than the gym. We would just need to get approval to set up and get the generators out there."

"See?" She smiled, proud in her perpetual rightness.

"Okay, smarty pants. You came up with the idea, you write up the proposal to give to the principal, and help organize the whole thing."

Her jaw dropped open and she started shaking her head in disbelief. "No, no, no, don't put that on me!"

I stood abruptly from my seat and held a pencil to her shoulder. "By the power vested in me, I, student council president Jason Monroe, name you, Margo Juneteli, the head of the prom committee."

The rest of the students that had shuffled in began to laugh, including Damon, our teacher. Poor Margo looked furious but I knew she would enjoy it. I had known her and Davie all my life and if there was one thing I knew, it was that she loved being in charge, especially when it came to putting together parties, organizing the little details. She would thank me by the end of it.

My own smile fell when I saw, standing in the doorway, the girl from the water fountain. She was watching me as most of the class was, but not with a smile on her face. Her pink glossed lips were turned down into a frown and slightly puckered, brows drawn together as if she were trying to figure out some sort of math problem.

I assume others noticed my staring when Damon stood from his desk and walked up to her. "May I help you?"

Damon Kline was the youngest looking teacher in our school. Appearing at most twenty-six years old, a lot of the girls and a few of the guys in our school had a crush on him. He was also my cousin. And judging by the blush spreading across the girl's cheeks, she wasn't immune to his good looks or the charm that oozed off him.

"Is this English Literature?" she asked.

He smiled. "That it is. Are you the new transfer I was told about this morning?"

"I am," she murmured. I watched as she fidgeted with one of the straps of her backpack. She kept glancing over at the rest of the class before shooting her eyes back to Damon.

"Well." He shuffled over to his desk and picked up a packet of paper, turning to hand it to her. "It's too late in the year for me to really give you a run for your money, but If you don't mind, I have a test I would like you to take, to gauge your knowledge."

The strong confident girl I had seen in the hall was smothered now, shy and fidgety in the face of all the eyes in the classroom watching her. She nodded and took the packet.

"For the sake of our new student, today is a reading day. Talk amongst yourselves or read, though I would prefer you read. In fact, extra credit for those who actually read one of the stories in our book and can give me a summary of what they read by the end of class."

The students began to meander about, either starting pockets of conversations or pulling out their text books while our new student awkwardly looked for a new seat.

"Oh blimey, I nearly forgot. I'm sorry, I didn't ask your name," Damon commented on the way back to his desk.

The girl stiffened when conversation stopped again as everyone realized this as well.

"Atalanta North," she whispered just loud enough for us to hear.

"Atalanta! Like the Greek hero who slew the Caledonian boar! Okay then, Miss North. You may call me Dr. Kline, or Mr. K if that's easier. Though, no need to call me Dr. K, as I don't care much for the formality of the doctor part. I'm also noticing we don't have enough desks. Jason, go get one for our new student from storage, please."

I rolled my eyes and walked to the front. "There are other students, you know."

"Yes, but you're our best errand boy," He smiled back, his retort double sided.

I shoved down the argument that bubbled up in my throat. It wasn't worth it. Grabbing the hall pass lanyard off the door hook, I began to shuffle out of the room when I was stopped by the sound of a small voice.

"Here, let me help you,"

I looked back to see our new student walking towards me. I was a little touched, but I shook my head anyway.

"It's alright, I got it." I declined with a shake of my head before leaving to go get a desk and chair.

When I got back, I found half of the small class, including Margo, circled around Atalanta as she sat awkwardly at what was once my desk and tried to answer the hundred and six questions that were being thrown at her.

The little minx hadn't had the decency to wait until I brought her back a chair?

Huffing in mild frustration, I placed the desk and chair down near the front of the classroom against the wall and flopped into it. For a while I sat silently, scrolling through my phone, listening to the students ask her question after question. But it was obvious to me that she was uncomfortable with all of the questions. No sense in trying to stop the curious students though, they would ask these questions eventually anyway.

Reaching into my bag, I pulled out my bottle and took in a long swig of the briny fluid.

With another glance at the new girl before leaning back to close my eyes, I noticed she was staring directly at me, that shy shadow in her eyes being pushed back by the spark of curiosity.

I smiled and held the bottle up to her in salute.

The little annoyed scowl she got on her face was really cute and I had the urge to poke fun at her till she was steaming from the ears. Though I also had a flash in my mind of scooping her up into my arms and kissing away her anger.

I shook my head to clear the image from my mind.

I tried to remind myself that she was human, therefore off limits to me. Besides, the image of a certain librarian came to mind. I didn't really need to be developing another crush I shouldn't be having.

Chapter Five

Atalanta

"So, what's it like to live in a city? Is it as noisy as people say?"

I nodded and continued to stare down at the next question on the packet. "Yeah, it can be pretty noisy."

Who were the main characters in F. Scott Fitzgerald's *The Great Gatsby?* That was easy.

I scribbled down the answer before one of the other students shot out the next question.

"And then you moved to Forks?"

"Yep."

Please, please, please. Stop asking questions. It was probably the only thing I hated about small towns; people always noticed the new kid and they *always* asked too many questions. I tried to grin and bear it, but every time I was surrounded by all these kids throwing questions at me left and right, I was glad to be well rehearsed by now. There was no point in lying about where we had been, but I was not going to divulge the reason we had left. But this was my fourth class today, and I was starting to sound like a broken record.

At least they weren't asking anything super personal. Dad had only just given me the new packet this morning to study, and I honestly didn't know much about Atalanta North beyond her being born in

Michigan on November 9th. And I think she liked horses.

"So why did your family leave? It's only like an hour away."

I turned my face down in an attempt at melancholy. "My dad moves around a lot for work and he's pretty superstitious. So when he heard that the town was being overrun by vampires, he packed us right up."

That shut them right up for a solid minute before I started laughing to break the tension and apologized for the joke. They awkwardly laughed it off but I got my wish and the questions died down after that. People shied away from awkward and weird. Though, I did mentally scold myself as being considered the weird girl wasn't a very good way to blend in. I was just really tired of the questions.

I shot another look over to the guy, Jason, I had heard Mr. K call him. There had to be something in the water in this town because between him, the librarian, and the English teacher, there was too much good-looking for one space. All of them belonged on a cover of GQ somewhere. Though, I'd say the teacher was a bit more Cal's type than my own. He had that prince charming thing going on, with the odd mix of decorum and familiarity with an accent I couldn't decipher.

Jason, on the other hand, who seemed to be a bit of a goof ball, was more my speed, if you could look past all that perfection: a bit on the jock side with his square jaw, bulky frame from probably hours of workouts, and close mousy brown hair cut. Then if I heard him

INTO THE SEAS EMBRACE

correctly earlier, he was actually the student council president and if I had to take a guess, I bet he was on some sort of sports team as well. I could not handle that much perfect in one place.

There was something fishy going on here, and it definitely had something to do with that water bottle.

It hadn't passed my notice that half the student body and some of the staff I had seen today happened to carry around these giant jugs of water. At first, I just thought the water fountains here were something to be feared. That was, until I had come out of the bathroom to see Mr. Perfect over there dumping a freaking cup of salt into his bottle.

And there he was mocking me with it.

"Hey, are you already crushing on my homeboy Jason?"

I jumped a little and turned to the seat next to me to see the girl Jason had been talking to when I had walked into class. She was sweet looking, with brownish red curls and adorable freckles running across her nose.

"Uhh, no?"

She smiled. "It's just that you keep staring at him. Not that there's anything wrong with that. Most of the girls do. But I just wanted to give you a heads up that you'll have half his fan club on your butt if you go after him."

I shook my head frantically. "No, no, I'm not crushing. He's not my type."

"Hot blooded males aren't your type? Then I guess you're more of the sweet guy kind of girl? You're right, though. I shouldn't assume," She leaned in close to me and very loudly whispered, "Are you lesbian?"

Like a bloody fish out of water I just gasped at her, opening and closing my mouth with absolutely nothing to say to that. When my eyes naturally darted around, looking for some sort of help or an answer, I realized that the class what staring at me. Including Jason.

In the panic of the spotlight I just spouted the first thing that came to mind. "No, I'm strictly dickly!"

I personally wanted to crawl into a hole and stay there for the rest of eternity, but everyone else found it hilarious as they burst into laughter.

"Saved by the bell," I muttered as all the students started getting up and shuffling out of the classroom at the sound of the chime.

"I'm sorry if I put you on the spot like that. Sometimes I just put my foot in my mouth," The girl smiled apologetically.

I covered my face with my hands, groaning. "That's alright. I don't think I handled it much better."

"I don't know, it was pretty funny," came a smooth baritone.

Looking up, I saw Jason standing next to us, staring down at me with that cocky smile he'd worn the entire class.

"Only an asshole would think something like that was funny. I was only put on the spot like that because of you and your water bottle," I snapped.

"Jason does love his water," The girl laughed nervously, her eyes flicking back and forth between the two of us. "He drinks so much of it, our other friend Davie calls him Fish. It doesn't help when Jason's the captain of the swim team and his parents are marine biologists."

"Geez. Tell her my life story why don't you, Margo," Jason growled.

She laughed nervously again. "Sorry."

Ah, so my hunch was correct. Mr. Perfect was on a sports team. And he was the captain! It was no wonder he supposedly had a fan club.

"Well, we better get to our next classes," Jason said before looking down at me expectantly.

"What?" I shot at him.

He pointed to the seat I was sitting in. "You're sitting on my coat."

I turned and immediately felt horrible that I didn't even realize that there had been a coat draped over the back of the seat. I had stolen his seat!

I mentally face palmed myself. Of course I had stolen his seat. He had gone to get one for me. I had just gotten so distracted with the bombardment of questions that I sat in the first empty seat I saw, completely forgetting it was his.

I shot up out of the desk like it had bitten me. "I am so sorry!"

He chuckled and picked up the coat, draping it over his arm. "It's fine, you kept it warm for me."

I felt that damn blush creeping up the back of my neck again. I couldn't let the blush win. With a swift goodbye, I rushed out of the room and down the hall to where I knew my next class would be, since I had spent lunch mapping out the school.

Like the rest of the town, the school was a bit worse for wear. The only new building I'd noticed so far was the library.

Thoughts about the library brought my mind back to the librarian, Percy. I wondered if he had started reading the book I had given him. A part of me wanted to stop by after school and see, but I tried to squash that part as it wasn't smart to get attached. Besides, I needed to go by the community center on the way home and see about that job. Though...the community center was right next door to the library.

I groaned. "No, Atalanta. No library for you."

Walking into the new classroom for math, I talked to the teacher, a rather old man by the name of Mr. Stevens, to confirm I was in the right room and to inform him that I was the new student. Of course, like all the other classes that day, I got the same curious stares and about 102 questions before Mr. Stevens saved me by insisting on actually teaching a lesson.

God, he made imaginary numbers seem so boring. And I liked math!

A few minutes before the bell was supposed to ring, I pulled the schedule sheet out of my hoodie pocket. Folded, refolded, and fiddled with several times, the paper was already worn despite having just received it this morning. But I did confirm that my next and second to last class of the day was gym.

I hadn't had the chance to check out the gym yet, but hopefully they wouldn't make us climb some frayed old rope or play basketball with nearly stripped balls which had a tendency to slip out of peoples hands and often hit me in the face.

At the sound of the bell, I waited a few moments for the rest of the students to corral themselves out the door and into the hall before following after them. It wasn't very packed in the halls like some of the schools I had attended in the past, which really helped my nerves. I only had to deal with the occasional bump of a stranger rather than packed sardines shoving and pushing each other to get to their next lesson.

I spotted Jason standing by one of the open classroom doors, chatting with the girl Margo and another boy. Lanky with tight curly hair and glasses. Judging by how close he stood to Margo, he must have been the boyfriend she mentioned earlier. They looked cute together.

It was interesting to see Mr. Perfect not stereotypically hanging out with the group of jock looking kids that were laughing loudly and pushing each other in the hall up ahead.

Jason laughed at something Margo had said, the sound of it rolling over to where I stood not a few feet away and sending goosebumps up my arms. Suddenly, I had the incredible urge to go over to him, talk to him, be close to him, touch him.

Before I had even taken a step in his direction, I was shoved from the side. Hard. Whoever it was sent me completely off balance and, well, floor meet butt, butt meet pain.

I yelped in surprise and pain as the hard linoleum floor met with my backside and shocked me out of whatever stupor I had been in. I blinked and shook my head.

"Oh shoot, I'm so sorry! Are you okay?" came a voice that was seemingly panicked and honey rich.

A tan hand appeared in my line of vision to help me up. Not taking it, I stood on my own, straightened my clothes, and took stock of any missing limbs. Looking at my attacker, I could only gape at the golden god.

"There is something in your freaking water," I muttered as I stared at the guy, wide eyed, slack jawed.

The first thing that drew me were his eyes. I couldn't exactly tell what color they were. At first they appeared to be maybe a brownish green, but as I continued to stare, he shifted back and they then looked more blue than brown. His hair was a brilliant golden blond, short at the sides and long and fluffy at the top. I resisted the urge to run my fingers through the soft looking locks.

He smiled, and oh, was it full of mischief. "That's just the mermaids."

I shook my head. "What? Did you just say mermaids?"

"You haven't noticed? It's the staple of our town. Brings in the tourists."

"You mean all those statues?" I asked, recalling the amazingly detailed sculptures I had seen all over the town.

"We'd better get to class," he said, tilting his head down the hall, his smile still in place.

I noticed he hadn't answered my question but nodded anyway and glanced back towards where Jason had been standing with his friends. He was there watching me as I had watched him. He looked concerned, his brows furrowed, causing his green eyes to darken and his lips were set in a thin line. Not really knowing how to respond to our awkward eye contact, I just broke it and shuffled along down the hall as quickly as possible, my head down.

"Where you headed, new girl?"

Startled, I looked up to see that the blond god had followed me.

"Um, gym," I replied.

"Well, then allow me to escort you. The least I can do for knocking you over," He said, offering his arm for me to take.

"No," I shook my head. "You don't have to do that."

"It's fine. Besides, I believe we are heading in the same direction."

Despite my insistence that I was fine, the guy didn't really take the hint and followed me all the way to the gymnasium which was on the other side of school. By the time we got there, a second bell had already chimed signaling that we were late. I groaned internally, hoping that I wouldn't get detention on my first day.

Off to the right of the gym's big brown double doors were signs leading to the locker rooms. Students were already filing out, dressed in simple gray t-shirts and blue basketballs shorts.

The guy held up his hand and began to walk towards the locker room door labeled Ladies. "Wait here, I'll get the coach."

"Won't you get in trouble for that? You're already late for your own class!" I called after him, but he only replied with a slightly toothy grin.

I was terrified he was about to make a fool of himself by walking in to the ladies locker room, but he only stuck his head through the door and called inside. A moment later, a tall, broad shouldered older woman in about her mid-thirties came out in a blue fitted track suit. Her long blonde hair was tied high in a ponytail through a baseball cap. Very coach.

"You're my new student? You're late," she said, her voice much higher-pitched and valley girl than I would have expected.

"I'm sorry. I had an accident on the way here," I unconsciously glanced over at the mischievous golden god.

She followed my eyes and groaned. "I should have known it was you, Mr. Clark. Well, since you made her late then you'll be punished as well."

"Punished?" I squeaked.

The guy chuckled. "I figured."

With a wink at me, he turned and walked into the men's locker room. Huh. I should have guessed he also had gym class. Otherwise, why would a guy like that escort me all the way here?

I flinched when someone lightly placed their hand on my shoulder. My eyes snapped from the locker room doors to the coach who smiled down at me, her salon tan skin crinkling along her laugh lines.

"It's alright. It's nothing too bad. Just a lap around the track," With her hand still on my shoulder, she steered me towards the ladies locker rooms. "It keeps the lazy bums from being late."

Behind the door, there was a mesh of metal and tile. The air smelled of stale sweat and an amalgamation of perfume that made my nose itch. The few girls that were finishing up getting dressed glanced up when the two of us entered.

"This way," the coach said, herding me towards an open door just inside the locker room.

The office was dark and there were boxes everywhere. The coach finally let go of my shoulder and moved to one of the boxes.

"What's your size? A medium?"

"I think so." I replied, absentmindedly rubbing my shoulder.

She nodded and rifled through one of the many boxes, pulling out two wrapped packages. She tossed them to me, the plastic crinkling loudly as they slapped against my chest and I fumbled not to drop them.

"Try those on, but be quick about it."

I nodded and scurried off back into the locker room, which was now empty. Heading to a back corner, I pulled my hoodie over my head, the two extra layers underneath trying to come with it but I kept them down with my other hand. Hurriedly, I unbuckled the belt that held up the insulated jeans I was wearing. They were hand-me-downs from my sister and a little too big for my frame.

Pulling the shorts out of the crinkly plastic, I slipped them on. They were a size too big, but it was good as they stopped just past my knees. I would have to be mindful when I sat down with them on, making sure they didn't ride up. I pulled the drawstrings tight and tied them to make the shorts fit. I suspected the shirt would probably be a size too big as well, but that was also okay. I pulled it out of the bag and swapped it out for the short sleeve shirt I had already over my close fitting maroon long-sleeve top.

Taking all of my clothes, I shoved them into my backpack and quickly stuck it into an empty locker. Hurrying out of the room, I was embarrassed when I realized I was still wearing my boots as compared to the other students who I'd seen wearing sneakers. But I didn't have anything else, so I tried to shrug it off as I crept discreetly through the gym doors.

The gym was ginormous! Immediately, I noticed my feet sank slightly into a rubber mesh, the same kind found at playgrounds. There was a track that circled the outer edges of a wooden court with stands reaching high up against the walls. It all looked rather new, at least compared to the rest of the school.

I spotted the class gathered at one end of the track, talking amongst themselves as the coach called roll.

I jogged up to them, my feet bouncing ever so slightly on the rubber of the track.

"That was quick," The coach said, pausing in her roll call. "Class, we have a new student. I believe your name's Atalanta?"

I nodded and tried not to focus on the rest of the class staring at me.

"Well, as I said before, students who are late to my class are punished with a lap around the track. Actually, Clark, why don't you get started while I go over the rules real quick with her."

The guy who had run into me stepped out of the crowd of students and set up at the starting line of the track. Several students were chuckling and I heard a couple mutterings of 'this will be good'. Curious at the commotion, I watched him shoot off and begin to jog around the track while the coach spoke to me.

"Every Monday we start with a lap around the track, but if you're late, you have to do an extra lap. You'll start here and I want to see you running. No lolly gagging...You didn't have any tennis shoes?"

I shook my head and whispered, "No. I only just got my schedule this morning. I didn't know I'd be having gym."

Clark stumbled about a quarter of the way around the track and almost fell face first before finding his balance and continuing his jog. A few of the students chuckled but the coach didn't pay it any mind.

"Well, I would recommend you bring in some next time but you should be fine to run in those, shouldn't you?"

"Yes," I nodded, fiddling with the sleeves of my long sleeved shirt and wishing she would just start the class.

"I would also recommend you just wear the T-shirt next time. You're going to be hot in that," She gestured to my undershirt.

I laughed internally. She would have to hold me down before I willingly wore short sleeves.

I watched as Clark stumbled THREE more times before finally falling face first and literally tumbling through the finish line. The class laughed hysterically as the coach groaned and berated the students for their rudeness.

So, he was just extremely clumsy. That was unfortunate. He was still handsome though.

"Okay Atalanta, your turn," the coach said, gesturing towards the starting line.

I frowned as I rolled my shoulders and shook out my legs. It had been a while since I ran on a track and hoped I wouldn't stumble around like Clark had.

Prepping in the crouched starting position, I took a deep breath and counted to down from ten in my head.

5...

4...

3...

2...

1...

And I took off down the track, my boots slapping hard against the rubber, my strides long and quick. Flying along the ground, for one short moment the euphoria of running washed away the stress of the day.

It ended all too quickly when I shot across the finish line and came to a walking halt.

Turning my head with a pant, I saw that everyone was staring at me with surprise on their faces. One of the guys whistled, making the blush I felt creeping up my neck burn hotter.

"You're quite the runner, Ms. North. It's a shame you're graduating this year and the season's over or I'd be begging you to join our track team," The coach praised, walking over to me.

I rubbed the back of my neck, a little bashful. "I used to compete back in middle school."

"You got schooled, Hip." A large boy with chubby cheeks and beady eyes chuckled.

I looked away from the teacher to see a group of boys a few feet away standing around Clark who was rubbing a red spot on his knee where he fell. They were all still laughing at him. Bullies. I hated bullies.

Mr. Golden God crossed his arms over his chest and grumbled, "Hey, I just needed to warm up."

Hip? I thought his name was Clark?

"She didn't need to warm up!" Beady-Eyes laughed, pointing a finger at me.

"Yeah, but you heard, she's a professional."

"Well, you're warmed up now and I bet you'd still fall on your ass." Beady-Eyes mocked.

"I would not." Hip growled, yet looking at him I saw mischief in his eyes rather than fire. "In fact, I bet you twenty bucks I could beat you in a race."

"Anyone could beat Jeremy in a race. He's as fast as a walrus. You should race the new girl," another guy piped up and all eyes turned towards me.

I shook my head. I did not want to be brought into this! The group of boys all stared at me expectantly.

INTO THE SEAS EMBRACE

Clark, or Hip, whatever his name was, looked at me with those big begging puppy dog eyes which were brown with hints of yellow and green in this light.

"Come on, Atalanta. We'll give you twenty bucks if you race Hip and win."

I perked up and held out my hand for the cash. "Alright, I'll do it."

"Hey, what about if I win?" Hip/Clark whined.

Beady-Eyes sneered. "Then you'll get the twenty bucks. But you're not gonna win."

At this point, I was tempted to let him win just to shut the asswipes up, but I could use the twenty bucks to buy a pair of sneakers, as I didn't actually have any money and honestly didn't want to ask Dad for it.

I looked back over to the coach who just shrugged. "I don't condone the betting, but I'll always say yes to a good race."

What the fuck? She would literally let students place bets as long as it encouraged us to do some form of exercise? How lazy was this class?

Setting up again at the starting line, I looked over at my opponent. "Good luck."

He nodded. "You as well."

The coach counted down:

3...

2...

1...

And she blew the whistle.

I once again shot off, sprinting around the track, my feet pumping against the rubber. I could feel Hip/Clark close behind me for a few moments before I heard him stumble and fall not even at the quarter mark of the track. Looking behind me, I saw him desperately trying to get up.

This would be an easy win! Those twenty bucks were mine!

Or so I thought, until I caught a glimpse of the class laughing again.

Curse my self-righteousness.

In the last half of the track, I purposefully slowed my strides, putting on a big show of being tired with loud panting and bending over, giving my opponent enough time to pass me till I picked up my speed again. Something weird happened when he passed me though, his strides weren't slow and clumsy as before but quick and sure-footed.

He was booking it down the rest of the track like a seasoned runner!

"Holy shit!" I gasped and picked up my speed, chasing after him now.

Even at my top speed, I was a good six feet behind him when he crossed the finish line. He had beaten me fair and square. Or had he?

I walked up to him and held out my hand. "Good race."

He smiled and took my outstretched hand, his was warm and calloused against mine. "Thanks. You too."

I let go, my fingers tingling with his residual warmth. "I gotta ask. What's your name? Is it Hip or is it Clark?"

"Both. My full name is Hip Clark. Really only the teachers call me Clark," He said, rubbing the back of his neck, his expression showing that he knew how weird of a name was.

I raised an eyebrow. "Is Hip short for something?"

"Maybe," He grinned and walked off, leaving me thoroughly confused and curious at what kind of person he was.

The rest of the class, I watched Hip carefully as he interacted with the students. If he were to live up to that golden godliness going, on he would be Loki. Despite acting like a bit of a bumbling baboon, this guy worked people like a skilled marionette. All of the students were his friends but they treated him as some sort of goofy sidekick. Like the town fool who could trick them out of the shirt on their back if he wanted. I watched the way he observed people, the same way I was observing him. His expression was serious and calculating.

Apparently, our little bet had drawn the attention of most of the class. They had all thrown in some cash to the pot, and they had all bet against him. I almost blew a gasket when I saw him pocket the wad of cash at the end of class as students walked out of the locker room.

Unable to keep quiet anymore, I stalked up to him and poked him in the back. "What was that?"

He turned and looked down at me, feigning innocence. "What was what?"

"Was your tripping an act or something?"

"I don't know what you're talking about," He chuckled and leaned his back against the wall. "I'm naturally clumsy."

"Are you sure? Because what I saw in there was a classic hustle."

"Listen Speedy, I'm just as surprised as you that I won that race. I got lucky. I'm sorry if it hurt your pride."

"I'm not upset about being beaten. I just don't like being used for your personal gain," I growled, getting as close to his face as my five foot frame could.

It was then I realized that he wasn't super tall, probably only 5'8", 5'9"? He was around the same height as my sister. But with that underestimation I also realized that me standing up on my tip toes this close to his face I was at the perfect height to kiss him, my lips only an inch or so from his.

I would be lying if I said I wasn't at least slightly tempted to go in for a kiss. Looking up into those ever-changing eyes of his, I saw that they were a deep brown green at the moment, almost as if they were reflecting my own. And he looked temped to kiss me too as I watched his eyes flicker down to my lips and back up again.

My anger superseded the urge to kiss him. Stepping back, I crossed my arms over my chest and stared him down.

For once, that easy smile fell into a real expression. Neutral, empty.

"You're right, I'm sorry. I saw a chance to make some extra money and I took it. Here," He took the wad of cash out of his pocket and counted out a few bills. "this should be enough to get you the tennis shoes you need. Go to Gail's in town. She'll sell them cheap to you. See it as payment for helping with my little scheme. Next time, I'll let you in on it first."

"How did you...?"

"I happen to know you got your schedule from the secretary yesterday. I heard her talking to my Gran about the new pierced up punk girl that moved to town. I also noticed your clothes are old and you jumped at the chance when they mentioned money. Ergo, you didn't forget your shoes. You just didn't have any."

I blinked, surprised by his deductive skills. Though that didn't really explain how he heard what the coach had said to me when he was jogging and tripping down the track at the time. I decided not to question him on it now.

Taking the cash he gave me, I clutched it closely to me. "Thank you."

He smiled and this time it was a real smile, one that reached his eyes. "You're welcome, Speedy."

My stomach flopped at seeing that smile. I almost had to resist one of my own.

"You know, while acting like an idiot may come with some advantages, it won't get you any real friends. See you tomorrow." With that, I jogged off down the hall to my next class.

Chapter Six

Atlalanta

Thankfully, the rest of my school day was uneventful. Jason was in my last class, Social Science, but we didn't really interact. His friend Davie was really sweet though, offering to share his notes from the past month so that I could take the test later that week.

Unfortunately, neither Cal nor Dad could pick me up from school as Dad was off at the dock to find a job and Cal was in town. So, walking home in the snow was my only option. First, though, was a trip to the community center to see about getting a job. Luckily, it wasn't a far journey.

I took a deep breath and closed my eyes. The wind flowed softly through the branches of trees that had lost their leaves this past fall and the resilient pines, whose bristles easily withstood the cold northern air. Argos was even closer to the beach than Forks and you could smell it on the air here. That crisp saltiness brought in by the waves.

I sneezed, my nose protesting the cold air.

I pulled up the hood of my hoodie and tugged the drawstrings tight. These clothes were definitely not for suited for a walk in half a foot of snow. I didn't even have any gloves. I wasn't able to find my old pair when I woke up this morning. It was probably in one of the boxes I hadn't bothered to open yet.

Picking up my pace, I briskly jogged the rest of the mile or so up the hill to the community center and the library next door. I hadn't paid it much mind the other day as it was a rather plain looking building at first glance: large with an overhang shadowing the steps to the doors, two columns supporting it. Upon second inspection I saw that the columns, like the library, had paintings on them. Two mermaids posed facing each other, a male and a female, the female's hair long and covering her naked chest. They were just a splash of color on the otherwise plain gray box of a building.

Shuffling closer, I got a better look at the two mythical creatures. Their tails, both a bluish-green color, were entangled around their columns. They were so lifelike. Each scale was painted in painstaking detail and the shadowing made it look like they were coming to life right off the columns. They had to be related, with matching golden hair and green eyes.

They also looked sad.

The style was certainly the same as the paintings on the library and I had to wonder who this mystery artist was who could paint like this.

I heard a door creek open and saw a small mousy woman with huge glasses that magnified her eyes, pop her head out of the entrance.

"Are you okay, dear?" She asked, her voice betraying her youthful appearance.

I plastered on a smile, my lips cracking a little. "Yes, I'm fine. Just admiring the paintings."

"Oh, they are beautiful, but you look half frozen. Please, come inside to warm up," She beckoned, opening one of the big metal doors further.

Nodding, I quickly jogged up the steps to the doors. I hadn't realized how much snow had piled onto me while I stood there admiring the mermaids until the kind woman began to briskly brush it off of me before I entered. I tried to stay still while she touched me, but it didn't stop my knees from going rigid.

"Like a popsicle, aren't ya? Oh, golly, you don't even have any gloves! Come in. Come in! Let's get you some nice hot cocoa."

I nodded again and shuffled inside after her, rubbing my arms back and forth.

Holy shit! Why hadn't I noticed I was this cold?

I brought my hands to my face and breathed hot air on them in hopes to get some feeling back. Stupid cold, I didn't have to deal with you when we lived in Florida.

I looked around, desperate to distract myself from my numb, shaking limbs. It was a little more impressive on the inside than the outside. It was like stepping into autumn, with warm brown walls with glimmers of orange and gold, fake flowers and plants scattered here and there. The air smelled of cinnamon, like those brooms you found stocking up shelves in the fall. We were in a small lobby area with a tall desk and a few cozy chairs propped near a window that looked out into the parking lot. On either side of the desk, I spied hallways leading off far into the building.

It was cozy.

The little mousy woman came hurriedly out from a door behind the desk, holding a steaming mug.

She handed me the mug. "I always have a fresh pot ready during this time of year. This will warm you right up."

The heat from the mug almost scorched my cold palms but I still held onto it tightly, taking tentative sips. The hot liquid settled into my stomach and slowly I felt my insides begin to thaw. It didn't just taste like hot chocolate though, as if there was something else in it.

"Is there cinnamon in this?" I asked the woman.

She smiled brightly at me. "Why, yes. I love cinnamon and I think putting a dash into the cocoa really makes the difference."

"It's delicious. Thank you."

"Of course, honey," She stared at me for a few silent and almost awkward moments before asking, "So what brings you here? It couldn't have been to just stare at those paintings."

I pulled the lifesaving liquid away from my mouth and shook my head. "No. I was at the library yesterday and the librarian told me that you might have job positions open."

"Oh! You must be one of the sisters I heard about. Yes, Percy mentioned you might be stopping by. He's such a sweet boy isn't he?"

I gave a wry smile, remembering the blunt, almost rude man I had met. Sweet?

"Word travels fast in this town," I commented, taking another sip from the mug.

"You're right, it does, especially when Charlotte and Mona are involved. They're the town gossips. I believe you met them when you asked for directions. Goodness, they called me right up after to tell me about the two beautiful dark-skinned girls that had pulled up in an old pickup to ask for directions."

Great work, Cal. Of course the first people you decided talk to would spread the word of our arrival like a pair of town criers.

She sighed. "Unfortunately, the mayor's daughter, Lidia, just took the position we had open in the daycare."

My shoulders drooped in disappointment.

Those big eyes studied me, scanning me up and down before saying, "However, if you need a job, Thesis could use some help cleaning around here. Lord knows he's stubborn and insists he do it all by himself."

Thesis? What kind of weird ass name is that?

"We wouldn't be able to pay you much, but I hope that you'll consider it."

"I'll do it," I said, probably a little too enthusiastically.

Cleaning was one thing I could do blindfolded and, unlike the daycare job, I wouldn't really have to interact with people while doing it.

She clapped her hands together. "That's great! Let me get the paperwork. My name is Dorris, by the way. I nearly forgot to introduce myself."

"My name's Atalanta, it's nice to meet you," I replied, tentatively taking the hand she held out to me.

"What a pretty name." With a smile, she went back into the room behind the desk before coming back out with a little pile of paperwork a few minutes later. "Is your sister your only sibling?"

"She is," I nodded.

Sadly, I drained the rest of my cup of cocoa. Not really knowing what to do with the mug, I gently put it on the desk in front of me.

"I always wanted siblings," She picked up the cup with a smile and put it away in that back room, speaking as she went. "I think growing up an only child is why I just love to gab with others. Did your parents move here with you? I know kids these days are just so independent. I mean, look at you, walking here yourself from school to get a job."

When she came back, she directed me to fill out the forms before she sat down in the chair behind the desk. Mostly, they were questions about myself: name, date of birth, address, social security number, phone number. If I was a convicted felon. A few of them, I had to take a moment to remember what it said on my new ID and info packet Dad gave me to study.

"My dad is here with us...My mom, she passed away," I mumbled as I squinted at the paperwork and tried to remember.

Atalanta North was born in Michigan on November 9th. She is not a convicted felon. Her new phone number is... She likes-

"Oh honey, I'm so sorry. I know it can be hard to lose a loved one. Why, I lost my Marv not three years ago. Miss him every day," she sniffed.

I paused to take a good look at Mrs. Dorris. She didn't look much older than thirty, but with the way she talked she might as well have been a great grandmother. Old at heart, I guessed.

Filling out the rest of the form, I gave a small sigh of relief, hoping that I remembered everything.

Dorris scrutinized the papers for a few moments before looking up. "These look good. Our computer system is old, you don't mind being paid with checks, do you? I know most people prefer that new direct deposit."

"Checks are fine."

I would just have to find a place to cash them.

"Good. Good. Now I believe Thesis is in the music hall if you want to meet him. He can give you a tour of the facility and tell you a little bit about your work here. I, unfortunately, need to go check on a few things but it's just down this hall to my left. Big sign, you can't miss it." She pointed to the hallway before fixing her glasses and leaning over to squint at the computer sitting on the desk.

Dorris threw a distracted reply of "you're welcome" to my whispered "thank you" as I made my way down the hall to find this Thesis.

The hallway had several doors along both sides. Each of them looked basically the same as the last when I peeked through the open doors, an empty room filled with chairs. A couple of them had art equipment like easels or what looked like pottery wheels. No music hall, though.

It wasn't until I reached the end of the hallway that I saw the sign. Peeking through the door, I noted that it was certainly larger than the others, a small auditorium with a stage. It was empty besides a guy, hunched over a baby grand piano wiping it down with a rag.

He was wearing cliché dark blue janitor overalls, spray bottles strapped to a belt around his waist. From what I could see, he had broad shoulders and a fiery red auburn mop of hair.

I could hear him humming softly to himself as he worked. The tone was melodious, drawing me in, and before I knew it I was stumbling down the aisle and up the stage to where he was.

He hadn't seemed to have noticed my presence, nor heard the loud racket I made when I accidentally knocked over a music stand in my tunnel-visioned walk to him. But the melodic sound of his voice, now louder, filled my head, turning it to fuzz. Like when I drank six shots of tequila that one time on a bet.

Without thinking, I reached out to touch this man, brushing my fingers lightly on his shoulder, startling him out of his work.

As if a drainage plug in my head had been pulled, all of the fuzziness seeped away, leaving me a little cold and shaky. Palms on either side of my head, I shook, confused as to what had just happened.

"Are you okay? Miss?"

A soft hand came to rest on my shoulder, making me jump, and the hand let go.

My eyes snapped up to meet a swirl of gray blue. The guy was standing in front of me, his arms extended towards me, palms up in the universal body language of someone approaching a dangerous animal.

I rubbed my face with my palms and replied though my hands, "I'm okay. I think I might just be coming down with something."

"I'm sorry, can you repeat that?"

I looked back up to him and repeated what I said, confused as to why he hadn't heard me the first time. I noticed how he watched my mouth instead of my eyes when I said it. Damn, the guy must be thirsty to be blatantly checking me out.

"That's not good, maybe you should sit down." Gently, he took my hand and guided me to the bench seat of the grand piano. "Your hands are freezing, and judging by your wet clothes I'd take a guess you were just out in the snow?"

I nodded. "Yeah, I walked here from the high school."

He crouched down to be eye level with me. "That's a two mile walk."

His voice was odd. Beautiful and soft, like the smooth tones of a harp but every few notes was a little off. As if he had some sort of speech impediment.

I shrugged. "I didn't really have another way of getting here."

It was in that moment that I realized his hand was still holding mine, its warmth seeping into me. I was torn, my nature wanting me to pull away but also not wanting to lose that warmth. With a squeeze, my attention was brought back to the man attached to that hand.

Getting a better look at him, I would say he was around the same age as Percy, early to mid twenties, with a nice dusting of scruff on his jaw. I wanted to touch that scruff, feel its prickliness against my palm. His eyes — which were again staring at my lips — looked tired and were accompanied by dark half-moon bags.

I gently tugged my hand out of his and scooted off the bench to gain some distance.

Looking at him I said, "My name's Atalanta. Dorris said I would be helping you with the cleaning starting today."

"Darn that woman. I told her I didn't want any help," He grumbled and stood.

"She said you were stubborn. Insisting you do all the work yourself when you didn't need to."

He blew an exasperated sigh and ran his fingers through his hair. "Of course she did."

"I promise I'll work hard. Besides, I already filled out the paperwork." I bit my lip and began to fiddle with the jacket sleeves.

He studied me for a few moments before sighing. "All right, let me show you around. My name is Theseus by the way."

"Theseus, that makes a little more sense," I chuckled.

He tilted his head like a curious puppy. "What did Dorris say my name was?"

"Thesis. Like the thesis of a paper," I smiled.

He returned the smile which quickly turned to laughter that he smothered with his hands. When his shoulders stopped shaking, he said, "Some people call me Thesis. I think it's easier for them to pronounce."

He collected a bucket off the floor and once again took my hand, guiding me down the steps of the stage and out of the music hall.

I wondered why he kept taking my hand, far too familiar with a stranger than he should be. I also wondered why I wasn't weirded out by his casual touching. Perhaps it was the warm tingles I kept getting with each touch, different to the shivers I usually received. My mind warred with my body on this. I wanted to pull away and berate him, but there was something that told me to continue holding that hand.

We wandered down the hall as he told me a little bit about the community center. How it was the gathering place for most of the town's activities, from health and safety classes to Friday night bingo. The high school swim team practiced here, as the center was the only place with a decent enough pool—and yes, part of my job would be to clean it.

He eventually let go of my hand as he pulled out keys to open up one of the art rooms I had seen earlier. "As for the art classes, we try to encourage them to clean up after themselves as they tend to get pretty messy, but trust me when I say that you'll still be mopping up plenty of paint and clay."

He moved into the room, his back towards me as he opened up a few of the cabinets to show me what went inside of them. "Often people don't put things back in the right space, so you might get a complaint every once in awhile asking 'where did you put this?' when really they are the ones that screwed up. Don't take it to heart, some of the older folk here don't have very good memories. I just politely show them where I put it. Though, the bratty ones I just let try and find it on their own."

"Do they hold art classes here every night?" I asked as I picked up a paintbrush out of a tin full of them and stroked its soft bristles.

But he didn't answer. Looking over at him, I noticed he had moved on to a storage closet, showing how they kept extra easels and a few folding chairs in there and how it wasn't something I really needed to pay much attention to, but might have to reorganize every once in a while.

"Theseus?" I called.

Again, no answer.

Brows scrunched in confusion, I tried something out of pure instinct. I gently knocked over the tin full of brushes. It clattered to the floor with a racket, the brushes scattering everywhere.

He didn't even flinch. Finally, he turned away from the closet to look at me and noticed the mess I had just created. His own brow furrowed to match mine, his mouth turning downward as well.

"What happened?" he asked.

I noticed that the moment he asked the question his eyes went from to the floor to my face, specifically my lips.

My eyebrows shot up, and I gaped at him, feeling like a complete idiot in my epiphany. "You're deaf, aren't you?"

He gave a weary smile and ran his hands through his hair. "That I am."

My mouth hung open in horror. "I'm so sorry! This whole time with the touching and the almost obsessive way you kept staring at my lips. I just thought you were…well…"

"A weirdo? Perhaps a creep? It's okay; it's partially my fault. I don't tend to tell people right off. It makes things more awkward. Hi, I'm Theseus, by the way, I can't hear. And then I just get gift baskets of pity, and it really slows down the conversation like what I'm ordering for lunch." He chuckled so light-heartedly it only made me feel worse.

"I mean, you speak so well. I thought deaf people couldn't—" God, there I went again putting my foot in my mouth.

"Some of us can, some of us can't." He shrugged. "It's harder for those who were born deaf. I wasn't. Lost my hearing about seven years ago in an accident. So, a couple of speech therapy lessons, lots of lip reading practice, and boom! You hearing folk are often none the wiser."

I couldn't help but laugh despite how horrible I felt. He had a refreshing sense of humor.

"I'm sorry if the touching weirded you out. I try not to automatically assume someone's following me. And with you not knowing your way around and me not being able to hear you…it was the easiest way…to, um."

"So you hold lots of girls hands?" I teased, trying to hold back a smile.

He tilted his head. "Well, maybe I just wanted to hold yours."

I nodded, bringing my sleeved hand up to cover my smile.

There was something about this guy that drew me in. I didn't know what, but for once I was looking forward to working.

After cleaning up my mess, we continued our tour of the facility. Over on the left side of the building, there was the sports center with the pool, a small gym, and a basketball court. Thesis showed me how to operate the pool vacuum and check the filter. Now that I knew he was deaf, I tried my hardest to remember to make sure we were looking directly at each other every time I asked a question. I had slipped up several times, luckily only embarrassing myself.

I was surprised to learn that the pool used a saltwater filtration system instead of the standard chlorine tablets. When I asked him why, he only shrugged it off, claiming that the town wanted a more natural pool. My father had done pool work for a while when we lived down south, and I knew the maintenance and cost to make a salt water pool that large had to be pretty expensive. For a town that struggled so much, I was surprised they would pour all their money into something like that rather than making the town look better for tourists.

I shook my head. Why would it matter to me where these people threw their money? I probably wouldn't be here for more than a few months anyway.

Finally done with my tour and subsequent teaching a couple of hours later, we ended up back in the front lobby. Dorris was typing away on her computer, but it was painstakingly obvious that she was spying on us. Every few moments or so, I would watch her out of the corner of my eye nonchalantly turn in our direction and pick up an empty glass, pretending to take a sip from it.

I felt a warm hand on my shoulder, bringing my attention back to the handsome man in front of me.

"So, I'll see you tomorrow? For work, I mean," He asked.

I smiled and nodded. "After I get out of school I'll be right over, and you can put me to work."

He matched my smile. "I wouldn't be so eager. I'll probably have you scrubbing toilets."

"Hey, money is money," I replied with a shrug.

"I'm surprised, though. I would have figured you would go for the daycare. I doubt most girls your age would choose being a janitor over playing with kids."

I shook my head, confused. "But I thought that the position was filled. By the mayor's daughter. At least, that's what Dorris told me."

"I did hear Lidia got dragged into working here, but there were two positions open."

I looked over my shoulder to see Dorris happily whistling to herself, pretending to be none the wiser to our conversation. That little sneak. I believe she was playing matchmaker.

When I looked back at Theseus, I think he realized it as well because he was avoiding looking at me, the peaks of his cheeks a rosy red.

I tapped his chest to get him to look back at me. "I would have rather been a janitor than change some kid's diapers anyway."

I watched as he read my lips. The smile he gave was infectious.

Looking out the window, I groaned when I saw that it was snowing pretty heavily now. I wouldn't be able to walk back. If I was lucky, Cal was still in town and hadn't reached the cabin yet.

"I need to call for my ride," I said before walking a few feet away and pulling the burner phone from my pocket.

"Snicker Doodles," came Cal's voice on the other end of the line.

"Fort Knox," I replied.

"Hey, little sis, what's up?"

"I wanted to know if you made it back to the cabin already. If not, you think you can give me a ride?" I asked hoping the answer was yes.

She hissed. "I'm sorry, hun. I got back to the cabin about an hour ago. But I can still come to get you."

"No, don't. It's snowing pretty hard right now. I'd rather hitch a ride than have you fling yourself off the road like last time."

"I did not fling myself off the road. I only skidded...a little."

"This is what we get for not having two cars. Do you know when we need to go get Dad from the fishing yard?" I asked, figuring I could stay here until she had to come back into town and hoped the weather was better by then.

She clicked her tongue. "He called me earlier to tell me he'd be out on some salmon run with this guy for a couple of days. Said the guy would give him seven hundred for helping him out."

"That's good that he found something, even if it is temporary."

"He mentioned seeing an old boat with a for-sale sign. Thought it might be a good idea to get it so he could go out on his own to catch instead of relying on someone's handout," She said, sounding a little exasperated.

I rolled my eyes. "He's too proud. You know that means we will probably have to help him if he does buy that boat right?"

"I hate fishing," she pouted.

"Yeah, but you like food on the table more," I added.

"You know I don't like it when you're right."

I pulled the phone away from my face to look at the date on the screen. Bringing it back I said, "It's okay, in a couple more weeks we will be able to get our allowance from Sam, and we won't have to worry about it as much."

"Oh, ye' old reliable Sam. I would assume that you got that job today?" she asked.

I glanced over at Thesis, who stood staring out the window with this peaceful smile. Seeing him like that, I couldn't help but smile as well.

"Yeah, I got the job."

"Good, get home safe, okay?"

"Okay," I replied, hanging up.

I groaned and walked over to Theseus.

Noticing me, he stopped looking out the window and faced me. "Judging by that frown, I'd say your ride isn't coming?"

"Unfortunately no," I said crossing my arms over my chest. "I'll have to hitch a ride. Do you think Dorris would-"

"I can take you," he offered.

My eyebrows shot up. "You can drive?"

He rolled his eyes. "Of course I can drive. Damn, and you were doing so good."

"So good with what?"

"Not asking the stupid questions. Most people ask all sorts of stupid questions and act weird when they realize I can't hear, like slowing their speech or speaking loudly, as if that would magically make me hear them," he mimicked, slowing his voice down and then raising his volume before returning to normal. "But you didn't do that. You even knew to look at me when I spoke to you."

"Oh," With a closed fist, thumb on the outside, I rubbed my chest clockwise in a circle. "I'm sorry if I seemed rude."

His eyes widened, and as he spoke he signed along with his words, "You know ASL?"

I shook my head. "Very little. Back in middle school, I had this girl in one of my classes who was born deaf. She couldn't speak, but it's how I knew not to do the slow speech thing and how to get your attention. I didn't really get much of a chance to learn sign language, though."

A smile spread slowly across his face. "Well, there's always a chance to learn, and I can teach you if you want."

"I'll look forward to it then."

He nodded, his face lighting up even brighter. "Let me just go get my keys, and I'll take you home."

He hurried off to the office behind the desk, and I certainly was not checking out his overall-clad ass. I certainly had more dignity than to do that. Slowly, my eyes traveled over to Dorris, who was staring at me with this sly smile.

With the blush slapping my face, I spun and faced the door.

INTO THE SEAS EMBRACE

I was not just caught checking out his ass! Nope. Because I'm not that kind of girl.

"Ready to go?" Thesis said after coming back out of the office and wiggling his keys at me.

I nodded and followed behind him out the door and to his car.

Okay! Okay! I WAS checking out his ass.

Chapter Seven

Theseus

Not for the first time in the last seven years was I disappointed by my condition. It had been a difficult transition from hearing to deaf, of course. Having to relearn how to live my life and such, but I had mostly adjusted. That was until I met someone new, someone I wanted to get to know and had to be reminded I would never hear their voice, never hear their laughter or their sorrow.

Atalanta was one of those people.

She seemed down to earth and I was drawn to her from the moment I saw her standing there with me on that stage.

Yet while she seemed to feel the same way towards me — as she kept close and didn't shy away from my touch — I knew it wasn't real.

She had heard my voice, heard me singing when she came to meet me in the music room, and there was no doubt in my mind she had been affected. That was to say I felt terrible for manipulating her will but I knew the effects would wear off in a few days. So that immediate trust I knew she felt would also fade.

I was determined to work extra hard to gain her trust the natural way, and the first step to that was insisting I take her home. There was no way I would allow for someone to walk God knows how far in this mess, especially when they weren't wearing clothes fit for the harsh winters of Argos.

Sauntering out of the community center, I headed towards my car in the parking lot, glancing behind me several times to make sure she had followed. I wanted to reach out and hold her hand, pull her close to me to be sure she stayed by my side, but I knew I needed to stop doing that.

Unlocking the car, I quickly moved to the passenger side to open the door for her. When I looked at her face, I saw that her eyes were somewhere off to my left. Following them, I spotted a man walking up the path from the forest behind the library.

"That's Percy, the librarian," I commented, my eyes flicking between Percy and Atalanta.

I caught her lips moving and focused on them.

'-The other day.'

"What about the other day?" I asked.

She turned her head back to face me. 'I met him the other day when I donated some books.'

I watched as her eyes moved away from mine to look back towards Percy. There was a pang of sadness in her eyes, and I couldn't help but get a little defensive for her. I knew Percival could be a brash man and had no doubt he said something to Atalanta to upset her within the first few moments of meeting him.

But then to my surprise, Atalanta waved at Percy, seeming to call his name to get his attention. Her smile was wide like a fox as she stared at him. It made my stomach drop. Perhaps she wasn't saddened by something he had said.

'Have you started reading that book I gave you?' she asked.

I looked back over to Percy who had spotted us by the car.

'No, I have not.' he replied.

My gaze flicked back and forth between the two to follow their conversation. She berated him, calling him a...book snob? Which he seemed to laugh at, considering the shaking of his chest. He proceeded to say something along the lines of 'I'm not a teenage girl, so why would you think I would like a book for one?'

I had never seen him look so happy. Oh. My. God. He was flirting with her! I could see the signs, clear as day, as he fidgeted awkwardly. His eyebrows were raised in a quizzical expression while he would go from both hands in his pockets to one hand messing with his hair, which was out of its usual ponytail and laying loose around his shoulders.

Damn it! My chances of getting Atalanta to notice me were slipping away in front of my eyes.

It was then that Percy seemed to have noticed me standing next to the car. That millimeter smile he wore dropped completely from his face, and the fidgeting stopped.

I watched as the same expression cycle he always had whenever he saw me crossed his face. Indignation, remembrance, then finally guilt.

With a curt nod to me, he said goodbye to Atalanta and fled back into his library.

Appearing confused at his sudden mood change, Atalanta turned back towards me. 'What's his problem?'

I shrugged, schooling my features so to not show my own guilt and annoyance. "I don't know. Maybe he remembered something he forgot."

I watched as she read me like an open book, her hazel brown eyes intense, seeing right into me with this expression that said she had seen plenty of shit in her life and my bullshit wasn't anything new. But then she shrugged, as if it ultimately didn't matter to her one way or another, and got into the car.

I sighed at the fact that this whole getting her to trust me thing didn't start off as well as I had hoped. I got in on the driver's side and pulled out of the parking lot.

Carefully, I watched her hand signals and the road to navigate us just out of town and up into the mountain heading towards the ocean. Once I realized what road she was taking us to, my eyebrows couldn't help but scrunch. It was the way to the Winchester Cabin. That place was a wreck, probably one of the oldest buildings in the area. I knew the mayor owned the property and the last I spoke to him about it, he had said he planned to tear down the shack and rebuild it.

When we pulled up to the driveway, I saw that the mayor hadn't done diddly squat with the cabin. It was still as rundown as the last time I heard about it.

"You know Atalanta, I know a few of the carpenters in town that would be happy to help you fix up the place," I said, unable to stop myself.

She stiffened. 'No. It's okay. My father is really handy and he likes fixing up old homes.'

"Alright, but if he wants any help with it, I'd be happy to."

The relaxed expression she had had until now was stony. I realized she was probably offended by me basically calling her new home a dump.

The damage done, she grabbed her backpack from between her legs and began to get out of the car.

'I'll tell him. Thank you for giving me a ride, hopefully it wont become a habit.' She said before slamming the door behind her, judging by how much the car rocked with the force of it.

I sighed. "You done goofed this one up man."

I made a point to try to think of ways to make it up to her tomorrow when she came in.

Chapter Eight

Atalanta

I practically sprinted to the door of the cabin before slipping behind the old wood and leaning against it.

"Way too intense," I sighed.

Today had been full of unexpected encounters. I was ready to just go to sleep on my cot and try to forget the whole thing.

"I'll say! Did you actually look at the guy you just ran from? Because he was H. O. T. Hot!"

I jumped a little and turned to see Cal standing near one of the windows, a wide grin plastered on her face.

My mouth agape, I replied, "I didn't...well, maybe. But I had a good reason!"

"And that would be?" She asked, one eyebrow cocked, hands on her hips.

"He was getting too curious. Wanted to help fix the house."

Her smile dropped. "Oh." She looked out the window, and we both watched as his car made an awkward U-turn and drove away. "Well, that's not too bad. At least he wasn't actually asking questions. You turned him down, right?"

I nodded. "Yeah. I feel a little bad though. I think I probably came off a bit harsh. I panicked. He might think I hate him now."

"I doubt that! I saw the way he stared at you. Practically devouring your mouth with his eyes." She said, wiggling her eyebrows suggestively.

"What, do you have eagle vision? He was checking out my mouth so he could read my lips. He's deaf."

Her eyebrows shot up. "Really?"

"Yeah, so don't get your hopes up."

I walked into the bare living room space and stuck my bag near the lit fireplace. The heat of the fire created a bubble of warmth inside the house that made me almost giddy to curl up in with a book and read. Then I remembered I didn't have any books to curl up with anymore and my sour mood darkened.

"I don't know, even if he was reading your lips there was interest on that boy's face."

"You're crazy. I doubt you could see that from here."

"Do you doubt the almighty Calilope?!" She boomed in an attempt at a god-like voice, her arms raised out at her sides.

I rolled my eyes. "Yes I do, you doofus. Now, come help me with dinner."

We worked in a comfortable camaraderie for a while as we meandered around the kitchen, opening and closing the fridge and the cupboard several times, trying to figure out what to make for dinner with what little we had. Eventually we got into an argument about salad or chicken fajitas before compromising to make a chicken fajita salad, which we managed not to burn or destroy! Go us!

As we ate our success of a meal together in Cal's room on her cot, I recounted to her the day's events. The weird salt thing with Jason, being tricked by Hip, and being utterly oblivious to Theseus's condition and making a fool of myself.

"You met a lot of guys today. You little minx," She teased, doing a little cat claw and 'meow' at me. "Do you think any of them are prom date-worthy?"

"Whoa, Cal, I just met these guys today! None of them under very romantic circumstances, I might add."

"Oh, perhaps that Percy guy then? He was pretty cute too. Maybe ask him?"

"You have a one track mind," I got up off her cot with my empty bowl and went to go put the dish in the sink. "I'm done talking about boys."

"Fine, fine. I'm sorry. You know I live vicariously through you," She pouted, following me into the kitchen.

I laughed. "Cal, you could easily get any guy you want. Why do you need to live through me?"

"Because I'm lazy?"

I tapped her on the tip of her nose. "Methinks you're afraid of commitment."

"Am not!" she shrieked.

"Sure, just keep telling yourself that," I said, patting her shoulder.

"Whatever," She shoved me, making us both break out into a fit of giggles.

"I spotted a path down the cliff to the beach. You wanna go check it out?" Cal asked after our laughter died down.

I thought about going back out there into the cold. I really didn't want to, but I found myself nodding anyway.

"Sure, let me just put on better clothes."

I had yet to change out of my slightly damp hoodie and was surprised I wasn't shivering to death. Rushing into my room, I pulled off the cold clothes and yelped when the even colder air hit me. Despite the clothes being damp, they collected my heat like a shitty furnace! Now shivering, I rummaged through the boxes and found one of Dad's coats, one of those giant poofy ones with the fur-lined hood. Shrugging, I pulled it on and changed my pants and socks. No sense in taking a shower yet.

We went outside, and I followed Cal towards the same spot I had been standing the other night when I saw the sea monster and its freaky glow. She directed us to a somewhat hidden path that led down the cliff face and onto an untamed beach.

Large hunks of driftwood scattered along the shore with rough boulders displaced against the soft peppery sand. The waves rushed in with a force that warned me to not to get too close. The sky was beginning to darken as the sun ticked closer to the water. I spied a dock not far off. If it was in good condition, it would make a good spot to fish at a safe distance from the rough waves.

Cal sprinted ahead of me towards the water laughing. "It's been so long since we went to the beach!"

"I wouldn't do that! I bet that water is freezing!" I called after her.

Disregarding me, she ran up to the water to touch it, only to come flying backwards spewing *"cold cold cold cold cold cold!"*, to which I only rolled my eyes at her stupidity.

We strolled along the shore for an hour or two before heading back to the cabin, too cold to stay out any longer.

I sat waiting on my cot for Cal to finish up her 45-MINUTE-LONG SHOWER.

"Cal, you didn't use all the hot water, right?" I called to her.

"Hop in and find out!" she shouted back.

"Bitch!"

That night after chasing Cal around in my towel for using all the hot water and causing me to take an icicle shower, we lay together on the floor of the living room after setting up an impromptu blanket fort. It was something we often did when our dad was gone.

I turned away from the crackling embers. "Do you ever think about Mom? Like what she might be doing right now?"

Cal was silent for several moments before she answered.

"...Go to sleep Atty."

With that, Cal turned her back to me, leaving me to fall into a fitful sleep featuring shadowy faces in dark corners.

***

So on it went, my first two weeks in the small town of Argos. A simple pattern: wake up at 6am to get ready for school, cursing the person who ever thought holding classes so early in the morning was a good idea as I chugged down a cup and a half of coffee before attending my first classes of the day. Once lunch rolled around, I would awkwardly huddle at a table in the back of the cafeteria observing the other students interact with each other.

There were a few times I saw Hip coming out of the lunch line. Often, he would spot me in my corner but then would only smile and give a small wave before going off with his friends. He would talk to me in class, making a point to include me with the others. I found out he lived on an apple farm, which was really cool. Once class was over, though, we would head our separate ways, me not wanting to admit I didn't want to see him go.

Jason, on the other hand, would just disappear any time I saw him, as if he was avoiding me like the plague, until he had no choice but to sit near me in class. I'd see him in the hall, we would make eye contact, and then he'd just spin in the other direction and walk off. Then it was an awkward eye dance in class. I would glance at him, but he would be already staring at me, and then quickly look away. If I tried to strike up a conversation, he would talk to me, but it was strained and filled with detachment.

He was probably put off by my attitude with him on that first day. I felt terrible. Yeah, the salt water thing was weird, but I shouldn't have been a bitch like that to him. It's not like he had actually done anything wrong.

It was lonely, but nothing I wasn't used to.

My real salvation was once school had ended, I would head to either the community center to work with Thesis or to the library to bug Percy.

"So, she just accepts that he's an alien? Just like that?" Percy asked incredulously, looking up from one of the books I had given him to read.

I shrugged, continuing to scan the pages of my chemistry textbook. "Well, by this point she's already in love with him even if she doesn't realize it. That, combined with the fact that she already suspected something, makes it easier for her to process the truth."

"What kind of asinine logic is that? Not only has he been lying to her this whole time, but he could end up killing her," he scoffed.

I looked up at him from my spot in the giant cozy leather chair I had claimed as my own. Percy was at his desk across from me looking somewhat exasperated. I couldn't help but giggle. He may not want to admit it yet, but he was getting hooked on these books.

"That's love. Accepting a person for who *and* what they are."

"Sounds like a fantasy to me," came a voice to my left.

My eyes snapped over to Jason, who stood with a cart full of disorganized books that needed to be put back in their place. The lanyard around his neck identified him as an employee at the library. Percy had a similar lanyard, though I'd only ever seen him wear it once.

"Fantasy is a necessary ingredient in living. It's a way of looking at life through the wrong end of a telescope, and that enables you to laugh at life's realities," I shot back at him.

He crossed his arms over his chest and quirked an eyebrow at me. "Did you just quote Dr. Seuss?"

"He was a real visionary," I smiled and continued to look him dead in the eyes, challenging him.

"I don't believe you've met," Percy inserted himself into our standoff. "This is my library assistant, Jason. He's been busy with student council this past week, so he hasn't been to work."

"We've met," Jason and I say at the same time. His voice filled with a little more hostility than I was expecting.

"We share a couple of classes together," I mumble, breaking eye contact with the jerk.

"Ah, I should have guessed. Well, I think I'm done with this piece of tra-" He quickly looked at me before continuing, "-fine literature. I think I'll go file some paperwork."

Percy stood from his chair and heaved up his arms in a very lazy stretch, which showed off the muscles in his torso far too well. I could hardly pull my eyes away until I glanced at Jason and caught something I probably shouldn't have. He was staring at Percy as well, and his expression was definitely not one of a straight man staring at another man.

My eyes strayed downwards, and no sir would a straight man have a hard-on while looking at Percy right now.

So, he was gay?

I felt a small pang of disappointment before shaking it off and standing as well.

"I should see about hitching a ride back to my house, then. If you're not gonna stick around for me to bother."

"Oh, I'll take you home if you would like," Percy offered.

I quirked an eyebrow at him. "Weren't you about to go file some papers or something?"

He waved his hand. "They can wait. I couldn't in good conscience let a young woman walk home alone in this weather."

I snorted and crossed my arms. "Such a gentleman. Where did that come from?"

"I've never not been a-"

His words were interrupted by a ringing phone on his desk. Quickly, Percy hurried over to pick it up, his tone no longer cordial and polite but taking on the harshness I had come to familiarize myself with. I guess you could say his voice was like felt; it was only smooth if you rubbed it the right way.

"I apologize, Atalanta, but I need to take care of this. Jason, can you take the young woman home?"

Jason stiffened and looked like he wanted to protest but decided against it and shuffled off to get his keys.

When he came back, I waved him off. "I can walk or get Theseus to take me home."

Theseus had been kind enough to take me home on the days that Cal hadn't been able to pick me up. Luckily, there were no hard feeling for the way I had acted that day. In fact, he had been extremely kind to me these past couple weeks, with taking me home, showing me the ropes at the community center, and he even brought me doughnuts once before my shift. I was starting to think that Cal had been right in assuming Theseus had some kind of crush on me.

"I'm taking you home," Jason grunted, walking out the door ahead of me.

INTO THE SEAS EMBRACE

I waved a goodbye to Percy and followed after Jason as he trudged his way toward a red sedan. Without a word, he opened up the door for me before jogging to the other side and hopping in. Slightly uncomfortable, I slid into his passenger seat and shut the door as softly as I could.

"I'm sorry about this, I know you didn't want to do this."

"Who said I didn't want to do this?" He asked, definitely looking annoyed.

I shrugged. "Well, I assumed with the...you know."

He turned his head towards me his brows turned downward. "No, I don't know."

"That, right there!" I pointed to his face. "That frown and the grumbly thing you've got going on."

"I don't have a grumbly thing going on!"

"Do too," I shot back.

He huffed. "I'm sorry. It's just that...you make me uncomfortable."

I blinked, taken aback. I made him uncomfortable? Was that why he had been avoiding me?

"Is this because of that first day? Because I am sorry about that, I shouldn't have acted like a bitch towards you."

"No," he exhaled. "Though you were a bit of a bitch, but no, that's not why."

"Is it because of Percy?" I asked, my voice small as I tried to broach the subject lightly, though I didn't possess much tact.

His head snapped to face me, his eyes wide. "What?"

"...Because you have a crush on him."

"How did you?!" He coughed, halting his words. "I mean, no I don't."

I rolled my eyes. "It's 2019, Jason. Being gay is probably the most normal thing you can be nowadays."

"I'm not gay," he said, his tone clipped.

"Jason, seriously, it's okay. Percy is a very good-looking guy, but if you have feelings for him, I won't encroach upon your territory, or at least try not to. I can't help if Percy feels anything for me, but I'll try not to...I just don't want you to feel intimidated by me or anything."

I knew I was rambling, but this was just so awkward, and I really didn't know what to say to the guy.

"Oh, for fuck's sake," he groaned.

Jason slammed on the breaks, jerking us to a stop, threw the car into park and turned towards me. Without any warning, he leaned forward and pressed his lips to mine.

His lips were so warm and far softer than I would have imagined. Then, when he touched my cheek and tilted my head to deepen the kiss? Oh, he tasted like chocolate.

I sunk into his touch and kissed him back with reverence, starved for this unthreatening intimacy. Gripping his shirt, I pulled him just a little bit closer. All too quickly he pulled away, his thumb stroking my cheek.

"That's why I've felt uncomfortable." His voice was breathy, eyes a little wide, and lips parted in such a way that made me want to tug him back to me.

"Because you wanted to kiss me?" I asked, my voice just as breathy.

He leaned back in, brushing his lips against mine for a much more chaste kiss.

"Because I...there are certain expectations in my family and I'm not really allowed," He sighed and cursed under his breath. "I can't really get into it."

My eyebrows shot up. "Oh my god. Is this because I'm black?"

"What?!" he shot ramrod straight and looked me dead in the eyes. "Of course not!"

"Then what?" I asked skeptically as I crossed my arms.

"I like you. You've got this...spark. My mother's family though, they are really strict and expect certain things from me."

"And you let your family control who you can and can't be interested in?"

"No."

"Really? Because that's what this sound like,"

He deflated. "Okay yes."

"I'm not about to tell you how to live your life, Jason. We hardly know each other. But I will say that letting other people control your life? It's not worth it. You'll be much happier taking hold of your own future."

He chuckled. "You say it like you have experience."

My brain stalled for a moment as I couldn't really tell him why I knew he would be happier without someone controlling his life. Luckily, the first thing that came to mind seemed to work.

"A reader lives a thousand lives before he dies. The man who never reads lives only one," I blurted out, sounding a lot wiser than I intended.

"Who said that one?" he asked, tilting his head, a small smile playing his lips.

"The great George R. R. Martin."

"Ah, the man of many stories…get it? Because he goes into the backstory of everything?"

I rolled my eyes. "Yes, I got it."

Jason giggled, yes, *giggled*, for a few moments at his own joke. When he stopped, he was looking at me like he wanted to devour me. He probably would have, if a car didn't honk at us to move. With a sigh, he shifted the car back into drive.

We sat in slightly uncomfortable silence for a few moments. My mind was racing thinking about Jason and his kiss, curious about what was up with his family. I wanted to ask, but it wasn't my place to go poking around even if I wanted to.

Not wanting to suffer in the awkward silence any longer, I spewed out the first thing that came to mind. "So, *do* you have a crush on Percy? I know you said you weren't gay, it's just that I kind of saw...well."

I bit my lip and pointed to his crotch.

He followed my finger and groaned. "Fucking hell, woman. Fine! Yes, I have a crush on Percy! Have for a long time."

"Does he know?"

He sighed. "This is really weird, you know. I just kissed you and you're focused on my crush on another man?"

"I'm sorry," I squeaked. "I don't get kissed often! Especially by guys I don't actually know that well, and I thought hated me until like a minute ago!"

Jason opened and closed his mouth several times, trying to look for something to say but coming up with nothing.

We were silent for a few more moments before he finally said. "I'm sorry. For avoiding you, I mean. I didn't really know what to do about the crush I was developing, so I just kind of ran like a coward," He licked his lips, drawing my attention to them. "As for Percy...no, he doesn't know. I'm pretty sure he sees me only as a kid, and I wouldn't really be allowed to date him anyway."

He looked really sad in that moment. I could only imagine what it was like to not only have the weight of your family rejecting your feelings, but also to have your crush thinking of you as a child.

I wanted to reach out and touch him. I felt that was a tad too intimate though, so instead I just smiled. "Thank you for apologizing." I paused before adding "I'm sorry about Percy."

The odd tension between us settled, and we drove the rest of the way back to my house in comfortable silence between my directions.

When we parked, he turned to me and said, "You're right."

"Of course I'm right... What am I right about?"

"I shouldn't let what my family might think get in the way of the things that I want. Atalanta, will you go out on a date with me this Saturday?" he asked, his face adorably bashful as his cheeks blushed and his mouth turned up into an adorable smile.

"A date?" I squeaked.

"Yeah, we could get to know each other better and I could show you that I'm more than just a jerk who lets his family push him around."

Seeing as how I had no real life, I was undoubtedly free this Saturday, but I needed to consider the implications of going on this date. He wanted me to get to know him better and, assuming there would be a quid pro quo, I would probably have to give something of myself in return. I could certainly pull it off if I was careful enough and studied Atalanta North's history packet. I really wanted to go on this date and, knowing Cal would certainly encourage it, I smiled and agreed.

Chapter Nine

Atalanta

The next day at school was a pleasant one. Instead of ignoring me, Jason actually sought me out between classes, including me in conversations during the classes I had with him and even invited me to sit with him, Margo, and Davie during lunch. They chose to sit outside for some strange reason, instead of inside where it was nice and warm. It was a lot quieter though, so that was a plus.

This was also the first time I really got to see Davie and Margo together. They were almost a sickly adorable. When they traded lunch with each other Jason and I shared a similar look that said, 'gag me, they're too cute'.

Jason had to ruin it when he noticed I didn't have lunch.

Jason tilted his head towards my backpack. "Did you not bring anything?"

"I, um, ate it during study hall." I said, trying to keep my face as natural as possible.

Of course, I wasn't going to tell him that all we had at my house were cup noodles, instant mac and cheese, a head of lettuce, and Pizza Bites. Luckily for the three of us, Cal and I would be getting paid this week, and we were also expecting a wire transfer from Sam. So, we would be able to fill our pantry with more than just crap. Right on time too, as Dad would be coming back from his third fishing voyage with that guy, whose name I finally learned was Larry.

Jason laughed. "That hungry, huh? Would you like a bite from my lunch?"

I took a quick look at his meal of a tuna sandwich, bag of chips and that damn jug of water he always carried. I may have forgone asking about it, but that didn't mean I didn't notice he still had it with him at all times.

I shook my head. "No, it's alright. I'm actually full from scarfing down my own lunch."

Of course, my stomach chose that moment to betray me with a loud growl. But I guess Jason didn't notice as he just nodded and went back to his meal. Stupid stomach, almost blowing my cover!

When lunch was over, Jason and Margo walked with me to English. Mr. K gave a long but thankfully interesting lecture on the differences between Old, Middle, and Modern English and why people kept mixing up that old garble that was Beowulf with modern Shakespeare. My stomach rumbled the whole class, and I regretted not taking Jason up on his offer, even if I disliked tuna.

"So, how are you liking Mr. Stevens and his invigorating lecture on radiants?" Jason asked, the sarcasm dripping off of him.

We had just finished English and Jason had kindly escorted me the five feet down the hallway to math.

115

I rolled my eyes. "It's so exciting. Can't you tell? I'm practically jumping to go in there and fall asleep."

As Jason smiled, his chest shook from trying to contain his laughter. "I bet. I think I have something to help keep you awake."

He reached into the ragged satchel around his shoulder and pulled out a book. As he passed it over to me, I read the title.

"I didn't expect you to be a vampire lover."

He crossed his arms, his smile turning into a playful pout. "So what if I am? Are you gonna make fun of me for it?"

"No," I shook my head. "Well, only if you like the kind of vampires that sparkle."

"Nope, I have higher standards than that. This one's a good book, I'm sure you'll like it," he said, tapping on the book's cover.

The minute bell rang, signaling us to hurry to class before the final ring.

"Hide it behind your textbook and Stevens will never notice," Jason said as he hurried away.

I waved him goodbye and headed into math. Jason was right, it was a good book. At least from what I read of it in class.

Before gym class started, I ran into Hip outside of the locker room. He was leaning against the wall, that easygoing smile plastered in place.

"Hey, Speedy, I didn't see you at lunch today," he said, his honey-rich voice dripping over me and warming my insides.

I smiled at the endearment, having gotten used to it pretty quickly. "I was having lunch with Jason and his friends."

"Jason, huh? Are you two an item now?"

Something sparked behind his eyes, which were a yellow green right now.

"Why ya' asking? Are you jealous?" I crooned.

"Perhaps I am," he said, his honey voice dropping an octave into seductive territory. His ever-changing eyes sparkled as he leaned in close to me. The smell of apples and wood wafted towards me.

Taken aback, I took a step away from him. Having him that close was overwhelming my senses and scrambling my brain.

For some reason, I felt this need to clarify.

"Jason and I aren't a thing," I actually saw Hip's shoulders sag ever so slightly in relief. Though I couldn't help the little jab of adding, "Yet."

"Well, I better up my game then," He said, taking my hand into his and leaning down to kiss it gently before turning around and walking into the male's locker room.

I held my sleeves up to my face because I couldn't stop smiling and walked into the girl's locker room. Hurrying along, I swapped my bag for the gym clothes and shoes I was able to get, thanks to Hip. Looking around, I could see that most of the girls were still here getting dressed.

Actually, a few of them were staring directly at me. The look on their faces weren't pleasant. A slight sneer to their lips and narrowing of the eyes made the happy feeling I had slowly leak away into trepidation. With quick glances back at them, I hastily made my way into the secluded and more private shower area of the locker room.

Tugging back the curtain, I shuffled into one of the shower stalls and made work of changing into my gym clothes. Luckily, there had been enough money left after getting the shoes to purchase some Under Armour online, so I wouldn't continue to get stares for wearing my long-sleeved shirts underneath the baggy gym shirt.

Pulling off my three layers, I swiftly got the form-fitting black nylon over my head fortunately before someone had the audacity to slide the privacy curtain back open.

Confused by the sound of the rings sliding against the metal bar, I turned around to see the three girls that had been glaring at me from the lockers.

"Can I help you?" I asked, being sure to tug the Under Armor all the way down.

"We just wanted to know why you were always coming back over here to change." One girl questioned. Her black hair was long and straight, like the woman from The Ring, her eyes like a snake's slits.

"I like my privacy," I muttered.

"But why do you always wear clothes under your uniform? It's not like it's cold in the gym," rebutted the girl to Snake Eyes' left.

Her hair was red but not a natural red, the deep store-bought kind, and she had way too much jewelry on. The clanking of bangles against rings and like ten other bracelets could be heard as she shifted.

The third girl was heavyset, a lot less bitchy-looking but her eyes said that she was out for blood. All three were annoyingly a good several inches taller than me.

What the hell did they want? Were they here to harass me about my changing preferences? Because that was some fucked up shit to be agitated about.

I shrugged nonchalantly. "The Under Armour helps with sweat. So I'm not walking around rest of the day smelling."

"You could just wear perfume," Snake Eyes leaned forward. "I'd say you could use some right now in fact. You smell like mold."

"I'll take that into consideration. Now, can I continue changing so we can get to class?"

"We want you to back off Jason. He's ours," Heavyset said, finally voicing the real reason for their intrusion.

I rolled my eyes. So that's what this was about? Were these some of the Jason fans Margo had been talking about?

I grabbed for the gym shirt and began to put it on. "I think Jason can decide who he hangs out with."

"Yeah, but you're only using him. We've seen the way you look at that clumsy idiot, Hip. Jason deserves better than some skank who doesn't know how to keep her pants on." Heavyset replied, her tone full of malice.

At that, Redhead, quick as a whip, reached out and tried to tug down my pants. But I was prepared. Just as fast, I grabbed the girl's wrist and twisted it at an awkward and most likely painful angle judging by the whimpering yelp she made.

"You bitch," Snake Eyes spat, grabbing for my hair and jerking me off my balance.

I let go of Redhead's wrist to dig my fingers into the hand, practically pulling my hair out of its scalp. Arms wrapped around my middle, constricting me and my movements. A feeling that was all too familiar bubbled up in my chest.

BANG!

'How does it feel, you little bitch?'

The vice-like arms wrapped around my torso were huge and covered in tattoos. The smell of freshly fired gun smoke singed my nostrils. Of course, that was before the pain of the bullet in my shoulder slammed into me, drowning out all my other senses.

I struggled against the arms that held me, desperately trying to get away from the pain in my shoulder, the pain of my hair being pulled. The arms weren't as strong as I remembered them. I jerked forward and back, feeling them loosen with my thrashing.

I have to get to Mom.

I have to stop them.

I kicked my left leg back like a horse, right into the stomach of my attacker.

Who was screaming? It certainly wasn't my captors.

A palm slammed hard into my cheek, the long fingernails scratching, leaving thin lines trailing behind. The shock of it made me pause, made me remember that I wasn't back in that house with Gypsy and her goons. I was in a shower with three crazy teenage girls no more threatening than baby sharks. Nothing compared to what I'd faced.

Head clear, I tightened my grip on Snake Eyes' hand, which was still gripping my hair, and spun my body, performing a similar maneuver to the one I had used on Redhead. The pain of her wrist twisting caused the bitch to let go of my hair. I kept my grip on that arm, and used it pull the girl towards me. With one well-aimed jab to her solar plexus, the girl was down for the count along with the other two, though I'm not entirely sure what happened to them.

I heaved a sigh, scooped up all my clothes, and walked out of the shower stall over the bodies of the three girls. I came face to face with at least ten other girls who were crowded together at the entrance to the showers, their eyes wide with fear and confusion. It was then that it hit me.

I had just assaulted three of my classmates, on school grounds, in front of a bunch of witnesses. It didn't matter that they started it, all that mattered was that I was walking away from their nearly unconscious forms with some minor scratches.

I was in deep shit.

Panic hitched into my lungs and I ran past the other girls clutching my clothes, not bothering to grab the rest of my stuff out of the locker as I dashed to the door. Banging the door open, I looked around seeing no one standing in the hallway, and just darted towards the exit sign. I thought I was in the clear, only to be stopped when someone walked out of the bathroom right into my frantic escape route. I slammed into a chest so hard I was thrown backward, landing hard on my ass.

"Ow! Watch where you're- Speedy?"

My head snapped up. Hip was standing in front of me, because my little weak self was the only damn one to get knocked over! I didn't have time for this. Scrambling to my feet, I continued my escape to the exit only to be tugged back by a calloused hand gripping mine.

"Whoa, whoa, where's the fire?" His smile fell, and eyes darkened as he looked at my face. "What happened to your cheek? Are you okay?"

His honey voice filled with concern, while mine was only filled with panic when I said, "Let go, Hip! I have to get out of here!"

INTO THE SEAS EMBRACE

His thumb stroked the back of my hand. "Not until you tell me what happened."

"Please," I begged, my eyes darting around. Sure that any second the teacher or other students would come out, looking for me, hunting me down.

I look up into his eyes which were now full of resolve.

"Let's go, then."

Hand still in mine, Hip turned towards the exit, tugging me along with him as we bolted down the hall and out of the school.

Chapter Ten

Hip

With her hand in mine, I pulled Atalanta out of the school. Anger bubbled in my stomach at seeing those red marks on her cheek. They would definitely bruise up.

Someone had attacked her, and once I got her to safety, I would find out who and I would turn their life into a living hell.

When I met her two weeks ago, I wouldn't have thought that I would be this protective of her. That first moment I spotted her in the hall mesmerized by Jason's voice, I was only trying to help out the poor new girl from making a fool of herself when I bumped her. But then I actually met Atalanta North. She was intelligent, and her observational skills almost rivaled my own.

Over the last couple of weeks, I tried to hold back from getting too close to her. I would see her sitting at the lunch table alone, watching everyone with those sharp eyes of hers and I would want to go over there and sit with her, but something would always stop me. Then today, I couldn't find her amongst the crowd and found out she had been with Jason. I couldn't really sit idly by without throwing my hat into the ring.

Tugging her along, I brought her over to my motorcycle. My pride and joy, a Honda Shadow I saved up for and bought from a guy in the next town over.

The poor thing had been in shambles, but with Grandpa's help I was able to fix her up.

Letting go of Atalanta's hand, I pulled my half helmet out of one of the saddle bags and placed it on her head, clipping the buckles.

Her eyes were wide, pupils dilated as she continued to panic.

"No, wait! Hip, my bag. My stuff. I can't."

"We can get it later."

"I'm in so much trouble," she groaned, her eyes darting back and forth, looking around for something that wasn't there. Like she thought wolves were after her.

I rubbed her arms and tried to get her to focus on me. "Hey, hey, hey. It's okay. Whatever happened, I'll take care of it. Now let me just get you out of here first."

"Okay," she nodded, her lip quivering. "I've never ridden a bike."

"You'll love it. Now just swing your leg over and I'll take your clothes,"

With trembling hands, she handed me her clothes and swung herself to straddle the back of the bike. Quickly, I shoved her clothes into one of saddle bags but then realized she was only in her thin gym clothes which was probably part of the reason for her shivering. Reaching into the opposite saddle bag, I dug out my riding jacket, black leather with a grey faux fur hoodie inside. Perfect for days like this.

I draped the jacket over her shoulders. After moments of watching her fumble with the zipper, her hands shaking, I put my hands gently over hers and assisted.

Hopping on the bike myself, I told her to hold on tight to me. At first, she hesitated, lightly gripping my sides. I rolled my eyes and with a smile I gripped her wrists and slid her hands around me, pulling her flush against my back.

Starting the bike, we took off out of the parking lot. I laughed at her initial squeal and clutching of my torso.

I loved it though, having her on the back of my bike. As we rode, I contemplated buying a helmet and jacket specifically for her. I ran the numbers in my head and I might be able to do it if I sold really well at the market these next couple of weeks.

I took Atalanta to one of my favorite places, a piece of land owned by my parents. In a small valley, between the sprawling hills and mountains of Argos, was an orchard full of apple trees. They were in hibernation for the winter, their leaves having already fallen, leaving the branches bare with the faint scent of apples still lingering in the air.

Not wanting to drive the bike through the soft snow-covered earth, I stopped along a pathway that lead through the orchard.

Hopping off the bike, I held out my hand for her. I was glad to see that while her eyes were still wide, they were beginning to fill with a little wonder, chasing away the panic and fear.

"Where are we?" she asked, taking my hand and casually sliding off my bike.

"One of the orchards my parents own."

She pulled the jacket closer to herself, almost hugging her middle. "Yes, you did tell me you lived on an apple farm. Not this one?"

"No, not this one. I think it's a bit too soon to be bringing you home just yet. I mean, this is our first date and all."

She chuckled, almost cracking a smile. "Aren't you supposed to give me flowers on the first date? You know, show up to my door with flowers, looking all nervous while my father glares at you with his shotgun. Please tell me you have some chocolate at least to make up for it."

I laughed and quickly scanned the ground in front of me. "Unfortunately, I didn't bring you any chocolate, buuut—" I snatched a flower off the ground and held it out to her. "I actually did bring some flowers for you."

The little white flower drooped ever so slightly, but the dew on it sparkled in the light.

"Oh, a snowdrop, I love snowdrops!" She exclaimed, her face finally lighting up.

 She took the little flower and held it to her chest lovingly.

"So that's what they're called?" I asked.

She nodded. "These little guys just pop right out of the snow just before it starts to melt for spring. One of the few kinds of flowers that can bloom in these conditions. This little fellow came out early."

"In the spring? I see these grow all over this valley in the winter," I said, gesturing to several other flowers that were beginning to break through the snow-covered earth.

"That's quite odd, they aren't really winter flowers," she replied, her brows furrowing.

I inhaled deeply and looked around. It was a beautiful sight. One of those rare days where you could see the blue in the sky as the gray and white clouds broke apart as they drifted across the sky. The breeze smelled like apples with a bite of winter air. Despite the branches of the trees being bare, the snow that lay on top of them twinkled in the small rays of sunlight, making them look just as breathtaking as when they were full of leaves and fruit.

"This land is full of magic," I whispered.

I gently placed my hand on the small of her back and guided her through the trees.

"So, do you want to tell me what happened?"

She inhaled and blew out a slow breath. "These girls in our class happened. They cornered me when I was changing, and it got violent."

"They are the ones that did that?" I asked, gesturing to the deep scratches along her cheek. They had swollen a bit in the last twenty minutes.

"Yeah," she gingerly touched her cheek. "Though you should have seen what I did to them."

I chuckled. "So, like a 'you think this is bad you should see the other guy' thing?"

A small smile graced her lips. "I guess."

Despite my lightheartedness, the anger continued to roil in my stomach. Oh, I would make these girls pay. Perhaps I would call in a favor and have them compelled to butcher their hair and post it all over their social media. Or perhaps read out their deepest secrets live for everyone to see.

Atalanta looked down at her shoes, biting her lip. "I'm going to be in so much trouble for what I did to those girls."

"But it was self-defense."

She shrugged. "Maybe, but no one was really there to prove it. All the other girls just sat outside the showers. The girls who did it could spin it to say I started all of it. And even if no one believed them...with how badly I hurt them, it might not matter."

She looked haunted, that little bit of happiness I had been able to coax from her fading back into the darkness.

She had that same look all the time. This tormented shadow following her around wherever she went. The smiles she gave rarely reached her eyes, and even though she was clearly a strong-willed girl, she would often hide behind the shy exterior she built. It was interesting, if not a bit concerning.

I watched her when people got too close, especially females. She would nearly jump out of her skin. There were a rare few times I'd seen her allow closeness, though. Her sister, for one. I'd seen her pick up Atalanta from the community center with real smiles and warm embraces, but she was family. Another being Theseus, who touched her quite easily and often. Can't say I wasn't a little jealous. Of course, there I was, often lurking in the shadows as I went to the community center for swim practice. I doubt she noticed I was there. Well, no more hiding.

I stopped walking and stood in front of her. I looked into those shadowy orbs of brown and green which reminded me of a lush forest. I couldn't help the impulse to lean down and kiss her on the cheek, so very close to her lips.

I lingered there for a moment before pulling away. "Don't worry Speedy. I'll take care of it, you don't need to worry about getting in trouble."

"But how?"

"I've got friends on the other side," I grinned, humming the tune to the song.

She tilted her head, looking at me with a confused smile. "Did you just make a Disney reference?"

"Perhaps."

Chapter Eleven

Atalanta

Hip had been right, the next day when I came to school, despite a few whispers of what happened, I never got called into the principal's office or cornered by a teacher. When I saw the coach in the hall, she acted like nothing was amiss! Thankfully, my bag had been untouched in my locker.

The three girls who had cornered me weren't at school and I was beginning to fear Hip was part of the Mob or something.

Cal had a conniption when I came home that night. She was ready to march down the school herself and go round two on those girls. But I advised her against it, pointing out that it would draw too much attention.

I tried to hide the bruising and scratches on my face with makeup, but I don't think I did a very good job as the only color I could find at the store was the wrong shade. On top of that, the scratches were raised, so they only stood out more with my botched coverup job.

This was yet another one of the many times I wished I had long, flowing hair that I could just hide behind.

When lunch rolled around, I was a little nervous to sit at the table with Jason like I had yesterday. I didn't want him to see me like this, and if I was being really honest with myself, I didn't know if I could face him after what had happened with Hip yesterday. So, once the bell rang for the high schoolers to go to lunch, I beelined for the cafeteria instead of the courtyard where I had sat the day before.

"Atalanta," a very familiar, very concerned voice called to me.

I groaned and spun around. "Jason."

"I've heard some rumors. Are you okay?" His eyes zoomed in on my cheek, his beautiful green eyes darkening the same way Hip's had.

"I'm alright, just a little banged up," I insisted.

His hand reached out, gently caressing my cheek. "I'm so sorry. This is all my fault."

"No, you shouldn't blame yourself for their actions," I said, shaking my head.

"But he should blame himself for not leashing his little fan girls sooner," came another familiar voice next to me.

I felt an arm drape itself across my shoulders. Looking up, I saw Hip standing next to me, his eyes trained on Jason. That easy smile he normally had was tight and eyes narrowed slightly with malice.

"This has nothing to do with you, Clark." Jason growled.

"Oh, I think it does, seeing as I was the one who had to clean up *your* mess and make sure that your fan squad didn't retaliate against Atalanta," Hip shot back.

I watched as Jason deflated, his anger seeping out like a balloon as his shoulders drooped.

I reached out for him, taking his hand in mine. "I don't blame you, it's okay."

"He's right though. I should have known something like this would happen. The girls at this school can be like vipers and I should have done something to stop them sooner. You're not the only one who's been pushed around just because I spoke to them for all of five seconds," his voice rose, loud enough for everyone in the always to hear. "And as the student council president, I will not tolerate bullying in my school."

Heads turned in our direction and I watched as a few girls looked as though they had just been slapped in the face. Wounded. Though a few of them still glared daggers at me because I was still holding Jason's hand.

I would say I was in a precarious position as Hip stood closely at my side, his arm over my shoulder warming me slowly while my hand held Jason's. Strangely, I didn't really feel like I was doing anything wrong. While both boys had shown their interest, they had no actual claim on me. And while those girls glared a hole into my skull, and I received curious eyes from the boys, I had no desire to let go of that hand.

"Let's go to lunch," I said, nudging the two towards the doors.

"I need to go buy my lunch," Hip replied, halting us.

I turned and looked up at him with puppy dog eyes. "You'll come join us, though?"

I could tell they weren't very comfortable right now, the tension between them still sparking in the air. A smart woman wouldn't have the two guys that had feelings for her, one of which she had kissed, eating lunch together. Well, I was a selfish woman. I didn't want Hip to leave my side, as I felt safe with him close to me like this. After yesterday I was on edge. The moment Hip had arrived, I had felt myself relax for the first time since he'd dropped me off at home yesterday.

Jason, on the other hand, clearly needed my presence as he felt responsible for my injuries, and probably wanted to go all caveman-protector on me. It was probably smarter to just give him what he wanted.

Those ever-changing eyes, which appeared to be blue in this light, stared into me, the malice I had seen before lessening. With a smile, Hip nodded and walked away.

I turned back to Jason. His expression landed somewhere between curiosity and confusion.

"I don't know what to make of him. I don't think I've ever seen him that hostile before. He's always been more of a jokester."

I shrugged. "He's one of those types with many layers, I think."

"Are we still on for this Saturday?" He asked.

I felt heat rise into my cheeks.

"I mean...I am if you still want to."

He squeezed my hand, his smile warm. "I wouldn't miss it for the world."

We made our way outside, where Davie and Margo were already sitting at the bench, swapping their lunches like the sickly cute couple they were. When they glanced up from each other, they shared similar frowns.

"What happened to you?" Margo asked, pointing to my cheek.

We sat down across from them and Jason pulled out that water bottle and his lunch. He really did love those tuna sandwiches, didn't he?

"You haven't heard the rumors?" I asked, trying not to look longingly at the food in front of me.

She shook her head. "I don't pay attention to the ramblings of these immature plebs."

"I had a run-in with some of Jason's admirers," I said, giving her a wry smile.

Their eyes went wide, and poor Jason deflated further. I leaned against his shoulder.

"And they just attacked you?" Davie asked.

"Technically yes, though it probably wouldn't have broken out into a brawl had I just let them have their way and not nearly break one of the girls' wrists when she tried to pull my pants down."

There was a plethora of differing reactions. Margo and Davie seeming impressed by my self-defense, calling me a ninja and a badass while Jason nearly shot up out of the chair in his anger, cursing up a storm.

"I want these girls' names!" Jason demanded.

I shook my head. "I don't know their names, I just know they are in my gym class."

"I'll have a talk with the coach. They can't get away with harassing you into a corner to the point that you have to defend yourself." Jason's face was turning so red that I thought steam might start coming out of his ears at any moment.

"Hip said he took care of it already. I haven't seen them in the halls and I haven't been called to the principal's office," I said, putting my hand on his shoulder trying to calm him down.

"Hip? That clumsy kid whose parents run the apple farm?" Margo asked, completely ignoring the fuming Jason.

"Yep, that Hip," I replied, continuing to rub Jason's arm hoping to calm him down off the ledge.

"Someone gossiping about me?"

Hip walked up to us, a tray piled high with food in his hands. Nonchalantly, he slid down on my other side, completely ignoring the looks of confusion from Jason's friends and the irritation from Jason himself. With a smile, he unwrapped a sandwich from his tray and began to eat it with gusto.

The group was uncomfortably quiet while Hip sat there, eating his sandwich. I watched Margo and Davie share questioning looks with Jason, but he only shook his head at them and slowly began to eat his own sandwich, finally calmed down. All eyes but mine watched Hip as everyone slowly began to eat their lunch.

Suddenly, something green and polished was placed in front of me. When my eyes came back into focus, in front of me was a small green apple. I blinked when moments later a plate of pasta piled with meat sauce slid into view. Following the hand that placed it there, I found Hip, who continued to munch on his sandwich. He looked at me out of the corner of his eye before picking up a can off his tray and putting it down in front of me with the other food.

"Eat your lunch during study hall again?" Jason asked as he also noticed Hip's odd gifts.

"Y-yeah," I lied and picked up the fork from the pasta and shoved a bite in my mouth.

"I wish I could eat as much as you and be that skinny," Margo said, her voice hinting at envy.

I felt a hand squeeze my left knee. I don't know how he had known, but I didn't take Hip's gesture lightly. Holding back my tears, I happily ate the food.

Somehow the tension faded, and the five of us broke into easy conversation through the rest of the lunch hour. Jason and Hip had discovered their similar love for video games and chatted about it through most of lunch. It only got bad when Hip had suddenly offered to drive me to work, which had opened up an argument between him and Jason. Jason claimed that he should drive me since he would be at the library after school anyway, and that motorcycles were too dangerous. Hip, of course, didn't take too kindly to his motorcycle being called dangerous. Jason won in the end though, since I didn't want Hip to be making the trip if he didn't have to.

As the bell rang, the five of us headed off to class, Hip and Davie breaking away once we were inside. As soon as they left, Margo was on me.

"So, what was that about? Are you and Hip an item now?" she asked, getting pretty close for my personal comfort.

I stepped away from her and closer to Jason. "No, he's just a really good friend. I have gym with him. He was there yesterday after everything happened with those girls and helped me out with getting away from everything."

"Aww, like a knight in shining armor! That's so cute!"

I felt Jason stiffen next to me. Glancing at him, I noticed that his jaw was clenched, his eyes staring ahead with fire in them.

There was no mistaking his expression as anything other than jealousy. I couldn't help the mini internal girly squeal at the idea. Yet, my logical side also recognized how tense he had been during lunch thanks to me, so I spent English trying to cheer him up. Mr. K gave us another reading period, so we talked about the book he had given me the day before and I helped him and Margo with ideas for prom.

INTO THE SEAS EMBRACE

A very sociable day for me, I would say. Cal would be proud.

After the bell for math rang, both Jason and Hip met me in the hall and escorted me to class. It was a little embarrassing to have both of them standing next to me like bodyguards. Their banter was entertaining to listen to, though.

"Kingdom Hearts One was way better than Two," Hip challenged Jason.

"But the gameplay in the second one was way better, and you have to admit that the art for the first one was pretty terrible."

"Are you crazy?!" Hip exclaimed, throwing his hands in the air. "Two was needlessly complicated and you needed to play the spin-off games to understand most of it!"

"It was only complicated because you probably suck at video games," Jason said pointedly.

"I'm awesome at video games," Hip shot back.

"I'm sure you were, if you thought the second game was too hard."

Hip growled. "I never said it was too hard, just too complicated."

I had to mentally roll my eyes. I love video games as much as the next person...when I could get my hands on one, but I didn't feel the need to constantly bicker about it like these two.

Tired of their verbal sparring, I chimed in. "I don't even know what you two are talking about."

They both gasped, looked at each other and then back at me.

"I can't even look at you right now," Jason teased.

Hip cliched his chest dramatically. "Look at her? I can't *even*. She's breaking my poor heart!"

"Seriously, guys?"

They both laughed at their antics before Jason said, "Kingdom Hearts is only one of the best video games of all time! How could you not know it?"

"I don't really play many video games," I shrugged.

"We'll have to rectify that, then." Hip smiled.

When we got to the gymnasium, Jason asked if I wanted him to wait until I was done changing but I told him I would be okay and didn't want him to be late to class. Reluctantly he left, looking back over his shoulder a few times as he hurried down the hall.

Hip waited for me, though. He'd seemingly stood by the door the whole time I was getting dressed before leaving to get changed himself. The girls weren't in the locker room, and beyond a few of them giving me wary looks during class, nothing happened. The coach acted none the wiser as well.

"What did you do, anyway? To make all of that go away?" I asked Hip as we sat doing stretches.

"I called in a favor."

And that was all he would say about it.

When the end of school came around, Jason waited with me as the initial rush of kids left the building. With his hand in mine, he escorted me to his car.

"Such a gentleman," I said as Jason opened the door for me.

He rolled his eyes. "Just get in."

I slid into the passenger seat, far more comfortable than I had been two days ago.

The drive to the community center was short and full of laughter as Jason mimicked the math teacher's boring monotonous voice.

"And that is the how the derivative of pi is equal to the square root of my love for all things cheese related," Jason droned, his face somehow managing not to crack a smile.

I snorted. "That doesn't even make sense!"

"Neither do half of his lessons," he replied.

We pulled into the joint parking lot of the two buildings. Over the last two weeks, I had noticed how ever so slowly the community center gained more and more color. Its bland walls were now painted with images similar to the library next to it. Even though I came here almost every day, I had yet to see the artist who could paint such exquisite work. Like the images just sort of appeared overnight.

Until today.

On a ladder stood a man. It was hard to make out any features from where I sat in Jason's car, but the guy was hulking like a bear. A bear with dark clothes and a paint brush in his hand.

"Oh my god, I feel like I've spotted the elusive Bigfoot," I whispered, my eyes fixed on the giant man as he swept his brush along the side of the building.

Curiously, Jason looked in the direction I was watching. "Who? Ajax?"

"That's his name?"

"Yeah, he's the town's artist. Keeps to himself mostly, but I'm surprised you haven't seen him around yet. He does jobs all over the town," Jason said matter-of-factly.

"What do you mean?" I asked. Thinking back, I hadn't seen any other buildings painted like these two.

"You know all those mermaid statues?" I nodded. "Well, he's the one who makes them. Along with the shops' name plates. *And* he had a hand in all of the renovations."

Wow, that was a lot of work. There were a good thirty statues I had noted placed all over the town. I wouldn't have guessed they were all done by the same person.

"That's really amazing," I said, awestruck.

"With how much work he does, I sometimes wonder if he ever sleeps."

INTO THE SEAS EMBRACE

I stared in wonder. Some people were just like that I guess— had their fingers in so many pies you can't help but wonder how they did it all.

Without my noticing, Jason got out of the car and opened the door to let me out.

"Do you need a ride home?"

I blinked, focusing my attention back to Jason. "I think I'll be okay today."

"Alright, well, I'm just next door if you need me."

With long strides, Jason made his way into the library. Turning towards the community center, I slowly approached the bear who seemed to be quite focused on painting what looked to be the start of a coral reef.

Coming closer, I could see a clear bin at his feet filled with small paint tubes and in his hand that wasn't holding the paintbrush was one of those round white boards with the hole in it for the thumb and small splotches of paint. The way he feverishly swashed his brush across the wall, the strokes rapid yet precise drew me in, like he was putting on some sort of show for an audience of one.

When I got close enough to begin to make out some of his finer features, he suddenly halted his painting and flinched, cupping the right side of his face. The fumbling movement causing his foot to knock against the bin of paint brushes and sent it crashing to the ground, the bright colorful tubes scattering everywhere.

I picked up my pace and bustled over to him, gathering up the tubes of paint as Ajax cursed and scrambled down his ladder.

"I've got it," he huffed, his voice as I would have expected, a low rumble that just made you want to curl up by the fire.

"No, no that's alright." I scooped the paint tubes and dumped them into the bin.

Gathering as many of them as I could, I took the bin and held it out to him to put his own tubes before handing it to him again.

"Here you go. Are you okay? You seemed like you were in pain before."

Standing face to face with the bear, I could confirm how large he was. Not only was Ajax extremely tall, hitting well into six and a half feet, he was also broad shouldered and bulky. Only wearing jeans and a black T-shirt, his muscles strained against the fabric, almost to the point where I bet if he flexed, he would pop a few stitches.

How the hell was he only wearing a shirt in this cold?!

Moving my eyes up his body to his face, I saw that he had that lumberjack look going on, scruffy brown beard and messy short hair to match. His eyes startled me in a way that was different than the others'. Jason, with his intense, dark green. Percy, with cold, calculative brown. Theseus, with a warm blue-gray, or even Hip's, with their ever-changing mischief. Ajax was unique, as he had heterochromia.

One eye was a striking icy blue while the other matched Percy's chocolate brown. And those eyes were filled with so much pain that I clenched my chest, my own pain and sorrow drawn to the surface.

He mirrored my movement as his eyes locked onto mine. "Too much."

"What?"

"What did they do to you?"

My stomach dropped as the shock and confusion settled. How could he know? He couldn't know. Flashes of those days bubbled into my mind. The terror, the pain, and God, there was so much blood. I clutched my chest harder, the tears flowing down my cheeks as the panic began to set in.

But suddenly my thoughts were pulled off their panicked track when the man, Ajax, doubled over and heaved up the contents of his stomach.

"Holy shit! Are you okay?!" I shouted.

He held up his hand for me to stop as I instinctively moved closer to him. He continued to throw up until there was nothing left, and he began dry heaving. I felt helpless, wanting to help him but not really knowing what to do. I scrambled up the steps of the center and swung the door open. Inside the lobby Dorris sat at her desk, chatting happily with Lidia whom I had only just met the other day.

"Dorris! I need help!" I shouted.

The two women jumped, and their eyes turned to me.

"What's wrong?" Dorris asked, standing up.

"The guy who was painting the walls, Ajax. He's really sick!"

She put her hand to her cheek. "Oh, dear. Lidia, can you go get some water and chocolate."

Lidia nodded and ran into the back room while Dorris shuffled out from behind her desk and made her way over to me.

"We've got it from here, Atalanta. Why don't you go find Theseus and start work?"

"But...are you sure?" I asked, my voice quivering.

I felt just as sick as he appeared, my whole body shaking from the afterthoughts of my past. I also couldn't help but somehow feel responsible for his sudden illness and wanted to help.

"Yes, Lidia and I will help Ajax. This happens every once in a while. He just needs some rest." She said, practically shoving me away from the door and towards one of the hallways.

Lidia came out of the office holding a giant bottle of water, a box of chocolate and... was that a bottle of salt? Yes, it freaking was! What was it with these people and their salt?

With another nudge from Dorris, I reluctantly went down the hallway to go and find Theseus.

A moment later I found him in the rec room, a room full of entertainment: a ping pong table, video game consoles, a whole wall of board games, and a huge projection screen surrounded by bean bags. Theseus was in the corner, vacuuming the carpet.

Approaching him, I tapped his shoulder.

He turned, his eyes lighting up when he realized it was me. "Atalanta." his face morphed into a concerned frown. "What's wrong?"

"I met Ajax outside, and he just started throwing up," I said. Might as well tell some of the truth, right?

His eyebrows shot up. "Oh, is he all right now?"

"Yeah, Dorris and Lidia went to go help him. She told me to come back here to find you, so I could start working." I said as I slowly began to sort some of the game board boxes.

He nodded. "Okay."

I turned my head so he could see my face easily. "They said that was normal for him? Like, should we be taking him to the doctor or something?"

"Don't worry, it normally only happens when..." He paused, studying me for a long moment. "Atalanta, what happened to your face?"

I gently touched the poorly covered up scratches. "Oh, these? I got into a fight at school yesterday."

"A fight?!" He shouted, his voice far louder than it should have been, but it wasn't like he could hear his volume.

"Yeah, it's alright now. The other girls came out of it worse than I did."

"Worse than you?" He spoke slowly as if not really understanding what he read for a second. "You're a bit of scrapper then? Taking on the whole school single-handedly?"

"I did not take on the whole school," I snorted and shoved him gently in the shoulder.

"But seriously, are you okay?" he asked, coming over and touching lightly on the spot on my face which was scratched up.

I nodded. "Yeah, I only came out of it with a few scrapes and bruises, nothing too serious."

"That's good," He said, his voice a hoarse whisper as his thumb stroked my check gently.

We stood there silently staring at each other like a couple of love-struck loons.

"You were saying something about Ajax? About him getting sick only happens when-?" I asked, wanting to find something to break the trance we had been under.

"Oh, uh, when he doesn't eat enough. He works too hard. Gets caught up in his art and doesn't eat," he replied, his tone a bit nervous, but I brushed it off.

"Do you know him well?" I asked.

He tilted his head "Just about the whole town knows Ajax."

"Jason said he tends to keep to himself," I pointed out.

"He doesn't talk much or interact with many people, but with how much he does for the town, it's kinda hard not to be well known, you know?"

No, I didn't, but I nodded anyway.

Theseus put his hands in his pockets and rocked back and forth on his heels. "Any-who, wanna help me finish dusting in here and then take out the trash?"

"Sure!" I said, going back to organizing the board games.

We cleaned the rest of the rec room in companionable silence. Most days were like this, it seemed. Together in a comfortable silence with little pockets of conversation here and there. With his condition, it was slightly difficult to work and talk at the same time, but I didn't mind it. It kept us from slowing down too much and we finished each room rather quickly.

He hadn't started teaching me sign language yet, but we didn't get much time as we hadn't hung out outside of work. Not for lack of trying though, as Theseus had invited me to hang out several times in the last couple of weeks. I had turned him down every time with excuses. 'I have a lot of homework', 'I need to help my sister with dinner', 'I need to go home to feed the cat and clean his litter box'. I didn't own a freaking cat.

I was torn, because I wanted to hang out with him more and get to know him better, but it was also easier not getting too attached to people. So every time he asked, I panicked and came up with some lame excuse. Not that I had been doing an excellent job of keeping my distance so far. The ride with Hip yesterday had been extremely intimate. On his motorcycle pressed up against him, and then later practically breaking down in his arms. Of course, there was Jason and that date on Saturday, and Percy...well, perhaps I wasn't going to the library just to read books. The not-so-well-mannered librarian was intelligent and funny to annoy.

The men in the town of Argos were far too tempting. Though as I thought about it, perhaps it wouldn't be too bad to get to know them a little. Dad and Cal had encouraged me to make friends and find a date to the Prom. So, when the end of my shift came, which was only four hours long, and Theseus asked me to hang out again I had a choice to make.

"Do you want to stay and hang out in the rec room? We can put on a movie or something," Theseus asked as we stashed our supplies away in the janitorial closet.

I turned to him, ready with some excuse, but looking up into those eyes I couldn't say no this time.

"Okay."

The way his face lit up made up for my slight discomfort at letting go.

We made our way into the rec room. There were a couple of younger kids in there; one was probably around thirteen or so while the other was at least three years younger. They were playing ping-pong. Theseus gestured for me to sit down in one of the bean bag chairs when I realized something.

"Are you going to be okay with watching the movie?" I asked with concern.

He rolled his eyes. "Noooo. You are losing brownie points here, woman!"

At my confused look, he said, "Subtitles."

I palmed my face and groaned. "Right."

Theseus laughed, the bright tone sounding like a chorus of bells.

My head spun at the sound, causing my thoughts to go all hazy for a moment. But I came back quickly, blinking in confusion when I realized I was leaning extremely close to Theseus, so close, a centimeter more and I would be kissing him.

I sprung back. "I'm sorry! I don't know what came over me!"

He shook his head. "It's all right. I wouldn't have necessarily minded being kissed by a cute girl."

He winked, the sly smile he gave me only serving to have my cheeks, which were already warm, intensify to flaming hot.

"Get a room!" One of the younger boys shouted.

Theseus, who hadn't heard the comment, only continued to stare at me, those gray-blue eyes growing darker. His eyes were fixated on my lips, but I didn't think he was watching for what I was going to say this time.

When he slowly began to lean in, I put a hand on his chest. "One of the boys just shouted for us to get a room."

His eyes broke away from mine to look at the boys who had stopped their game of ping-pong to ogle us.

"Maybe we will!" He called back to the boys lightheartedly.

"Ewww," the younger of the two said.

I couldn't help but giggle.

He turned his gaze back to me. "I just want you to know that I do really want to kiss you right now, but I don't think it's the perfect time. Not yet."

"What would be the perfect time?"

His hand lifted up to brush his fingers lightly against my cheek. "I don't know. But I will when it happens."

I wanted that time to be now. Yet, if he wasn't sure, it would be a bad idea to try and force it. Besides, I was curious about this perfect moment.

After getting the projector set up, we scrolled through Netflix before picking a DC movie. It turned out that Theseus was a bit of a nerd. When he found out I had yet to see most of the DC or Marvel movies, he was determined to christen me into the world of comic book movies. We started with an older Batman film. I thought the costume design was hilarious. I mean, nipples on top of armor?

Theseus was adorable, constantly explaining any little back story or alternate timeline stuff with each character that showed up. Of course, I became pretty confused when he explained how all these characters could possibly have different stories.

"Wait, wait, how many different versions Batman are there?" I asked, turning away from the movie to face Theseus.

He tilted his head in thought. "Well, you have Ninja Batman, Steampunk Batman, Zombie Batman, and then there was this version where Damian Wayne inherited the title of Batman, Batmage. Oh! And then there was this one time that Batman became a green lantern and was known as The Dawnbreaker."

I waved at him to stop, laughing I said, "Okay, okay, I get it. But why have these different versions?"

"Because once the character was created, lots of other writers wanted to write their story in their own way."

I pursed my lips and thought about it for a moment before saying, "So really, comic books are a bunch of fan-fictions of the original."

He laughed. "Yeah, basically."

I felt somewhat lightheaded again, but for a briefer moment this time and when I came out of it, I was leaning heavily against Theseus. I also realized what was finally causing these little dizzy spells and blips in my memory. It was his laughter.

His voice was what kept making my brain go all fuzzy. That hadn't been the first time either. On the day we met, he was singing, and suddenly I was up on stage with him, then again earlier when I almost kissed him. I realized he wasn't the only one too, the same thing happened the first time I heard Jason laugh! Though it hadn't happened with him since. At least that I knew of.

I sat back away from Theseus, studying him with narrowed eyes. What was going on?

It was one thing to be attracted to these men, but it was another thing for their voices and their laughter to literally put me in a trance.

"What was that?" I asked.

His face which was full of happiness morphed into one of confusion. "What was what?"

"This," I said, gesturing between the two of us, "it's not the first time it's happened. Every time you laugh, it's like my head is stuffed with cotton balls and the next thing I know I'm practically in your arms."

"Perhaps you're just that attracted to me?" he grinned.

"No, well, yes," At his smile, I reasserted, "But no! That's not what this is. This isn't the first time it's happened, and it wasn't only with you. And don't get me started on that!"

I pointed to the tall bottle of water at his side. Right before we started the movie he had gotten up and brought that back with him.

"A bottle of water?"

"Yes, a bottle of water. Half the people in town carry these giant bottles of water around with them, keeping them at their side like it's a freaking religion. I have had some of my teachers actually stop their lectures the moment they realized they were out of water! Not to mention the fact that I've seen several people pour freaking sea salt into their bottles! SEA SALT, THESEUS! Not only is that not normal, but it's downright dangerous!"

He shook his head slowly, his brow furrowed. "Atalanta, I don't know what to tell you. It's just a bottle of water."

I snatched his bottle off the ground, twisted the cap open, and put it to my lips and chugged, only to be running to the wastebasket seconds later to throw up. There was enough salt in that bottle to make the dead sea envious.

When I finished emptying the contents of my stomach into the bin, I stood up to see Theseus looking at me with a worried expression. Though I couldn't tell if that was worry for me or worry about me discovering his secret.

I stomped back over to him, shoving the bottle into his hands. "When you're ready to stop bullshitting me, maybe we can finally have that perfect moment."

Turning around, I left. My heart burned while my mind roiled. A perfectly good moment, ruined. It all started when I spotted that sea creature. That huge glowing mass which I had seen on the cliff that night, and then the stupid water bottles, Hip somehow getting me out of trouble, and every time I was placed under some sort of spell by these men.

That was *it*.

I would find out what was going on with this town.

Chapter Twelve

Atalanta

Beyond picking up my check from Dorris, I avoided the community center. Over the next two days, I kept my eyes wide open. Observing the residents of Argos both in and out of class. Instead of going to the library, I actually walked around the town for the first time, immersing myself with the townspeople.

I supposed, on the surface, they seemed quite normal. Huddling together and bustling about, running errands, chatting about fishing or the high school swim team. Normal people stuff.

Then there were these small instances.

A scrawny fellow moving what had to be a two-thousand-pound cement barrier. An older woman who stayed miraculously dry despite walking in the rain. Children running around near butt-naked in the snow doing perfect impersonations of dolphins. The last one might not have been supernatural, but it was weird.

Certainly not small-town stuff.

Cal thought I was crazy when I had asked if either of them had noticed anything strange at dinner the night before. My dad, on the other hand, didn't think I was crazy. In fact, he was just as suspicious about the goings on in this town as I was.

"The guys down at the docs. They aren't normal," he commented after taking a bite of salad.

"What do you mean they aren't normal?" I asked.

"Most of them have this way about them, like something is going on behind the scenes that they all know about yet are still trying to keep it secret. They will say odd stuff then get all hush-hush for a moment when someone walks up. A lot of them act like they are in these little individual gangs with their own territory and such. Abnormal is what I would call it."

"I think that's just small-town macho mentality," Cal rolled her eyes.

"Perhaps. Or maybe there's a cult in this town," Dad said, annoyance in his tone. Rightfully so, since he's dealt with them a few times in the past.

A cult? It wasn't something I had considered, yet, I had doubt there was a cult. Perhaps that was only wishful thinking as I had long ago learned to trust my father's intuition. He had this way of reading people. Always knowing when they were lying or hiding something, a skill that came with all those years that he had been a federal agent before the incident. He never lost that investigator mentality.

It was Friday, and the town was a bit busier than it had been the day before. I just came out of the coffee shop owned by the man I'd seen move the cement block.

His name was Gregory, and he appeared normal despite his abnormal strength. I may have played undercover detective and pretended to be a simple awed bystander who had seen him move the block. He just laughed it off, saying his mom had always called him Hercules for looking deceptively strong, but I had been mistaken. Claimed the cement barrier I'd seen him push was propped with a board with locking wheels, making it easier for them to move around when they couldn't get a crane to move it.

I made a mental note to go back and check the barrier as I sipped my hot cocoa. While that mystery might have been cracked, it didn't explain the woman or the children I had seen the day before. My logical side told me the woman could have been holding a clear umbrella, and I just hadn't noticed, and the kids might have just been playing some sort of strange game. Then what about the water bottles? Or the weird hypnotic voices?

Dad thought something was going on as well and I had learned to trust his gut instinct. So, I couldn't give up.

Walking across the street from the coffee shop, I sat on a bench and observed the townspeople again, casually sipping from my cocoa and pretending to play with my phone, skimming my eyes over the little shops surrounding the town square.

I spotted a familiar face on a ladder in front of one of the shops. The burley Ajax was hanging up a sign over the hardware store that read 'Build It, Fix It, Paint It. Joe's Hardware'.

Not knowing why, I stood up from my bench and jogged over to him. He was wearing a short sleeve shirt again, this one a deep green, and had a tool belt hanging around his hips. He had to be freezing, yet he couldn't bother with a coat?

Not wanting to startle him I called as I got closer. "Hey, Ajax, right?"

He stiffened on his ladder and slowly turned his head to look down at me. His eyes were so cool looking, I couldn't help but stare into their multi-colored depths.

"You."

I tilted my head. "Me?"

Ajax scrambled down the ladder and came to a halt in front of me.

"Wait here," he said, holding up his palm before jogging away.

Somewhere between confused and curious I stayed still, following his progression to a dark green truck. He opened the door and reached inside for something before shutting it and coming back over to me.

He held out what was in his hands. I looked down to see a red box wrapped in a tinted film.

"Chocolate?" I asked, the scale tipping more towards confused now.

He nodded. "For you."

"Uh, thank you? But why?"

"It always makes me feel better."

He was a very short worded person it seemed. Not that he was dumb, but just didn't say much, like speaking made him uncomfortable or something.

I gently took the box of chocolate into my hands. "And you're hoping that it will make me feel better? But I feel fine."

His brows crinkled a little as if he was trying to understand something before merely saying, "If you say so."

The silence between us was awkward. I held the box to my chest and rocked back and forth on my feet. I wasn't used to random strangers giving me gifts, let alone something that they believed would make me happier. He was a giant teddy bear, wasn't he? All huge and intimidating on the outside but sweet and cuddly in the middle.

Unable to take the silence anymore I asked, "Are *you* feeling better? The other day you got really sick when we met."

He nodded. "I wasn't prepared. I'm better now because I am prepared."

"Prepared for what?"

He was towering over me and I had to crane my neck to meet his eyes. I didn't really know what to think of him. His expression was blank but there was so much in his eyes that I couldn't decipher.

"You."

Shocked, my mouth fell open before snapping shut. "You got sick because of me?"

That didn't make any sense.

"No, not entirely your fault," he said, confusing me even more.

"But still somewhat my fault? How?"

A small smile cracked his lips. "Can't say. I don't know you."

"So, if you get to know me then you can tell me?"

He shrugged. "I suppose."

We were standing close now, his body a hair's breadth away from mine. My heart began to gallop in my chest as his eyes flicked down to my lips. Taking a deep breath in, I caught a whiff of the forest, earthy fresh wood with the odd faint layer of paint on top go it. I stepped back.

"Well. Then hi, my name is Atalanta." I held out my hand for him to shake. "I like reading, going fishing with my father, and secretly adore my older sister. But I hate pineapple, and please don't tell my sister I adore her."

Slowly, he took my hand into his own enormous one. It was warm and covered in heavy callouses. I felt so tiny as his whole hand basically engulfed mine. Everything about him, from his broad shoulders and well over six feet in height, dwarfed my small frame.

I bet he gave great hugs.

"Ajax. I like to paint and sculpt...I also don't like pineapple."

"Look at that, best friends already. Will you tell me why I made you sick now?" I said with a grin.

He smiled at that, his sad eyes lighting up with a bit of sparkle as a chuckle rumbled in his chest.

"Not yet."

I hadn't expected him to tell me anything, so at least I wasn't disappointed.

I snapped my fingers. "Well, darn."

"One day. Not today though. Today I have to put up this sign," He said pointing to the hardware sign half hanging off the building above our heads.

Ajax climbed back up the ladder and went back to working on the sign that looked to be hand-carved and painted. I remembered Jason telling me about how Ajax did a lot of work for the town, including their nameplates. This must have been what he meant. It would have taken a few days to make a sign like that. I wondered how he ever found the time.

I wanted to push for him to tell me the answer. I really did, but I could see he wasn't the type to divulge easily and I didn't want to waste time trying. Though, talking to him gave me an idea. Something I should have thought of before.

"Ajax. I was told you made all those mermaid sculptures around town. I'm guessing you also painted the mermaids on the front of the library."

"Yes. I did," He replied, his focus completely on getting the sign well-positioned to be screwed in.

"Why?"

"I was asked to." With one hand holding up the sign, he reached into his tool belt and pulled out some screws. Putting a few in his mouth, he grabbed for his screwdriver.

"By whom?"

He turned on his screwdriver, the fast whirring sound piercing the air before it stopped and he said, "The mayor."

"Because he wanted this to become a tourist town with the theme being mermaids?"

"Basically," he replied, driving in another screw.

Before he could start on the next one, I threw out, "Do you know why the mayor chose mermaids?"

He lowered his driver, making a point to stare directly at the sign before he replied.

"...No?" he asked.

He wasn't a very good liar, but I guess it worked for him since he was tight-lipped regardless.

I smiled. "Thank you for the chocolates, Ajax. I hope to see you around and get to know you better, so I can get the answer out of you one day."

He merely grunted as a reply.

INTO THE SEAS EMBRACE

With a new skip in my step and a box of chocolates, I headed towards the library. Percy might have the answers I was looking for. If not, I bet a book would.

I hadn't noticed Percy carrying around a giant water bottle and the few times I heard him laugh my brain hadn't gone all fuzzy. So whatever Jason, Theseus, and the rest of the town were, Percy didn't seem to be one of them. Which meant he might be willing to divulge anything he knew...I hoped.

It took about thirty minutes to trek up the road, through town square, and to the hill of the library. My mind wandering back and forth between the mysterious Ajax and the fun-to-irritate Percy.

Luckily it wasn't snowing, and the weather was somewhat warm, so it wasn't too bad.

Reaching the parking lot, I halted in my tracks when I saw Theseus walking out of the community center to his car. I cursed. I didn't want him to see me, but it wasn't like I could hide. The nearest set of trees was a good hundred feet away and running to them would only attract more attention. So, head held high, I trudged the rest of the way through the parking lot, not making eye contact when I knew without a doubt that he had spotted me.

"Atalanta!" He called.

I ignored him, still hurt and mad at him for the other day. It was one thing to not tell me the truth, but another to play off my confusion and questions as if I was nuts.

My nostrils flared in anger, and I picked up my pace to the library doors.

"Atalanta, please!"

Screw him. I still had a day or so before I would let my anger abate and face him. Till then he would just have to deal. I would not look back no matter how much hurt was in his voice. Nope, certainly wouldn't.

As I reached the doors with one hand on the handle, I looked back.

Damn it! I had NO self-control with these boys.

He looked so desperate and upset. His moppy curls of red were frazzled, and his eyes had deeper shadows underneath them. I wanted to run to him and both slap him for his behavior and apologize for mine. I knew I wasn't wrong, though. With what little amount of willpower I pretended to have, I gripped the handle tighter, pulled the door open, and slipped inside.

I took a deep breath and waited to see if he would follow. After a minute or two, it was clear he wasn't going to, so I relaxed and moved further into the library.

It was a little busier than normal with it being a Friday. There were at least twenty people that I could see milling about, several of them students, perhaps studying, and a few other regulars who were fellow book lovers like me. Percy wasn't at his desk like usual. Instead, Jason sat in the chair, staring deeply into the computer in front of him.

I walked up. "Hey Jason."

"Atalanta, hey," He said, scrambling about in a dance of 'oh shit, a girl! Do I look good? My hair must be a mess. No, stop fidgeting, she's staring. Act natural', before settling with his elbow propped up on the desk, his head resting against his fist.

It was rather cute to see him lose his cool for a few moments. He always acted like the confident jock, always having the right answer or staying calm and collected. Besides the time I had called him out on his crush on Percy, I hadn't ever seen him get all flustered like this in the weeks I'd known him. Seeing Mr. Perfect all flustered at my simple presence was priceless.

"Whatcha doing?" I asked, leaning over the desk to try and see the computer.

He quickly turned the screen away from me.

"Uhhh, paperwork?" He asked, not stated. Asked.

We had ourselves another lousy liar, folks.

I grinned. "You know, I don't think you're telling me the truth. So, I'm just gonna assume it was porn."

"It's not porn!" He spluttered.

"Iiiif you say so," I sang, laying on the sarcasm.

He was about as fun to mess with as Percy. Speaking of the stoic librarian, he chose that moment to walk out of the aisles of books with an empty cart. He must have been putting books back. That seemed odd, as I had assumed that was Jason's job.

"Ah, Ms. North, come to hound me again with another trash book suggestion? I finished the last one you gave me."

"And did you like it?"

He pursed his lips. "It was okay. The one before it was better."

"But you totally liked it. See, they aren't all bad."

His usual frown deepened. "I suppose."

I couldn't help the smile that spread wide across my face. He was so falling in love with these books. Even if he didn't want to admit it.

He cleared his throat. "So, what can we help you with today?"

"I was wondering if you had any books on mythical creatures?" I asked.

He paused and studied me for a long moment before saying, "We do."

"Great, can you direct me to them?"

He nodded and simply walked off. I chanced a glance at Jason who seemed to be schooling his features but failing. There was worry in those eyes. I waved to him and followed Percy into the books. The heady smell of paper engulfed me as I walked through the shelves, comforting and familiar.

Percy came upon a section and gestured to the shelves. "These are all on mythologies and their creatures. Though this one right here might be what you're looking for."

He pulled a book off a shelf and held it out to me.

The cover read *Cryptozoology: A Study of Hidden Creatures in Our World*. The cover was colorful with a bunch of mythical creatures: a unicorn on its hind legs, a centaur crossing swords with an elf, and a mermaid perched on a rock, singing.

I ran my fingers over the mermaid and whispered, "Percy. Why is the mayor choosing to turn this into a tourist town featuring mermaids?"

"I think you know the reason." His voice was smooth and deep, like black velvet.

"Well, why don't you tell me? Confirm my theory."

He stepped into my personal space, the smell of old books and pine trees settling over me. I'd never been this close to him before. Like Ajax, except being this close to him I didn't get the feeling of comfort, but a feeling of safety, a feeling of being protected. I stared into those pools of brown behind the glasses. They were sharp, seeing right through the barriers I built around myself.

"I will when you tell me about the girl with no name," He whispered.

I stiffened, my jaw dropping open. "You saw that, huh?"

He nodded. "It certainly piqued my interest. Why a woman who is as self-confident as you would go with a title that screams a lack of identity."

"I'm not that self-confident," I murmured.

"I don't think you're seeing yourself well enough," He replied, his hand reaching up to cup my neck, his thumb running the line of my jaw.

"Oh, and what do you see?" I asked, trying not to sound breathy at his touch.

He leaned in closer, his lips just millimeters from mine. "I see a woman who's been through something. Something most people wouldn't have survived and came out the other end, somewhat broken. Despite that, you've kept yourself together and pulled yourself through the trenches to come out the other end stronger than before."

I could feel the tears falling down my face as my body shook. I pulled back from him, the temptation to lean the rest of the way into that kiss strong, but I was also scared. Scared that he was peering far too deep into my soul.

He kept his hand on my neck, not letting me go far. Instead of backing away or running from my tears as most men seemed to do when a girl cried, Percy kissed my tear-soaked cheeks and held me closer, humming softly as his other hand ran up and down my back in comfort.

"You can let people in, you know."

I shook my head. "I can't."

"Why? You're smart, you know bottling everything up won't help you."

"This is about more than me. I have to keep my family safe."

"I can protect you, Atalanta."

I frowned. "I hardly know you."

"What, and that means you're not deserving of my protection?" he asked, an eyebrow cocked.

"It means I don't know you; therefore my secrets stay mine."

He nodded, conceding. "That's fair enough. Though my invitation for protection will stay."

"I don't understand. What about me would make me worthy of such a thing?"

"You intrigue me and aren't afraid to challenge me."

I chuckled. "So does a good math problem."

"You're not wrong. But a math problem doesn't look so kissable. A math problem doesn't make me wonder what it would sound like as it screamed my name in pleasure."

My eyebrows shot up. "Wow, you don't pull your punches."

"No, I don't."

I hadn't realized one of his hands had settled at my hip until he pulled me towards him, my hips resting flush against his. The other hand was at my neck pulling my face forward into his lips in a hard, claiming kiss.

I didn't sink into it immediately, shocked for a few moments but then his hand ran up and delved into my hair. A warm pit gathered in my center, demanding for me to pull him closer, claim him right back. Percy was a fantastic kisser; his lips were soft yet demanding. Perhaps even better than Jason.

I gasped and pushed him away. "Jason!"

"Jason? What about him."

"I can't be kissing you. I have a date with him tomorrow. And he-"

"And he what?"

I bit my lip, still feeling tingly. "He has feelings for you."

Percy nodded and crossed his hands over his chest, leaning his shoulder against the bookcase.

My brows furrowed as I studied him. "You're not surprised?"

"No, I'm not. I've known about Mr. Monroe's feelings for me for a while. He's not very good at hiding it." His tone was matter-of-fact, back to the cold, calculative librarian.

"Then you know that I shouldn't be here kissing you, especially when he's nearby."

He shrugged. "You mentioned having a date with him tomorrow. It seems that he is moving on from me. As he should."

"Because you're straight?"

"Because he's too young."

"You don't look much older than 23 or so."

"Looks can be deceiving," He leaned back in to give me a small peck on the lips before walking off back towards the front.

I was left standing there, a jumble of confused emotions and heated need.

It took me several minutes to calm down and focus on the book that I so clumsily dropped during Percy's plundering of my lips. Making my way to a study table in the back, I cracked open the book and skimmed through the table of contents before finding the chapter I was looking for.

Mermaids.

Appearing in mythologies worldwide, these cryptids possess the top half of a human female and the bottom half of a fish. Known in Greek mythology as sirens, they are sneaky creatures who use their alluring voices to entrance men into their waters to drown them and devour their flesh.

"Ick, their flesh? Oh yeah, Homer's *Odyssey*." I recalled the story of the character tying himself to the mast of his ship so he could listen to the sound of the sirens singing without throwing himself into the water.

I continued to read, skimming the book's pages. There were several photos, some were ugly fish-like creatures with skeletal faces and huge fangs and claws. While others depicted beautiful women with long golden hair and shiny tails, beckoning to men on ships.

"In some myths, their tears turned to pearls and their blood or flesh could make you immortal," I mumbled aloud.

There were a few myths about them being able to take on a fully human form to come to shore and find human mates, though it seemed the human would often meet a watery death after providing the mermaid with a child. Most of the older stories about them were quite violent, sometimes telling of vengeful sprits or gods who would drown people for their sheer amusement. But there were a few accounts that depicted them as benevolent water spirits who would guide lost boats or save children abandoned by the riverside.

It really seemed that mermaids were like humans, not all good or bad. The bad ones were a bit scary though. I mean, drowning you and devouring your flesh? Like freaking crocodiles.

Near the end of the chapter, there was a much smaller section titled:

Mermen

Drawn to the section, I pulled the book closer and muttered the words aloud, "The male counterpart of the mermaid, Mermen are often depicted as ugly creatures with green skin and seaweed like hair. Their temperament varies from myth to myth, some being horrid creatures who enjoy calling huge storms to sink ships, while in other stories they are much kinder than their female counterparts, said to be wise teachers and amazing caregivers. However, like the female counterparts, Mermen are also said to have the ability to entrance humans with their voice and are just as dangerous because of this ability..."

Just like the mermaid section, there were photos, a few of which were ugly looking like the book said but there were a couple that were gorgeous specimens. Tall and well-muscled with beautiful faces.

I sat back and stared at the ceiling. This can't be real. They can't be mermaids, or mermen or whatever. This was just a book, they were just mythical creatures. But I also couldn't just ignore the signs that were there, even if others were quick to brush them off. Percy didn't though; he knew and basically handed me the answer, even if he didn't say it out loud.

I had read enough stories and mythology to know that the ideas for these creatures had to have come from somewhere...Yet for them to be real, and I had possibly kissed one?

No, I had to be crazy.

I giggled nervously to myself, closed the book, and put it back on the shelf. Stiffly, I walked back to the front of the library. Jason was still sitting at the desk, his face scrunched as he stared at the computer, lips pursed like those girls who made duck faces on Instagram.

That sweet little duck face couldn't be some mythical flesh-eating monster. Nah.

Percy walked out of his office holding another YA novel in his hands. I couldn't help the blush that spread across my face as I remembered our shared kiss. That blush spread further when he walked up to Jason and bent over his shoulder to stare at the computer screen. I had kissed both of these men.

"That won't do. You want to impress her, not bore her to death," Percy said as he stared at the screen.

Jason glanced back at him. "What? Baseball isn't boring."

"She's not the type to be okay just watching sports, she's more likely to enjoy playing them."

"Huh," He typed something up on the computer. "Then what about this?"

"That's perfect," Percy nodded.

Were they talking about me? Picking out what I might find fun?

I walked up to the desk, trying to calm my nerves and keep my face as calm as possible. "Hey, guys."

"Hey, Atalanta. Find what you were looking for?" Jason asked, his eyes twinkling and his smile wide. Much different than the worried look he had before.

I glanced over at Percy who gave me a small nod.

"Yeah, I did. So, what are you up to?" I asked.

INTO THE SEAS EMBRACE

A small blush appeared across Jason's cheeks. "Percy was helping me go through date ideas for tomorrow."

"That was nice of him. Um, I'm not feeling all that well though, so I think I'm going to go home and sleep it off. I don't want to be sick for our date."

Jason frowned, then offered, "Want me to drive you home?"

I shook my head. "No, no, you keep doing what you were doing. Percy doesn't look all that busy, I'm gonna have his lazy butt take me."

Jason looked a little disappointed, but he nodded anyway. "Feel better. I'll come to pick you up around noon, okay? And don't worry if you're sick, we'll just have a night in or something."

I could help smile at his sweetness. "Okay. Ready to go, Percy?"

Percy readjusted his glasses. "I find it interesting that you didn't actually bother to ask if I wanted to take you home or not."

"Yes, but you wouldn't leave a girl to walk home alone, would you? Especially if she wasn't feeling well. I might develop pneumonia and die, and all your hard work on planning my date with Jason will go to waste."

His lips turned down in a scowl. "Fine. Come on."

I followed him out into the parking lot, relieved Theseus wasn't there. Of course, he wouldn't be there, but it was nice that there wouldn't be another awkward standoff between him and Percy. The few times I had ever seen them in the same vicinity, there was always this uncomfortable moment of standing there watching them stare at each other. Definitely some lost love between the two of them.

Hopping in Percy's black sports car, I snuggled into his heated leather seats. It was a bit odd thinking about how most of my intimate time spent with these men was them taking me home. Something I would have to start changing...well, if they didn't turn out to be some sort of mythical monsters. Which brought me to the real reason I talked Percy into taking me home.

"Are Jason and Ajax Mermaids? Well, Mermen?" I asked Percy.

His calm expression didn't change. "It's not really my place to divulge someone else's secrets, Atalanta."

"But they are something. It's why you handed me the book. Isn't it?"

"I handed you the book because you were looking for it," He said, glancing at me. His mouth quirked in a millimeter smile.

Ugh, he was so tight-lipped.

I sat back and thought about it for a moment before saying. "Just answer me this."

He flicked his gaze toward me. "I'm listening."

I fiddled with the sleeves of my jacket before asking, "Will they hurt me? If I continue to be around them?"

His grip on the steering wheel got tighter, and he let a slow breath out through his nose.

"No one in this town will hurt you. Not while I'm around," his expression softened. "But I know that none of them will hurt you. They are all good men. Even Theseus."

I never mentioned Theseus, but considering Percy knew my involvement with him it was no surprise he suspected I was wondering about Theseus as well.

"Okay, one more question." I said holding up a finger.

I could see his eyes roll wide behind his glasses. "One more."

"When you kissed me," I paused biting my lip and gathering courage. "does it bother you that I'm close with the others? You know I'm friends with Hip...and going on a date with Jason...And Theseus and I, well, there's something there."

He was silent for a few heartbeats. When he replied his voice was soft. "You are your own person. I may be interested in you, but it is not my place to dictate who you see or kiss. Especially since we aren't exclusive."

"And if we become more...involved?"

He let go of the steering wheel and placed his hand on my knee. "One thing at a time, Atalanta."

We were silent the rest of the ride back to the house.

Chapter Thirteen

Percy

I returned from dropping Atalanta off at her home. Jason sat at the front desk talking to Lidia, who I assumed just got off her shift with the toddlers based on the general disarray of her person. Clothes crumpled and covered in suspicious stains, and her hair which was always up in a neat bun any time we crossed paths was a mess. Despite this, she was still making the moves on Jason. Leaning heavily against the counter to show off her admittedly impressive cleavage and batting her eyelashes at whatever Jason was saying.

My first thought was to believe that Jason was oblivious to her obvious advances as that was who I had known him to be. However, something made me overanalyze it.

Perhaps Jason was not blind to the girl's attraction to him, rather, he was encouraging it or at the very least not discouraging her behavior. Considering the conversation I had just had with him about his upcoming date with Atalanta, watching this display set aflame a small pit of anger in my stomach.

Walking up to them, I did my best to keep my tone neutral. "Ms. Davenport. So nice to see you. I hope your job at the daycare is going well."

She turned to me, her eyes sparkling with interest. "Hey, Percy! Yes, it's going really well, I was just telling Jason all about it."

It was hard to miss the way she ran her eyes blatantly up and down my body, checking me out. Lidia Davenport, while somewhat of a brat, with not much dignity in her pursuit of any male she deemed worthy, was not a horrible girl. Unlike some of Jason's other fans.

The pit of anger in my stomach flared at the thought of those girls who had laid a hand on Atalanta. After hearing about what happened from Jason the day before yesterday and then actually seeing the fading bruises and scratches on her face today, my protective instincts were kicked into overdrive.

It's what pushed me to finally claim her. To pull her close and claim those lips as mine and damn had it stirred something in me that I thought had been dead long ago. I had felt the sting of rejection when she pushed me away but was somewhat comforted to know it was because of her loyalty to Jason and his feelings towards me. Not because she did not carry the same level of attraction that I held towards her.

I admired that loyalty, though I hoped it wouldn't constantly come between us in the future.

I wondered if perhaps I should discuss this with Jason, but first I had to get rid of Lidia.

I snapped my attention back to the girl who was still checking me out and placed a mask of authority on.

"I'm sure Jason would love to hear more about your day with the children, but unfortunately I need him for some paperwork in my office," I said walking the rest of the way to them and behind the desk with Jason. His computer was still open to the site that discussed the details of the date I had suggested he and Atalanta go on.

"What paperwork?" Jason asked, his tone nothing but indignant.

I wanted to kick him out of that chair.

"The paperwork for the new shipment of books I have coming in tomorrow," I said, glad that I was able to maintain my calm tone.

"Oh, alright…"

He nodded a goodbye to Lidia, got up, and went to the back room. I gave Lidia my own curt nod before heading in after him. She did not look happy to have her eye candy taken.

My office was still…cluttered. As I had not had either the opportunity or drive to tidy up, there were still piles of books everywhere along with stacks of papers. It was a bit too dim for Jason's eyes, so I flicked up the dimmer.

"Your office is a wreck, Percy."

I shrugged off his comment. It was organized chaos.

"I believe we have other things to worry about beyond the condition of my office."

"Atalanta?" He asked.

"She's intelligent and has pretty much figured out what's going on. I haven't said anything directly, but our next move should be figuring out what to tell her. Whether we brush this off or bring her in."

Technically it wasn't a lie as I had not actually told Atalanta anything about our true identities.

"I don't want her to know."

My eyebrows shot up, surprised at this insecure version of the man I had known. "Are you ashamed of yourself, Jason? Because you should be proud of what you are."

Our truth wasn't a completely guarded secret. We did not go around shouting it to everyone we met, typically only telling a select few we cared for deeply. The humans in town preferred not to get involved. While a small number knew the truth and most had an idea, they kept it to themselves rather than being tagged as nut jobs by the media.

Every so often, some overzealous snoop poked around, trying to find evidence to support their suspicions but with a few suggestive words, almost all of them disappeared. And the few that did not? Oh, the advantages of this modern day. Anything they ever got out to the world was seen as some sort of hoax, leaving them discredited.

"I like her, and I don't want her freaking out before I've even gotten the chance to really know her." He slumped into one of the high back chairs I had propped near the wall for reading. "Besides, if we tell her, then there might come a time where my family gets involved and we both don't want that."

He was correct. I loathed Jason's family as much as he was subservient to them. Telling Atalanta would get their attention if they were not already privy to the human girl who was asking too many questions.

But still.

"She already knows something is going on. If you want to stay in her good graces, I would advise you to tell her the truth," I pointed out.

"Why don't you tell her then if you're so insistent on it," he said defensively.

"Because you are the first one she has actually given a chance and the one who first seemed to arouse her suspicions. Therefore, the truth will be better coming from you."

Jason had told me about his first moments of meeting Atalanta. Having grown up in a town so familiar with our oddities that no one questions them anymore made him careless. At first, I thought that the girl had simply let it go, perhaps even forgotten about it, but today she had shattered our comfort and delved right in to try and discover our secrets.

Jason sprung out of his self-pitying slouch, his eyes wide.

"The first one? There are others? Who?" He studied me for a long moment. "Percy. Do you like Atalanta?"

I held back a chuckle, amused by the fact that he had only seemed to focus on the suitor part of my statement.

"Yes, I fancy her. She intrigues me," I admitted, knowing that hiding the truth would make this harder on him.

I watched his heart break before my very eyes. The question was whether his sadness was from my confession that he was not the only one after the girl's heart or that I was interested in someone other than him.

Jason was a good kid whom I had watched grow into a handsome young man over the decade I had lived on the surface. And while I had felt some attraction to him once he came into his own and I was made aware of his crush towards me, he was my employee and still had a lot of life to live. Atalanta was the first person besides me that he seemed to show interest and I felt inclined to make sure he did not screw it up. However, that did not mean I would sit back and let him have her all to himself.

I knelt down in front of him. "Jason. I have known you for many years at this point. And while you are my employee, I feel that I should tell you I know about your feelings for me."

His cheeks reddened immensely and slowly his eyes came up to meet mine, wide like a deer in headlights.

"When? How?"

"Probably before you even realized. But what is crucial is that this girl is important, and you shouldn't let the idea of other suitors stand in your way."

"But it's hopeless. You're...well, amazing, and if I'm up against you in a race for her affection...trust me, it's going to be you every time."

My mind flashed back to earlier when she had pushed me away for his sake despite the lust and hunger I had seen in her eyes.

A small smile spread across my lips. "Don't count yourself out of the running yet."

I stood up and made my way to the door, wanting to give him a moment to process the things I had said.

Before I left, I turned back to him. "I would start by telling her the truth."

Chapter Fourteen

Jason

Tell her the truth? But how could I do that?

It was the next day, and I stood on the steps of Atalanta's rundown cabin. At least it looked like someone had replaced the missing window panes. I was nervous, more nervous than I'd ever been on a date. Of course, this was the first time I'd ever gone out with someone I actually liked instead of just keeping up appearances.

Yesterday had been a rolling thunderstorm of emotions for me. Percy insisting I tell her the truth, and then revealing I wasn't the only one after her, *and* confessing he knew about my feelings?

Fuck.

Fucking fuck me up the tailpipe without lube.

Nothing is more embarrassing than your longtime crush admitting they know about your feelings and admitting they have feelings for your new crush.

Like, I would have rather streaked across the school in my birthday suit than dealt with the awkwardness that was yesterday.

And now I was here for my date with Atalanta, and Percy was expecting me to tell her the truth. Which was probably a lot harder for me than him. Percy didn't grow up on the surface with constant warnings of 'don't reveal yourself to the humans' and 'humans would hunt you for your blood and flesh'. Gah!

No, Percy got here and saw how happy we coexisted with the humans in the town, but he didn't realize how difficult it was for our people when we first started settling here in what was now Washington. Granted I wasn't old enough to have experienced it first-hand, but my mother was, and her stories weren't jolly bedtime tales. She had a happy ending though; she found my father and they had been happily mated for the last two hundred some-odd years.

I didn't necessarily think that Atalanta would be the type to sacrifice me for my flesh or sell me off to someone who would, but it was hard to shake the feeling of dread whenever I thought about telling her the truth.

And then there was my family. I really—

My thoughts were interrupted when a very large man opened the door. My first instinct was to be afraid of the man, as fathers in movies were usually shotgun toting, 'hurt my daughter and I'll hurt you,' kind of people and this man wasn't all that different. Face turned down in a scowl, his large muscles flexed as he crossed his arms.

"And who might you be?" He drawled with a slight, surprisingly southern, twang.

Atlanta had no such accent.

"My name's Jason, sir. I'm here to pick up Atalanta. We have a date."

Immediately his big bad wolf persona broke as an excited smile lit up his face.

"Oh, it's so nice to see my baby girl finally bringing some boys home! Come on in. I apologize for the lack of furniture. We move around so much, it's hard to keep the larger pieces. Normally, we try to get a furnished place but something about this old cabin called to me. Maybe it was the price," he chuckled to himself.

He welcomed me through the door and I tried not to let my jaw hang open. Lack of furniture was right. There was absolutely *no* furniture that I could see. The entry led to a living room space which was devoid of everything but the fireplace and a milk crate in the corner. 'Bare bones' is what my mother would have called it.

"Mr. North—" I started.

He interrupted, waving me off. "Please, call me Titus."

"Titus, I don't mean to sound rude but if you want, I'm sure I could ask around for any spare furniture people are looking to get rid of. The townsfolk here are the type that would be more than happy to help if you need anything."

"Oh, no, that's alright. I wouldn't want to let all the furniture go to waste if we ended up having to move again," he replied, shaking his head. "Awfully kind of you to offer, though."

If? If he wasn't sure about them moving, why live like this? I wondered if maybe he didn't want to feel indebted to anyone in the town. I had thought that Atalanta and her family might struggle a little when it came to money, but not this badly. I would have to talk to Dorris about giving her a raise.

I heard hurried footsteps on wood and looked towards the hallway to see Atalanta rushing forward in probably the sexiest outfit I had ever seen her in. Skin tight jeans that clung to every curve with a light purple off the shoulder long sleeve blouse that flattered her figure as opposed to the oversized clothes that she usually wore to school. Her short hair was dripping as if she had just gotten out of the shower, the droplets falling enticingly onto her light espresso skin.

I shifted, a little uncomfortable, pulling down my hoodie as I tried to hide the erection that was starting to form.

"Sorry, I woke up late and didn't realize what time it was until I heard you pull up outside. I'll be done in a minute, okay?"

I nodded, the frog in my throat stealing my ability to speak.

She scurried back down the hall. Her ass swaying back and forth drew my eyes like they were magnets.

Shit, I would not be sporting a hard-on in front of her father!

Ummm, sea plankton. Baseball. Dolphins. Chewbacca.

My muscles relaxed somewhat as I felt the blood slowly seep back into my brain.

INTO THE SEAS EMBRACE

I glanced at the father who just stood there with a wide shit-eating grin. He had totally just caught me checking out his daughter.

"So, Jason, tell me a little about yourself," He said, his arms crossed.

I rubbed the back of my neck. "Well, um, I've lived here in Argos my whole life. I'm the student body president as well as captain of the swim team."

"A high achiever." He nodded approvingly and made his way into the kitchen. "Your parents must be proud. What do they do?"

"They work at the nearby university as marine biologists," I replied.

He pulled a couple of vegetables out of the fridge. "Any siblings?"

It was in this moment that I had realized that the kind overexcited father was slowly morphing into one of the serious investigators I had seen on TV. Despite appearing focused on whatever he was working on in the kitchen, it felt like he was keeping a sharp eye on me over the counter.

"No...only child, sir."

"I was an only child myself. It can be lonely, which is why I was so determined to have at least two children. Atalanta has an older sister, Cal. Have you met her?" He asked as he pulled out a knife and began to roughly chop the veggies.

I had seen the more spirited of the sisters around a couple of times. She was quite gorgeous too, as they looked very much alike.

"We haven't been formally introduced, but I've seen her around town, and she's come to pick up Atalanta a couple of times after work."

"Oh, are you one of her friends from work? Is that how you met?" he asked.

I shook my head. "No, I work at the library next to the community center, but I met Atalanta at school. We have a couple of classes together."

"That explains why she likes you."

I tilted my head. "Sir?"

He grinned. "You work in a library. If there is one thing you should know about my little girl, it's that books mean everything to her. If she could, she would probably sleep at the library."

I chuckled. I did notice she liked books, though I had figured she might have been going there to see Percy and study.

A few moments later, I heard soft footsteps make their way up the patio. Turning, I saw the sister entering through the door. She paused when she saw me standing in the living room before a wide smile spread across her face.

"You must be Jason!" She came over to shake my hand. "Atalanta told me all about you. My, your eyes really are as beautiful as she said."

I couldn't help the red that tinted my cheeks, but I gave her a sly grin. "Well now I have a bit of ammunition against her."

"Against me?"

I jolted a bit at Atalanta's sudden appearance next to me. She was a sneaky one. Her hair was now dry, and I think she was wearing makeup. Looking a bit closer it was more obvious by the fact that the fading bruises and scratches on her cheek were well hidden. I felt a little dip in my gut when I remembered hearing about what happened to her. It was my fault those girls confronted her.

Shaking myself back into the present I leaned closer to her and crooned, "Yep. Now I know you think my eyes are beautiful."

"Your smile is beautiful too," she said matter-of-factly.

"Well, damn. If you're going to be so upfront about it, how can I use it against you?"

"That's the point," she replied, all proud of herself with that little smile.

It was cute and made me want to kiss her. I almost did until I heard a throat clearing and remembered her family was in the room.

Backing up, I pointed towards the door. "Come on, we have a day of getting to know each other and fun adventure ahead of us."

She nodded, her smile lighting up the room.

"You be good, now," her sister purred.

"I want her back by ten, or it will be your head on a platter," The father chimed in, back to being the big bad wolf again.

I didn't really know what to make of the man. One moment he was a happy, doting father playing tough; the next he was a trained investigator, and then back again. Regardless, he seemed to care a great deal about his daughters.

I jogged ahead of her to open the passenger door and helped her in. Hopping into my own side and buckling up, I began the trek of the first destination: a cozy family diner in the next town over. I had been there several times in the past and thought it would be a good place to get a decent meal before I took her to the date location Percy had suggested.

"Please tell me my family didn't embarrass you," she said a few minutes into the drive.

"Your father interrogated me like a trained professional," I chuckled. Then I got a little curious and asked, "Was he a cop at some point?"

"No, he's been a fisherman all his life," she said.

"Well, he certainly would have made a good one." I replied.

It took about a half hour to reach our destination. The whole way, we played twenty questions. I found out she loved mac and cheese and was afraid of spiders. So scared of them, in fact, that she refused to buy bananas from the store because she was terrified of being attacked by a banana spider. I told her about my forbidden love of all things cake, and how my mom would have to hide any sweets she bought because my father and I would eat them all. I told her about my hatred for jellybeans. She told me about how she always wished she owned a bunny rabbit, because they were super cuddly and their intelligence was wholly underestimated.

I kept the fact that I had a rabbit to myself, thinking it would make for a great second date. She would be so excited meeting Rocket and his cute fluffy butt.

She wasn't wrong about them being intelligent. That little jerk could get out of any cage we put him in, somehow opening the latches or locks to let himself out and paying us back by leaving small poop pellets on our beds. We eventually stopped trying and now the little eight-pound white menace ruled the house. He loved to cuddle up in anyone's lap and watch TV with them, so that made up for it.

The diner was well-packed for a Saturday afternoon. Luckily, we were seated quickly. The menu was extensive, but I knew exactly what I wanted. I ordered the fried fish sandwich while she ordered fried chicken and waffles.

"You really like fish, don't you?" she asked, once the waitress walked away.

"I guess I do."

"You've had a tuna sandwich for lunch every day this week," She pointed out.

I pouted. "Its super easy to make in the morning."

She nodded, conceding my excuse, but she still looked a tad suspicious. I left my water bottle in the car for this exact reason, making sure to chug as much of the salty liquid as I could before knocking on her door. Again, I had waited too long before quenching my need to be in the ocean. My skin was beginning to crawl and dry out in spots. I really hated this need.

Our food arrived, and we ate in contented silence. She seemed to share my habit of stuffing as much food as she could into her mouth, only coming up for air a couple of times.

Halfway through the meal, we both leaned back in the red pleather bench seats and took a breath. We broke into laughter when we realized our mirrored actions. It was nice to let go a little around her knowing that she should have gotten used to my voice by now and it shouldn't affect her anymore.

"I'm glad you're not a stick eater," I said.

"A stick eater? What the heck is that?" She snorted.

I waved my hand. "You know, those girls who will only eat salad and then pick at their food the whole time claiming they're full or on some sort of diet."

"I love food too much to torture myself like that," She looked down at her stomach. "Though I do think I need to shed a few pounds."

I shot her a glare. "You look fine. I'd actually say you need to gain rather than lose."

Now that she was wearing form-fitting clothes, it was a little concerning to see how skinny she was, especially knowing how much she ate.

My train of thought came to a screeching halt, and realization washed over me. I hadn't seen her bring lunch at all that week. I brushed it off when she kept saying that she would eat it in her study period. Yet in the last few days, Hip had been bringing and sharing his lunch with her. I thought she was possibly eating it out of kindness, but now realized that she would scarf that food down like someone who was starving. She wasn't eating her lunch beforehand because she didn't have any.

God, I was such an idiot.

I vowed to myself that I would start paying attention to this girl more. But I was also burning with the curiosity of why she wasn't bringing lunch.

"Atalanta...how badly is your family struggling?" I asked trying to keep my voice low and nonthreatening.

She began to fidget with the sleeves of her shirt.

Not meeting my eyes and with a small voice she said, "We get by."

"Is there anything I can help with, maybe?"

She shook her head vigorously. "No, Jason, please no. We are fine, seriously. Money gets a little tight sometimes, but we all got paid this week so... yeah."

I was making her extremely uncomfortable with this line of questioning as her eyes were beginning to look like a deer in headlights and she nervously kept tugging at her sleeves. So, against my better judgement, I changed the subject.

"Hip mentioned you were a real athlete?"

The tension in her shoulders broke as she began to tell me about her experience on one of her schools' track teams. It was a surprise to see that we shared a similar love for that rush, despite our sports literally being polar opposites of land and water. That moment when you're totally in the zone, and it feels like you're flying, the world is whizzing past you, and nothing else matters in those seconds but pushing your body to the fullest.

It seemed she liked the competition side more than me though. I had an unfair advantage that most people didn't, so there was never that drive to always win when I knew I would likely always come in first.

When we finished our lunch and I paid the check, I held out my hand for her to take. Without hesitation, she slipped her small hand into mine. It was a lot warmer than I was expecting and extremely soft.

I felt a surge of contentment holding that hand and for a few moments as we walked out of the diner and watched as the snow slowly drift from the sky, I thought to myself that I could be happy holding this hand for a very long time. It was over all too quickly when I helped her into the car.

Ten minutes later we arrived at the lake. The parking lot was packed, and people were walking back and forth from their cars or chilling on tailgates. There was a food truck at one end of the parking lot opposite the bathrooms.

Hopping out of the car, I rushed to open her door. Getting out, she looked around curiously, taking everything in.

"Where are we?" She asked.

I smiled. "Why, only the best ice-skating park in the whole world."

"Ice skating?" She asked, her face lighting up with excitement before morphing into a confused frown. "But wait, we're outside?"

I couldn't help but start laughing. What kind of person only ever skated indoors?

Trying to calm down my sniggering I held out my hand. "Come on, I'll show you."

Taking her hand in mine, I pulled us through the throng of cars and people until they made way for the view of Ashter Lake.

It was a decent sized lake which I personally knew could be well over fifteen feet deep in some spots, but right now it was completely frozen over. People were skating across its icy surface. Some were light and graceful on the blades, while others were hardly steady. Off to the sides, there were kids and their family playing in the giant piles of snow that had been scooped off the shore. It was a jolly sight, only missing the Christmas lights that some people would string from the trees in December.

I looked down at Atalanta who watched with a bit of wonder and excitement.

"I've only ever seen indoor rinks. This is amazing!" She was nearly jumping up and down with joy until her face fell into a frown and halted. "Is it safe? Won't the ice crack?"

"This deep into the winter, no. Once it starts to warm up some, it will be too dangerous." When her face began to morph into one of concern, I added "The locals know the lake pretty well, so they'll start blocking it off to tourists when the time comes."

She nodded. "That's good."

I took her up to a temporary trailer which was manned by an old couple who rented out skates by the hour. After I paid for the skates, we strapped them on and made our way down the bank to the ice. I was pretty steady on my feet walking through the padding someone had laid down, having done this for many years. Atalanta, on the other hand, was a bit wobbly. She held onto me tightly as she tried to maintain her balance. Hey, I wasn't complaining about having her hands all over me and neither was the erection in my pants.

When we hit the edge of the lake, I glided effortlessly out into the ice. Spinning, I watched as Atalanta made it a couple feet out on wobbly legs until losing her balance and falling on her delectable ass.

I glided over to her, trying to suppress my smile. "Would you like some help, my lady?"

"Nope! I got this," She held up her hand for me to stop, then flailed around for a few moments attempting to stand before falling right back on her butt. "Okay, yes, I need help."

I chuckled, took her hand, and pulled her to her feet. "Come on, nice and steady."

We went like that for a while, me holding her hand as she tried to maintain her footing on the slippery ice. Whenever she would start to fall, I would just keep her steady until she was good to go. Eventually she got the hang of it, not needing me to hold her anymore. I'd have to say within a good twenty or thirty minutes, it was as if she were born on this ice. She wasn't able to do tricks or anything like the few professionals that were here, but she stopped falling and skated around with ease.

"I don't know whether to be jealous or proud that you're a natural at this," I commented as she skated gracefully in a circle.

"Apparently I have figure skating in my blood," she said.

"Really? From your mother?" I asked, curious. She had yet to mention her mother.

She nodded. "She died when I was really little though."

A pang of empathy shot through me and I reached for her hand. "I'm sorry."

"It's alright. I hardly remember her," she said, slipping her hand out of mine.

I probably wouldn't have caught it if I wasn't so focused on her, but her voice was a bit strained, and she bit at the corner of her lip when she said that. I didn't understand why she would feel the need to lie about something like that. I thought long and hard on it for a moment before I realized I had seen her bite her lip like that several times today, not giving it much thought.

When I talked about her father acting like a cop.

When I asked about her birthday.

Several times when we talked about our likes and dislikes.

...When she first said she ate her lunch in study hall.

I had brushed it off as a nervous tic, but now I realized...she didn't trust me with the truth.

Anger flared in my chest. The point of today was for us to get to know each other and she had more than likely been lying the entire time! Was anything she said true? I know she had been lying about eating lunch. What else had she been lying about?

"I just remembered something. I'll be right back," I said through clenched teeth.

Turning around, I skated off towards the parking lot, leaving Atlanta standing there all alone in the middle of the lake.

I stomped up the padded path and towards the bathrooms, too angry to even take off the boots once I hit the gravel. I would have to buy them now that I was chipping the blades, but at this moment I didn't care.

The heat of rage continued to boil in the pit of my stomach. I wanted to go back there and scream at her, call her out on all of it!

Trudging into the men's bathroom, I locked myself in the handicap stall. Breathing heavily, I moved to the sink, leaning myself on it. Looking up into the mirror, I could see the color of my irises spread, blocking out both my pupils and sclera until my eyes looked like iridescent blue orbs.

Growling, I raised my fist and smashed the glass, shattering my image. I knew I should have cut open my hands doing that but the scales under my skin were rippling, meaning the small ones which covered the tops of my hands protected the skin from the impact. I knew that if I didn't calm down, the fins on my back, legs, and ulna would be tearing through my clothes.

I took a deep breath, willing myself to calm my shift.

In through the nose and slowly out through my fanged mouth.

When I felt my scales settle and fangs recede back into my gums, I opened my eyes and looked at myself through the shattered remains of the mirror. My eyes were back to normal.

Sighing, I slumped against the wall and slid down to the floor.

"At least I didn't lose it in front of her," I mumbled to myself.

I felt ashamed of myself for losing control like that. I had no right to be mad at her for keeping secrets. I had several huge ones of my own that I was too afraid to share with her. Percy was right. I knew she suspected something, and if I wanted to continue what I was doing, I would need to tell her the truth.

I was scared, though. That side of me was a monster, a mythical creature which belonged in the ocean, not on land with the rest of the people I cared about. The others never seemed to struggle with that part of themselves as much as I did. Even Percy, who was so strong and hadn't grown up on the surface, seemed fine. Never losing his temper and fazing, never seeming to need the ocean as much as I craved it.

Perhaps it was because they hadn't grown up the way I had.

Or perhaps it was because I was weak.

Chapter Fifteen

Atalanta

"Jason?"

I called into the men's bathroom. I had seen him practically sprinting this way when he suddenly bailed on me on the lake. I didn't know what was up with him. One moment we were talking and the next he went all rigid and booked it.

I worried he had caught me in my lie. The lie that my mother was dead, when in reality she was alive, probably behind bars or padded walls. Yet, the normal reaction I was used to when caught in a lie was to be confronted about it or ignored. Not running away.

So, after several minutes of waiting on the slippery ice, I followed him, being sure to swap out my skates for my normal boots that we had left at a spot near the shore.

It was a little upsetting as up until now the date had been pretty magical. Well, besides the interrogating questions I had to answer knowing that I really couldn't give the full truth for a lot of them.

I knocked on the side of the wall, the dull thudding just barely echoing into space.

I called again, "Jason, are you in here?"

This time he did answer, his voice guttural. "Yeah, I'm sorry...I kind of had a bout of... diarrhea?"

I don't know why I would have thought he would have learned how to lie in the last twenty-four hours, but I decided to go along with it nonetheless.

"I hope you didn't get food poisoning from lunch."

"I might have...do you mind? I should be done in a minute," he said, his voice slowly returning to its normal tone.

"Okay, I'll be outside," I replied.

I backed away from the bathroom's entrance and leaned against the concrete. I could only hope I was overthinking, and he was telling the truth.

I bit the corner of my lip. He didn't owe me any truths because I hadn't done much to deserve it. Yet the little flame of curiosity inside me wondered if he ran because of what I said, or if it had something to do with what I learned yesterday.

Initially, I had thought to use today as a way to get some answers out of him. But then he was sweet and charming, bringing me to this lake and helping me get my footing on the icy ground. He was noticing the oddness of my situation. The money struggles, Dad's experience as an investigator, and unlike Percy and Hip, who seemed to see things instantly but kept quiet, slowly trying to coax answers out of me naturally, Jason was more upfront, asking me directly what was up. I was afraid that if I began to poke around with his situation, he would do the same and next thing you know we'd be having to pack up again.

"Sorry about that." I looked up to see Jason coming out of the bathroom.

He looked alright, if a little pale.

"Are you feeling okay?" I asked, concerned.

"Yeah, I didn't mean to run off like that. I just didn't want to shout out my sudden need for the toilet," he replied with a shaky smile.

I laughed. "Well, poop is poop. We all do it, it's nothing to be embarrassed about."

Jason looked down at the skates in my hand and then to the ones that were still strapped to his feet. The blades were dented and chipped from his run across the hard, rocky ground.

I grimaced. "I don't think they'll be happy about you destroying their skates."

"No, probably not. Hey, if I tell them I had food poisoning, do you think they'll have pity on me?"

"I doubt it," I said with a snort.

It turned out the couple was forgiving, as they had replacement blades for most of their skates along with a sharpener. They came prepared, saying that this happened a lot more than we would think. Jason still had to pay them twenty bucks for damages.

As we made our way out to the car, I wondered if we would be ending the date here or if he had something else in mind.

As we got in the car Jason said, "As penance for cutting our ice-skating date short, I have a surprise for you,"

"Is it a million dollars?" I asked, batting my eyelashes at him.

He snorted. "Hell no, if I won a million dollars, I'd be keeping that to myself!"

"No fair," I crossed my arms over my chest and pouted. "didn't your parents ever teach you to share?"

"Didn't your dad ever tell you finders keepers losers weepers?"

I stuck my tongue out at him like a bloody two-year-old. I was delighted when he stuck his tongue right back at me, adding a raspberry to it, causing us both to break out into a fit of giggles.

Once our giggle fit began to break, Jason said, "Besides, if I were the one to win a million dollars, I could take you on nicer dates."

"I thought this date was perfect, Jason. Besides, I pride myself on being a cheap date."

"I feel like that's not something you should be proud of. Or at least don't word it like that," He said, breaking out into laughter again.

"I see nothing wrong with being a cheap date," I shrugged. "It just proves that we can have a good time with or without money."

"True. Though you do realize what it also implies right?"

"Why, yes, I do. And trust me, Mr. Monroe, you'll have to work a lot harder to get into my pants," I said wiggling my eyebrows at him.

He replied with a low, sensuous growl which heated up my core and encouraged me to tease him more. But we were driving, and I honestly didn't want us to crash if I distracted him too much. So, I sat back and studied him.

He looked really good in his olive-green canvas jacket and dark jeans. His brown hair looked soft and fluffy, and I wanted to touch it so badly that I slid my hands underneath me to keep them still. I also wanted to kiss him again. However, I wondered for a moment if it was because I liked him or because I was subconsciously trying to distract myself from the lies that I was giving him and the lies that I was getting back in return.

He looked over to me and gave me this devastatingly perfect smile that sent little butterflies fluttering about in my stomach. Oh, yeah, I definitely wanted to kiss him because I liked him.

I turned away from him and stared out the window. The trees we passed were tall and surprisingly green despite the snow that laid on top of them. I liked the forest. Cities were often too loud, too full of people. They made me nervous. I often wondered if the reason we stuck to small towns was not that they were obscure but because my father and Clint knew about my issues.

We would hear from our handler soon. I liked this one. When we moved from the south, despite having the same head, our handler changed several times. The last one was a bit of a dick and didn't get that we had been doing this for years and didn't need to be babied.

One day I would be free, and I could go back to my life. Though I wondered what that life was. A girl who loved to go shopping at the mall on Sundays, cared about the latest fashions and drooled over boy bands. That girl was a star on the junior track team and had thirty friends but wasn't close to any of them.

A girl that didn't know what it was like to have a bullet stuck in their shoulder.

A girl with a functional, smiling mother.

Who was that girl? Because I wasn't that girl anymore. At least I didn't think so.

The car drove over a rough spot, pulling me from my thoughts and back to where I was. Back to being Atalanta North in the car with a cute but mysterious guy.

I smiled. "I know you said it was a surprise but are you at least going to give me a hint as to where we are going?"

Jason pursed his lips and thought about it for a moment. "Elation."

I tilted my head. "Elation?"

"Yep," he grinned.

"That's all I get? A single word? Not even really a word but a feeling?"

"Yeppers."

I pouted and sat back in the seat. "You're no fun."

He laughed but refused to give me any more hints as to where we were going.

About ten minutes later, we pulled up into the driveway of a house. It was a beautiful house, two stories, modern, painted beige with a red roof. There was a gigantic tree in the front yard, its gnarled branches stretching high up and across, passing by a few windows. It looked like the perfect tree to build a treehouse in, or perhaps to sneak out at night through the windows. I noted that there were no other cars out front in the circular driveway, indicating that it was unlikely anyone was home.

Jason turned off the car and looked excitedly at me. "Come on."

He didn't open my door this time, hopping out of his seat and rushing to the front door of the home.

"Are we at your house?" I called to him.

"That we are."

"What could cause elation at your place? A little presumptuous don't you think?"

"I'm not going to try and get into your pants," He inserted a key into the door and turned to give me a panty-melting wink. "Though, I do like how you think having sex with me will cause you that much joy. Now, come on, it's about to rain!"

I rolled my eyes wide, trying to suppress the smile that was trying to reach the surface along with a slight blush. Hopping out of the car I scampered over to the door right before the first drops hit the ground.

He held open the door for me to walk through.

I stared back at the heavy drops that pitter-pattered against the ground. "How did you know it was about to rain?"

"One of my many talents," he smiled.

The inside of the house was, well, homey. The floor was white tile, and from where I stood in this little hallway entrance, I could see that it opened to a living room with two cushy looking couches in an L shape, one of which was facing a wide flat screen atop a black stand. Colors of black, white, and beige popped out at me. Looking around, I noticed that there were oriental knickknacks and decor everywhere. An ancient looking dagger sat on a pedestal atop a table in the entryway. The table in front of the TV was black and had intricate designs like many of the classic Asian paintings I'd seen in books. In fact, several paintings like that were hung up on the walls, and next to the TV stand stood a small terracotta warrior.

"Is one of your parents Asian?" I asked, somewhat puzzled by the decor.

"No, my mom just loves Oriental stuff," he gestured around to all the decor. "This is all her doing."

He dropped his keys into a bowl that sat next to the dagger and placed a hand gently on my shoulder.

INTO THE SEAS EMBRACE

I looked up at him. His face was lit up with even more excitement than when we were at the lake. He turned his head, looking out towards the living room and with his free hand tapped his fingers against the wall.

I scrunched my eyebrows, thoroughly confused as to what was going on. I pulled my eyes away from him to look around.

I caught movement out of the corner of my eyes and followed it. A small white ball poked its head out from a hallway up ahead. My eyes grew wide as the small white ball came further out into my view.

"BUNNY!!!!" I exclaimed, squealing like a little girl who was just given a pony for Christmas.

The bunny froze, standing stark still as its upright white ears swiveled around to find the danger, its nose twitching. I silenced my squeals not wanting to scare the most adorable thing I had ever seen.

"Come here Rocket. We've got company," Jason said, patting his knee, I assumed to get its attention.

At the sound of Jason's voice, the bunny looked directly at us, its blue eyes wide. Jason whistled, tapping his fingers against the wall again. The bunny broke from its frozen state, his back feet thumped hard against the ground before he hopped excitedly towards us. Jason scooped him up off the ground and turned to me.

"Atalanta, meet Rocket. Rocket, meet Atalanta," He said as he scratched the top of the rabbit's head.

I don't think any amount of will could contain my smile at that moment. Jason had been right, elation was a good word for what I was feeling. I was bouncing up and down with excitement, my hands curled into fists waving back and forth in front of me.

"Oh my God, you have a bunny!"

"Yes, I do," He chuckled.

"Aaand, why did you not introduce us sooner?"

"Because I thought this would make a good second date."

I couldn't contain myself any longer. With my hands out I asked, "Can I hold him?"

"Sure. If he squirms, just hold him like a baby. He likes that."

Jason shifted the rabbit in his arms and held him out to me. He squirmed at first, uncomfortable with the new position but he didn't look scared as I gently took him.

He was so small, no bigger than a bowling ball and covered in bright white fur from head to toe. Well, not completely head to toe. The fluffy pads of his feet which sported some wicked claws were tinted yellow. When he snuggled into me, I just about died.

"I want you to know you're not getting him back," I stated matter-of-factly.

"I figured as much," he laughed. "which is why I thought it would be a good idea to watch a movie while you held him."

We moved further into the house, opening more of it up to me. I could see the stairs that I presumed led to the second floor, down the hall that Rocket came out of. The kitchen, which was right next to the entryway that we came through, wasn't very large. At least not as large as I would've expected from a house this size. There were more Oriental decorations than a shop in Chinatown, including a porcelain doll in a yukata, a Japanese-style dress.

"Won't he get bored and start squirming around?" I asked as I scratched the top of Rocket's head.

"Maybe, but he likes to watch movies."

My eyes shot up to Jason who was watching me with a serene expression.

"Seriously?"

"Yeah. We don't really know why but he could sit there with you for hours beyond a few potty breaks."

"Does that mean he's gonna poop on me or something?" I couldn't help my disgusted frown.

I loved the rabbit already, but nobody liked being used as a litter box.

He shook his head. "He's trained to go to the bathroom in a small spot in his cage."

"I didn't know rabbits could be litter trained."

"Most people don't."

He walked over to the TV and started rifling through the DVD selection. "Any particular genre?"

"Do you have any satire?"

He pulled out a DVD and held it up to me. "Stardust?"

"That works." I nodded.

Jason popped in the movie and sauntered over to the larger of the two couches and flopped down. He looked up at me and patted the space beside him. Nervously, I shuffled over with Rocket in my arms and gingerly sat down on the cushions next to him.

Initially, I sat there stiff as a board, nervous about being this close to him completely alone in the house. But once the movie began, I settled a little, petting Rocket gently between his ears.

Jason wasn't lying when he said that Rocket liked watching the movie. He snuggled into my lap, only getting up to, I assume, go to the bathroom. He would hop away down the hall and then come back a few minutes later and hop back up on the couch with us. Sometimes he settled into my lap and other times into Jason's. Whenever he chose me, Jason and I would look over at each other and share giddy little smiles.

About halfway through the movie, I finally fully relaxed into the couch, Jason's arm slung over the back behind me. He was mere inches from me, and I was constantly aware of his slow, even breaths and deep barrel-chested laughter at the comedic drama of the movie. I was also aware of every time his gaze slid to me, and his hands twitched, probably wanting to touch me.

INTO THE SEAS EMBRACE

By the high point of the movie's climax, I was leaning fully into the crook of his arm, my body relaxed, while my heart pounded. Testing my boundaries, I rested my hand over his chest feigning an attempt to snuggle closer. I could feel his heart racing underneath my fingertips. I was glad to know I wasn't the only one affected by our close proximity. Rocket lay sprawled across the two of us, a long noodle of fluff. His eyes were closed. Evidently, he was completely unaffected by the electrical tension that sparked the air.

As the movie wrapped up, I slowly began to run my hand up and down his chest. I could feel the hard muscle beneath the turtleneck sweater he wore. I could also feel him twitching at my touch. A little bit of triumph flickered through me at the thought of evoking a reaction from him. As the credits scrolled down the screen, I slowly turned my eyes toward Jason. He was already looking at me. His pupils were dilated, and he was probably breathing about as hard as I was.

"Atalanta, you're certainly not making it easy to be a gentleman," he whispered.

"A gentleman wouldn't have kissed me like you did the other day," I pointed out.

He licked his lips. "True, but I knew that was wrong of me to spring myself on you like that. So, I'm trying to be more courteous this time."

"And who said I wanted you to be a gentleman?"

Taking a leap of faith, I slid my fingers up into his hair, pulling a groan from him before tugging his lips down to meet mine. The moment our lips touched,

Jason surged forward, startling poor Rocket out of our laps. His hands found their way to my hips as he leaned heavily into the kiss. It was desperate, needy. Hands mapping out each other's bodies over our clothing, mouths meeting feverishly. When his tongue swiped across my bottom lip seeking invitation, I gave it. When his tongue delved into my mouth, my body, which was already warming up, set itself on fire. I arched into him, wanting more attention from his hands, his mouth, him.

I reached around his waist to cup his jean-covered ass, wanting him closer. He leaned into me, gently pushing me down until I was sprawled across the couch with him on top of me.

We broke the kiss, panting, meeting each other's eyes for a split second. I gasped. His eyes were shining brightly. It almost looked as if the green of his iris was fading into other parts of his eye. I only caught a quick look before he leaned to the side and nipped at my ear, distracting my mind with the tingles that ran down my body to my core.

His lips and teeth nipped and licked, making their way down to the crook of my neck. I moaned when he suckled there, arching into him further. My right leg, which was between his, pressed against the hard bulge that was in his pants. He felt rather large, and I wanted to explore his length more. Slowly I ran my hand down his chest making my way to his crotch. When I cupped him through his pants, he groaned and broke away from my neck.

"Atalanta," he whispered, his voice low and harsh.

I hummed as I continued to rub his cock, feeling proud when he moaned and thrust further into my touch, clearly wanting more. His own hands, which had been supporting him on either side of me, repositioned, the left one shifting under my head, fingers tangling themselves in my hair while the right one pulled up to lightly cup my breast on the outside of my blouse. He was gentle, testing me to see if I would deny him. In response, I pressed my hand harder into his cock.

He jerked his crotch forward, thrusting into my hand once more before leaning his face back down into the crook of my neck.

This all felt too good. My body was hot and needy, wanting his hands to sink below the waistband of my pants but also not wanting him to stop his slow kneading of my breast. I knew I was wet, I could feel it as I began to dampen my underwear. When his legs moved closer, one of them pressing into me, I found my solution. I ground myself against his thigh.

"Someone wants something," he chuckled into my neck, his hot breath causing me to shiver.

"Maybe," I breathed.

"Well, I can't leave you unsatisfied."

He shifted again, his leg moving away from my grinding hips, the hand which had been focused on my breast making its way down.

It was right before those fingers touched the top of my pants that I felt myself slipping. Before I realized what was happening it was too late. I fell off the couch with a yelp, dragging Jason down with me as we tumbled and smacked into the coffee table next to us.

It didn't hurt, but it definitely startled me out of my lust-induced haze.

"Holy shit, are you okay?" Jason asked. He was still on top of me, and I was unable to get a good look at his face.

"Yeah, I'm fine," I replied. I placed my hand on his shoulder, urging for him to get up.

He didn't for several moments, both of us panting heavily. I turned my head and looked at the table. We had knocked it over in our fall, the stuff that was on top spilled to the floor.

Whoops.

Finally, Jason sat up. When I looked at his face, he was flushed and grinning like a fool. I also noticed that his eyes looked normal. I guess it had to be my sex-crazed brain seeing things.

"Well, that was enlightening," he said before standing, pulling me up with him.

"What do you mean enlightening?"

"Well, I just mean that--"

"Oh my God, I think I broke your table!" I interrupted him with a shout.

INTO THE SEAS EMBRACE

The table wasn't just knocked over, one of its legs had bowed inward. Frowning, Jason looked down at the table as well. Walking over to it he picked up the corner with the broken leg. It dangled there for a moment, a few splinters holding the piece of wood on before it fully snapped off and fell with a thud to the floor.

Jason stared at it for a moment before he broke into laughter. I, on the other hand, was completely mortified.

Holding my face in my hands, I groaned. "I am so sorry."

"Why? It's not like this is your fault. Besides, it's an easy fix."

"But I was the one who fell into it. Oh, your parents are going to be so upset! They're going to hate me, and I haven't even met them yet!" I rubbed my face back and forth, so frustrated with myself.

Putting the table down, he came over to me and gently pulled my hands away from my face. "Atalanta, it's okay. I'll fix it up good as new before they even get home tonight. They aren't going to be mad when no real damage was done."

"I don't know," I said, staring at the table.

I felt Jason's fingers gently touch my chin and pull my face away from the broken table to look up at him.

"It's going to be okay. Let's get you home and I promise I'll send you a text with the photo of the fixed table."

I nodded. I felt horrible about breaking the table. Yet, I would admit I didn't mind what lead up to it. My insides shivered thinking about his lips on mine and what could have been if I hadn't fallen over.

That pleasure and warmth was doused by a bucket of ice water when we were leaving.

As I had passed by the mirror and caught a glimpse of myself, I noticed that I looked really cute in the off the shoulder long sleeve Cal let me borrow. My eyes had widened when I realized the shirt had gotten messed up during our frantic make-out session and a sliver of white scar was poking out from beneath the low neckline of the shirt. Quickly, I fixed the shirt and looked over to Jason who was grabbing his keys and our coats. A flutter of relief spread through me when I realized he probably didn't see anything.

Of course, the reality of what could have happened slapped me in the face. If I had let him go any further, he would have seen. How could I possibly explain it to him? I couldn't.

I would have to be more careful from now on.

We drove back in a comfortable silence. He had one hand on the wheel, the other wrapped around mine. When he pulled up outside, I noticed Dad was gone. With any hope, he had gone to get groceries with the money from our paychecks and some more supplies to fix the house.

I turned to look at him, my free hand on the door handle. "I'd invite you in, but if you hadn't noticed before we don't have any furniture. And you need to head back to fix that table."

He nodded. "I noticed. I told your dad that I'd be able to help him find furniture around town, that the townspeople might have some spare furniture for you guys to use. But he said he didn't want to take their furniture if he wasn't sure you guys would have to move again."

"Yeah. Some places we've stayed only a month or two."

"Why?"

I shrugged nonchalantly. "My dad's work moves him a lot."

"Doesn't he work down at the fishing yard?"

I stiffened and said through gritted teeth. "Yep. I gotta get going. I'll see you at school on Monday?"

Before I even got a reply, I was out of the car, waving back at him with a smile. He looked confused if a little disgruntled, but waved back nonetheless.

I really would have to come up with a different reason for why we moved a lot. I had forgotten that I told him my dad had always been a fisherman.

Stupid. Stupid. Stupid.

I was really messing up with these guys.

Slipping through the cabin door, I stomped to my bedroom. My cot was set up underneath the window. A deep blue sleeping bag lay on top, deflated without a body in it. The muted winter's light that streamed through the large window made the room feel relaxing and comfortable.

I made my way over to the cot and slid my hand underneath the sleeping bag to pull out a blue file with the word "North" written on it.

Pulling off the pen that was attached to it, I opened the file which contained everything I needed to know about Atalanta North: where she went to school during kindergarten, her favorite teacher, pet, subject, what type of movies she liked, the name of her first crush, and the kind of clothes she liked to wear. Her entire life history in a file. We unfortunately had to ignore the last one most of the time, as we weren't getting enough money in to constantly be swapping out our clothes.

With the pen, I marked down over the minor section of the father's history:

'Worked as a fisherman whole life. Moved around a lot?'

Closing the file, I slid it back underneath the sleeping bag.

With a sigh, I stared out my window. The day had been a good one. A couple of ups and downs, but overall good. Jason was kind and handsome, and he really seemed to like me, or at least was attracted to me based on what happened earlier.

I suddenly felt the weight of depression lay itself over my shoulders. Why? I didn't know. If I had to guess, it was all of the hidden truths. The beautiful lies we gave to protect ourselves.

I hoped that one day I wouldn't need to lie anymore.

But I was also aware that the sadness also could have just been there, inviting itself into my mind for no reason, as it was with depression. It was best to wait it out sometimes. Perhaps I would go for a walk. Just then, I felt content to simply look out the window and watch the snow drift softly through the trees, the little flakes perching themselves on branches. When I skimmed my eyes to the right, the ocean churned and waved to its own rhythm, separate from the drifting of the snow.

By the time my father and Cal came home, it was sundown and the clouds blocked out any light from the moon or stars. I had sat there the whole time, my mind slowly swaying back and forth like the ocean. Moments of mindless bliss turned into stormy dark thoughts before diving back into nothing as I stared out that window.

I could hear them talking as they brought groceries and whatnot back and forth into the house. I could help them, but I honestly just felt like staying in my room.

I missed my books.

They were my constant. The stories written in their pages never changing, always revealing their characters' souls open for me to escape into, to occupy my restless mind.

At the sound of a knock at my door, I turned my eyes away from the window to see my father. His eyes were scrunched to reveal the laugh lines of his age as his mouth spread into a smile.

"How's my baby girl doing?" he asked softly.

"A little down," I said honestly. No sense in hiding it from him.

His brow furrowed. "Did your date end badly?"

"No." I shook my head. "It actually went really well. Jason was amazing. We went ice skating and watched a movie. Besides the fact that he got to know someone who technically wasn't me, it was perfect."

"Oh, honey," he crooned and came over, sitting at the edge of the cot. "It is you. Yes, while some of the facts of your life are different, you're the same woman inside and that's who I'm betting this boy is falling for. The person, not the facts. This Atalanta North might hate pineapple, but I bet she's not funny like you, bet she doesn't have your tenacity. You brought that to her persona."

I felt tears well up in my eyes. With a sniff I held them back. "I know, Dad."

He leaned over and kissed my forehead. "I love you Bun-Bun. Now, why don't you go on a walk and clear your head. I know that can sometimes make you feel better."

He stood and held out his hand for me.

I took it, letting him help pull me up and guide me towards the door.

Chapter Sixteen

Ajax

The day had been another long one. The mayor had wanted me to try and finish up the mural I had begun on the community center. I don't think he realized how long it was going to take to do the whole building, but I simply let him babble on about it. After that, I helped Mr. Norrison fix the shelves in his house and delivered one of my paintings to a collector in the next town over. Now that it was dark out, I had the chance to head out into the woods by my house and find a good tree to cut up and drag back to use in my next piece.

Who needed sleep when there were things to do?

I yawned as I trekked through the forest, the lantern in my hand swinging gently back and forth.

The crunch of my feet as I broke through the snow and twigs underneath was loud in the quiet crop of trees. I could still hear the ocean's call not far off. I knew it was a mile and a half to my left, just as I knew every tree in this section of woods. You walk around them long enough like I had, and they started to become familiar.

After several minutes of searching, I found it. A young picea sitchensis, a spruce which had fallen several days before. The woods in this part were too dense, and the roots didn't get the chance to spread wide enough. One hard gust of wind with the cold, wet ground and the poor thing just toppled right over. But it would make for good carving wood.

I put my lantern down near the base of the stump, the light casting odd, mangled shadows all around me. Pulling out the axe from the bag on my back, I got to work stripping sections of it. I knew it was too large to take back all at once, so I mentally broke the tree into manageable parts, and once I cleared away all the smaller branches, I swung my axe high.

Whack!

Whack!

The work was good, it allowed for my mind to be distracted. The people of Argos had been good to me when I hadn't deserved their kindness, and it was only fair that I returned the favor. Which was why this particular piece of wood was going to go to Dorris, who had helped me the other day when I went through an attack.

Whack!

Whack!

Whack!

My mind wandered to the reason for the attack. A girl, or perhaps a woman, had caught me off guard while I had been focused on painting the mural.

Atalanta. Her name was Atalanta. And I had given her chocolates.

When she first approached, her emotions had come crashing down on me like a tidal wave. Fear, pain, confusion, curiosity, sadness, and a distinct pain in my right cheek. Confused, I had dropped my supplies onto the ground below me. When I went down to retrieve them and saw the girl that was causing such strong emotions, I was surprised. She was young, perhaps in her late teens to early twenties, with gorgeous chocolatey skin and short, colorful hair. I felt her pain, both new and old.

I studied her and spied what was hidden: bruising beneath makeup. Someone had hit her, and knowing this I felt a surge of my own anger amongst her concoction of emotion.

It had proven too much when our eyes met. I caught a glimpse of enchanting brown and green eyes before all I could see was blood, lots of blood, and screaming. There was a voice crying out to 'Stop, please stop!'.

I knew the images weren't mine. Memories which were imprinted so deep into her subconscious that they leaked out of her soul with the rest of her feelings.

The next thing I knew I was throwing up, emptying my stomach onto the ground in front of me.

Rather embarrassing, to be honest.

I hadn't been affected by someone's emotions like that in a long time. Having gained control over my abilities years ago, I had finally come to see my powers of empathy as less of a curse and more of a mild burden. Yet, I could still remember when being near anyone caused my stomach to clench as my mind was overwhelmed by theirs. Chocolate always helped to soothe the attacks.

Whack!

I paused in my chopping to take a deep breath. I hadn't yet broken a sweat. It would take a lot more to do that, especially in this cool, crisp air.

When I finally recovered with Dorris' help the other day, I felt the immediate need to seek out the girl again. Despite knowing it wasn't a good idea so soon after getting sick, I felt the innate need to help her. To understand her pain and want to heal it as my abilities demanded. Dorris had convinced me, however, to go home instead.

On the way back, I had stopped by Tim's and asked for some chocolate to settle my nerves. He was more than happy to help and even gave me an extra box to take home. The box was pretty with a thin, colorful film. Holding it, I thought back to the girl and thought she could use it more than I.

When she had approached me two days later, I was more prepared. Her emotions slammed into the wall I had built up to prepare being in a town surrounded by so many people. I was prompt about giving the chocolate to her. Her happiness at receiving the gift warmed my insides like a small fire. I wanted her to feel that again.

Whack!

She was interesting.

Whack!

And gorgeous.

INTO THE SEAS EMBRACE

Whack!

And she was standing two hundred yards in front of me.

I looked up as I felt her unique signature pass at the edge of my radius. Startled, the axe slipped from my hands in my downswing and went flying into a tree not far from her.

"Holy shit!" She shouted.

Eyes wide, I rushed towards her to make sure she was okay.

She turned to run, only to stumble on a root and fall. When she turned and saw me still coming, she curled up into a ball, whimpering. I halted and reassessed the situation. She was scared.

I realized that to her, a large form was racing towards her in the middle of the night after throwing an axe at her.

"Atalanta," I called.

I felt her surprise and realization at my familiar voice.

I approached slowly. Pulling out my phone, I turned on the flashlight to add extra light for her to see. She looked up at me, her beautiful eyes meeting mine. Prepared this time, I put up my mental walls to block the full extent of her emotions.

"Ajax?"

I crouched down next to her and leaned forward, wanting to comfort her and make her feel safe. "It's me. I'm here."

"What the fuck are you doing out here at night with a fucking axe!?" she shouted, causing me to sit back away from her with my eyebrows raised.

I opened and closed my mouth a couple of times before coming up with, "Cutting wood."

"In the middle of the night?" she asked, her voice rising in pitch, cracking.

"It's my only free time."

"Oh, that's all the better, to be walking around at night with a creepy lantern and hacking at wood with an axe!" She waved her hands wildly in the air. "Here I was, minding my own business, trying to get some air when I see your lantern! Then I hear the creepy chopping, and of course against my better judgement I freaking get closer to the sound! Next thing I know, an axe is flying at my face! You know how freaking scary that is?! You threw an axe at me!"

She talked quite a lot. It was obvious that she was a tad upset.

"I'm sorry," I apologized as I helped her to her feet. "My hand slipped."

She laughed. "Slipped? Slipped?! Christ, Ajax, you could have killed me!"

Strike that, she was just a bit hysterical. Her emotions were all over the place as she continued to rant about how scared she was and how it was extremely weird and stupid for me to be out here cutting down trees in the dark."

I felt bad for causing her to feel such fear. Wanting that feeling gone from her, I instinctually reached forward and brushed my hand along her cheek and pulled her fear into me. I felt the pain spear through me like an icicle through the heart, causing a shiver to run down my spine before I brushed it away.

Almost immediately, the fumes I could practically see coming out of her ears stopped. Her hands, which were waving all over the place and pointing fingers at me, calmed. Her ramblings slowed to a stop, leaving her panting.

She let out a heavy breath. "Okay. I feel much better now."

I nodded, doubting she realized that I had pulled the negative feeling from her. Most didn't, unless they knew about my ability beforehand.

"That's good," I commented, staring into her eyes with what little light we had.

She stepped up close to me and poked me in the chest. "You need to be more careful, Mister. Out cutting wood in the dark and throwing axes at girls."

"Again, my apologies. It slipped." I said as I stopped her finger from poking my chest by gently wrapping my hand around hers.

She blinked her beautiful wild eyes up at me, drawing me into her. She was wearing a heavy coat that looked far too big on her and…*super* tight jeans.

Before I realized it, I was too close into her personal space, leaning over her as if I was about to kiss her. She was looking up at me, her mouth open ever so slightly. When she licked her lips nervously, I had to step back.

As a distraction, I walked over to the tree that my axe had buried itself into. With one hand, I pulled it out and began to walk back towards the tree trunk. I knew she was following behind me. Being a bit of a show off, I swung the axe high and slammed it hard down on the wood, chopping off the rest of the section.

Standing up straight, I saw her at the edge of my space watching me as she leaned against one of the nearby trees.

"That was rather impressive," she said, her voice a little breathy.

I smiled, pride prickling in my chest.

"Now how are you going to move it?" she asked, crossing her arms over her chest with a cocky expression on her face.

Without a word, I walked back over to my backpack and pulled out some rope. I tied the rope around the piece of trunk, snatched up my bag and lantern, then used the rope to pull the hunk of wood onto my back.

She whistled.

Curious to see if she would follow me, I took one careful step at a time as I walked back to my house with the wood. It wasn't particularly heavy, just awkward, and the bark scratched against my back.

With a quick glance behind me, I saw that Atalanta was indeed following.

Discreetly, I let the scales on my back rise to the surface, acting as an efficient barrier to the rough bark.

"Here, let me at least hold this for you," she said, hurrying over and scooping up my backpack and lantern.

"Thanks," I muttered, warmed by her offer to help.

We walked through the forest for a few minutes in comfortable silence before she broke it.

"You don't talk very much. I noticed it earlier, but I don't know. I felt the need to bring it up now."

I shrugged. "Not a lot to say."

I had never been much of a talker. I didn't understand why people felt the need to fill the peaceful, quiet void with useless small talk. Though, Atalanta was female, and most of them had always seemed prone to talking needlessly.

"So, do you think that with helping you, you'll finally tell me that secret?"

Not that I completely minded her constant chatter. Her voice was lyrical, similar to a few of the others in town despite her being human. I found myself enjoying it.

I shook my head. "Not yet."

In spite of of not knowing her very well, I liked her, and as if she were a planet, I felt drawn towards her. But this was a secret I kept close to my chest. Humans couldn't know about my abilities, and I had only agreed to tell her once I had gotten to know her better as an excuse. She was a curious person, and if I had something she wanted to know, it would keep her interested in seeking out my company.

At least for a while.

Suddenly I could feel her sadness like a heavy blanket laid on my shoulders, and before I could stop myself, I asked, "Why are you upset?"

"You mean besides almost getting my head cut off?" she teased.

I simply nodded, suppressing the need to roll my eyes. I was worried that my not telling her had been what upset her.

She shrugged. "I just get sad sometimes…do I look that upset to you?"

I studied her. She looked strong and confident, out in the woods with a virtual stranger who had just thrown an axe at her.

But I said "Yes" anyway.

She looked down at the ground in front of her. "Oh."

She stayed silent after that, and for once I felt the need to be the one to fill that silence. But I didn't, I just kept trucking along through the forest until we reached my cabin.

It was large, having built it myself many, many, years ago. It had everything I needed. A wide porch, a good bed, and plenty of space for my work.

I placed the hunk of wood down and dusted off the wood splinters and bark off my shirt.

Without a word, Atalanta ran her hands up and down my back to clear away the areas I couldn't reach. Although the contact was brief, her hands felt good on me. Warm, sending tingles down my spine.

"Whoa, what do you have under that shirt? Armor or something?" She asked, brimming with curiosity.

My eyes widened and my insides dropped as I felt her tug at the hem of my black t-shirt. Quickly, I retracted my scales just as she lifted the back of my shirt. Standing stock still, I let her inspect my back, praying to the Gods she hadn't seen anything.

I internally relaxed when she murmured, "That's strange, I could have sworn I felt something hard under your shirt."

I shrugged, hoping she would play it off as just my muscle density or something. It wasn't like I was a small man by any means. Thanks to long hours of heavy labor, I easily rivaled those guys who spent hours at the gym.

When I felt her fingers gently stroke the muscles of my back, I also felt a stirring in my cock that I hadn't felt at another person's touch in a long time. Spinning around, I grabbed her hand and pulled her close to me.

"You shouldn't touch a man like that."

"You mean like how you shouldn't be pulling a woman up against a growing hard-on?" She challenged me.

I didn't like backing down from a challenge.

"Yes, but this is exactly why you shouldn't touch a man like that. They could take advantage."

She grinned, confidence rolling off of her. "I'm not scared of you, Ajax. You're a fluffy teddy bear."

I was not a teddy bear!

I growled. "You should be."

She tilted her head back and let out a snort. "That is such a cliché line to say! Like you're some big scary vampire lord from a romance novel? What's next? Are you going to tell me that falling for a man like you could be dangerous? That my poor virgin soul will be devoured by your tainted body?"

My brows scrunched as she laughed hysterically. She was a strange human. As I watched her continue to poke fun at my words, my initial intentions were lost. I didn't know if I was just trying to be sexy, like she said, or warn her to stay away from me. Yet I saw no point in trying to warn her. She could handle herself, if not physically then she could confuse an attacker into letting her go.

Chapter Seventeen

Atalanta

"Wait! And then he said what?" Cal exclaimed, as we sat in our blanket fort by the fire.

Our dad was passed out in his room. The poor guy was tuckered out, and even though Cal insisted he go to bed, saying she would stay up and wait for me to get back, he was sitting on the porch pretending he wasn't super relieved when I came home. Acting all nonchalant, sketching in his sketchbook like it was normal to want to sit out in three-degree weather.

"Like I said, his voice got all dark and ominous and then he goes 'You should be'."

Cal rolled around, laughing. "That's like straight out of some gothic romance or something!"

I popped a grape into my mouth. "That's basically what I said."

"I swear, Atty. I leave you alone to go traipsing through the woods at night and you not only get an axe thrown at you but a giant hunk of gorgeous, being all 18th-century vampire on your butt. What kind of messed up harem are you living in right now?"

"Harem?"

"You know, when a bunch of girls are with one man? You've got that, but reversed."

"I am not living in a harem."

"Oh, really? Let's see," she sat up and began to count off on her fingers. "You've got Hip, the cute golden one with the mischievous smile; Jason, who you totally macked out with today; Percy, who you said devoured you like a man starved; that cute guy Thesis who looks at you like a pining puppy dog; and now dark and giant Ajax? You said that was his name, right?"

I nodded.

"Yep, so now you got a giant bear of a man Ajax who's going all Edward Cullen on your butt. And if I had to guess, you like all of them right back." Her grin was so wide, she looked like the Cheshire Cat.

If you had asked me several weeks ago if you could melt ice cream purely from the heat rushing to your cheeks alone, I would have said you were crazy. Yet, here I sat with a spoonful of melted rocky road and cheeks as hot as the sun.

I opened and closed my mouth several times. I honestly didn't know what to say. She wasn't wrong. All five of these men had shown interest in me, and while I went on a date with Jason, I still felt something for the other four. And I didn't feel the need to become fully exclusive with Jason.

That wasn't normal, was it? Being interested in so many men, not feeling the need to settle with one?

How would they feel when they learned this? Percy seemed okay knowing I had gone on a date with Jason, but there had been this tension between Hip and Jason all week. It didn't look like they hated each other, but there was a general discomfort. And the weird thing with Theseus and Percy? That's not even including Ajax.

My head was spinning.

"What do I do?" I groaned and flopped backward onto the pillows.

Cal laughed. "Well, the first step is always admitting that you have a...well it's not really a problem, per se. But at least you're acknowledging that something's going on. You should talk to them about it. Who knows, maybe they won't care about sharing you."

I turned to look at her. She looked downright jolly with my predicament, her green eyes twinkling, and lips spread in a mischievous smile that would rival even Hip.

I pouted. "I would have thought you would act like the responsible and wise older sibling and tell me who to choose."

"Why choose?" She asked before taking a large bite out of her Neapolitan ice cream sandwich.

She wasn't very helpful.

That night, I lay awake thinking about the guys. They were all mysterious and hiding something. Granted, it seemed the whole town had something to hide. Jason, Theseus, and now Ajax were definitely on my 'suspicious' list, but I didn't think that they were up to no good. They seemed like genuine people...well, possibly people.

The nagging mermaid theory was still floating in the back of my brain. However, my logic said that maybe they were practicing hypnotists and part of some magician's cult. Because that made *so* much more sense than magical creatures.

I snorted to myself and shifted over in my cot to stare up at the ceiling. Some of the roof was rotted away in places, but at least it wasn't bad enough to leak water through. Yet.

I wondered where Hip and Percy fell into all of this. Were they in on it too, or just Average Joes who just happened to know more than they should?

Percy definitely knew something, but his lips were sealed tight. Monday, I would have to test Hip. See if he would be the one to slip up.

Thinking up a plan, my mind finally settled, and I was able to drift off to sleep.

***

Sunday was a lazy day. Cal, Dad, and I all had the day off, so we took our fishing rods and went down the cliff to go fishing. Someone, probably the original owner of the cabin, built a tall dock that went far out into to waves.

Dad inspected it and gave it his seal of approval before allowing us to step foot on it.

The three of us sat at the end of the dock, sometimes sitting in a comfortable silence, sometimes in joyful banter, with our fishing lines cast far out into the water.

I was practically pulling in a smorgasbord. Within the first 30 minutes of casting my line out in the water, I pulled in my first fish. Unhooking it, we placed it in a bucket filled with ocean water. About 45 minutes later, I caught my second fish. And then my third. Cal and Dad weren't so lucky. At the end of it all, they each only caught one fish while I reeled in six!

I was dubbed 'Queen of the Rod' by Cal, much to my chagrin and my father's discomfort.

As the sun began to sink lower, we collected our winnings and made our way back up to the house. Dad spent the evening cleaning and storing the fish in the large freezer box we found around back.

I was surprised to see that I had gotten a text from an unknown number. In the text was a photo of a very familiar table.

I brought the phone close to my face and texted the number back.

"Jason?"

"Yep. I realized after I dropped you off yesterday that I didn't have your number. I hope you don't mind but I finagled it from Dorris."

I personally didn't mind, but I hoped she didn't make a habit of handing my number out to people.

I texted him back.

"I'm glad to see the table is fixed. Did you tell your parents?"

"I did not. I'm curious to see if they will ever notice. I think I did a great patch job."

With that text came a close-up photo of what I assumed was the leg that I broke. I could see a thin line of glue running across the leg, but otherwise it looked fine.

"It looks great."

"Glad you like it. I think I'd be happy to break it all over again ;)"

I paused before replying, remembering our lust filled make-out session from yesterday. Just thinking about having his hands on me warmed my core. I wanted to do it again. Before I could tell him as much, the phone buzzed in my hands again.

"How was your day?"

"It was good, went fishing. I caught the most fish :)"

"That's awesome! Queen of the sea!"

"My sister dubbed me Queen of the Rod"

"Lol. Hope I get to have you rule over my rod someday."

My mouth dropped open and the small warmth that had been burning in my core shot up to a blaze. I licked at my dry lips as I stared down at the words on the screen.

"Too much?"

"No! It's just-

I bit my lip, wanting to tell him he was making me horny, but I didn't know if I could be that bold. But I had to say *something*. I squeezed my eyes shut and hit send.

"No! You're just making me horny is all."

"That's good to hear >:)"

He sent a text immediately after, cranking the heat level from a three to an eight.

"I like the idea of making you wet for me. Especially since I didn't get a chance to touch you there yesterday."

I was sure that if I slid my hand into my underwear right now, I would be wet. And while I was extremely tempted to touch myself and calm the burning that had begun in my center, I smiled at the thought of having one of the guys taking care of it for me and decided to wait it out.

"Soon."

I texted back to him, before turning off my phone and closing my eyes. Eventually, I drifted off to sexy dreams of half-naked men.

***

Monday came and before I knew it, school was over. Not nearly as successful as I had hoped it to be. All my attempts to pull something out of Hip were thwarted when he either conveniently remembered he had to do something or somehow would drive the conversation in the complete opposite direction without me even realizing it.

I would get my chance, though. The swim team would be meeting at the community center after school tomorrow, and I had an inkling that it would be my chance to catch Jason or Hip in the act. In the act of what, I didn't know, but I bet something strange was going to happen.

I was at the library again. Not having work today, I laid sprawled in one of the reading chairs with a good book. Percy was off doing some organizing and Jason had a student body president thing, so he was stuck at school. Hip sat across from me in one of the other chairs, bobbing his head up and down to music pouring from his large headset. He had given me a ride today, offering after Jason told us about his after-school meeting.

At first, I thought it would be another chance to weasel something out of him, but once we got here, he put on those headphones and hadn't said much since. He didn't seem to be ignoring me, just drifting off his own little world. Occasionally, we would make eye contact and he would give a little smile. His eyes, which looked like mine at the moment, brown with hints of green, sparkled with their usual mischief.

I sighed and turned my mind back towards the book. It was a steamy cliché romance book that you'd typically pick up at a Walmart or something, where the characters had no real connection or depth. But it wasn't horrible, and still entertaining. Downright hilarious in some places, doing a good job of keeping my thoughts distracted. It did have one downside, though. The sex scenes were doing a good job of keeping my arousal level sitting at a solid five.

I knew my cheeks were probably a bit flushed. Thank the Gods for my skin tone making it at least a little difficult to see the redness that graced my cheeks.

I shifted as the slickness I felt in my panties only served the purpose of making me more uncomfortable.

"Perhaps I should stop reading this." I muttered to myself under my breath.

"Why? Is it not good?" a voice asked from above me.

My eyes shot up and my head tilted back, bringing me to face level with a jean-clad crotch. The man attached to that crotch smelled of the forest and paint.

Ajax stared down at me, and the moment he realized how close his cock was to my face he stepped back a little, allowing me to get a better look of him.

"No, it's just fine it's just...umm..."

He tilted his head, confused.

"She's uncomfortable because the book has sex in it and it's making her horny." Hip said, as he took off his headphones and looked at the two of us.

I squealed and threw the book in my hand at him. "Crude much!?"

He caught the book easily and smirked. "It's true. Nothing to be ashamed of."

"So, the book was making you horny?" Ajax asked, holding out his hand for the book.

Hip handed it to him, and Ajax began to flip through its pages, studying it. He paused, and if I had to guess he came upon a sex scene. I bit my lip, looking nervously between him and Hip, who just stared at me with a hungry expression. His eyes darkened like I'd seen them do before.

Ajax looked up. "This isn't very realistic. They would have had to be on drugs to cum that fast."

"Let me see?" Hip replied, sliding out of his chair and walking over to look at the book.

Next to Ajax, Hip looked significantly shorter, but I supposed most people look super short next to a bear.

Hip skimmed the words before looking over at me. "He's right. During real sex, there's much more foreplay, touching, stroking."

He moved away from Ajax, coming closer to me in my chair. Leaning in, he whispered into my ear, his voice dropping down into the sexy zone.

"Nipping, licking, biting." On the last word he nipped the top of my ear before moving away.

A shiver ran down my body. While I didn't want to admit it, my breathing became heavier as my arousal shot up to a seven. My core clenched just a little, begging for one of them to touch me more. Damn, I knew I shouldn't have read that book.

I sat up in the chair, hoping like hell my clothes were thick enough to cover my hard nipples.

Both were staring at me like predators who had just found their next meal, and I was torn between giving into them or running like a scared little rabbit.

Much to my disappointment, the sexual tension wasn't broken when Percy walked in on the stare-down not moments later. If anything, he made it worse. Those sharp eyes observing the situation before instant understanding came across his face and his frown morphed into a sexy millimeter smile.

"It seems that my suspicions were correct in that I wasn't the only one who was interested in Miss North," Percy said, readjusting his glasses.

Both Ajax and Hip blinked, as if realizing in that moment that they had basically been double teaming me. They looked at each other in question before looking at Percy.

"You too, Percival? Who else?" Ajax asked.

"Well, if I'm correct it would be the three of us here along with Mr. Monroe...and Theseus."

Ajax pursed his lips and tilted his head up. Quiet. Contemplating.

Hip, on the other hand, looked from me to Percy, then to Ajax, and then back to me, his eyes showing a mixture of hurt and concern. "But, wait. I knew Jason and Thesis, but there are five of us? How am I supposed to compete against four other men?"

I tensed up and was about to give a rebuttal, a little annoyed that they were talking about me and my feelings like I wasn't right in front of them. But Percy cut me off before I could.

"I don't believe you have to, Mr. Clark." Percy's eyes met mine. "I'm pretty sure she holds affection for all of us. Equally."

I could not be any more embarrassed at that moment. The three of them all focused their attention back on me, making me feel like a cornered animal. They weren't wrong. Cal had said as much the other night. She also had said I needed to talk to them. I just didn't think I actually would...Or that they would find out.

It was something I was just going to take to my grave, God damn it!

"This isn't normal though, right?" Hip asked.

A sharp slice went right though my heart at his words. It was true, it wasn't normal.

Percy nodded. "It's not normal. But that doesn't mean it doesn't happen, it's just uncommon. For humans at least."

My preverbal scared rabbit ears perked up at that. "What do you mean for humans?"

"I meant animals. Like gorillas, elephant seals, some species of bat, a few types of fish. Lots of species of animals live in non-monograms relationships," Percy replied, cool as a cucumber as he adjusted his glasses on his face.

INTO THE SEAS EMBRACE

I narrowed my eyes at him, not fully believing his reasoning. He only stared right back at me, that cockiness practically radiating off of him. But I wasn't fooled.

"I'm *so* sure that's what you meant." Having found my bravery, I swung up out of my chair. "Perhaps I do have a crush on all of you."

I'm pretty sure my voice was not as bold as I hoped it sounded.

Percy met my eyes in an unwavering challenge. "What are you going to do about it?"

Yep, there went my three seconds of bravery as I stared at the three men before me, all watching me with hunger in their eyes.

With a nervous smile, I slowly backed away. "For now...I escape!"

With that, I ran like the frightened little bunny I was, scrambling away from the three men that were making my blood boil. I could have sworn I heard a few chuckles.

A hop, skip, and a jump out of the library doors threw me right into the arms of another one of the guys.

Warm hands wrapped around my arms, trying to stop me before my momentum slammed me into his broad chest. Looking up, I met stormy blue-gray eyes.

"T-Theseus?" I stammered.

Fuck. Of the few people I wanted to avoid, I just happened to run into number one on my list while fleeing numbers three, four, and five.

He looked good, if a little disheveled. His red mop of hair blew wildly around as the wind whipped powerfully. He wore a warm looking gray jacket and dark blue jeans, and this was probably the first time I saw him out of those work overalls.

"Hey, Atalanta," He said, his beautiful odd bell tone voice washing over me, causing more shivers to run down my body.

I licked my lips. "H-hey."

He looked down at my lips for a moment, the storm in his eyes churning as he watched me.

He cleared his throat. "Listen, I was just coming over here to try and find you. I wanted to apologize for my behavior."

I stepped back, out of his arms. "It's not really okay. But I'm not all that mad at you anymore."

"It was wrong to pretend you were crazy. You're not. But the thing is," He sighed, clearly a bit stressed. "While you aren't wrong, I can't really tell you the truth. At least not yet."

I crossed my arms over my chest and cocked a brow at him. "And why is that? Don't want to share your big important secret with the outsider?"

"It's not that at all!" he shouted, his voice awkwardly loud, making me wince. Seeing his mistake, he lowered his voice. "I'm really starting to care about you, okay? There's just more going on here than you realize. I just want to keep you safe."

He was bouncing a little as he stared at me, eyes scrunching as he bit his lip. Oh, the poor boy was so nervous I couldn't help but feel my heart melt for him.

I was closing in on their secret whether he wanted me to or not. And it wasn't like I didn't have secrets of my own. At least he was apologizing and admitting that I wasn't crazy. If I were being honest, that's what had bothered me the most. Probably what bothered me the most about this whole thing. I hated being called crazy, and it only drove me to want to know the truth even more.

"No more trying to play it off like nothing's happening, okay? If you can't tell me, just say it," I said, pointing at him sternly.

He nodded vigorously. "Okay."

With a small smile I pointed at myself and then ran my right hand along my left palm and then pointed at him, in an attempt to sign 'I forgive you'.

He stopped bouncing immediately and a relieved smile spread across his face. He took my hands and pulled me close into a hug.

He really was a marshmallow.

After letting go, he invited me out to dinner, to which I said yes. I did not internally squeal like a little girl. Nope, I did not.

As we walked to his car, I glanced back at the library. In one of the windows I saw the three men I had run from talking. Ajax, who was facing in my direction, caught my eye, studying me before flicking his eyes over to Theseus, his expression questioning if I was okay. I nodded slightly, and his shoulders relaxed, but he continued to watch me until we drove away. Like a stone sentinel, ever vigilant.

Theseus took me to one of the few restaurants in town. A little hole in the wall Italian place that every town needed. It was called Tino's and was classic brick and mortar that stood out from the wood of the surrounding buildings. Bill, the owner, was a classic New York Italian. Very loud, friendly, and made sure I had enough to eat. I ordered probably the creamiest fettuccine alfredo I have ever had, while Theseus had a seafood medley. Bill, who had visited our table multiple times despite being the head chef, was calling me doll by the end of the meal.

I'd have to say that I loved it. The only time I felt overly uncomfortable was when Bill would get too close into my personal space, sitting down next to me in the booth and chatting all about his years growing up in Brooklyn. He said that when he came to Argos, he completely fell in love, even if they didn't have any tall stone buildings like he was used to. He said it's why he made a point to make his place the first brick building established in the area.

It wasn't that I minded his stories; they were pretty interesting. It was how he would lay his arm over the back of my seat and with his other hand gesture closely and animatedly towards me.

INTO THE SEAS EMBRACE

Luckily, Theseus noticed my discomfort. Making a quip about favoritism, he scooted over to make space for Bill. At first Bill looked a little confused, but he shrugged and simply hopped over to Theseus' side.

My belly full of fresh baked garlic bread and creamy pasta, I practically waddled out of Bill's restaurant, a big fat smile on my face.

Instead of taking me back home immediately, Theseus suggested we walk down the square. We strolled alongside the little park which sat in the center of all the town's main shops. There were plenty of people about, either enjoying their day or doing some last-minute shopping. Those same kids I had spotted the other day were back at the park. Still in little to nothing, chasing each other around and playing in the snow that had lightly piled up on top of the grass. But right now, I wasn't supersleuth Atalanta. I was well-fed and sated Atalanta with a warm heart and belly.

I tapped Theseus on the shoulder. "If the owner's name is Bill, why is the restaurant called Tino's?"

"He once told me that it was because the name Bill just didn't sound Italian enough." Theseus replied.

I giggled. "I mean, he's not wrong. I still find it silly. If I owned a restaurant, I would want it to have my name."

"Is that what you want to do with your life? Be a chef or own a restaurant?" he asked.

255

I pursed my lips. "If I'm being honest, I don't really know what I want to do with my life." I chuckled. "I know I can't cook, though."

"I can't cook either," He smiled. His gaze was tender and warmed my heart.

"What about you?" I asked. "Do you want to be a janitor your whole life, or do you have some big plans for your future? Not that being a janitor isn't a good profession! But you don't strike me as the type to settle with that kind of job."

"Well, I wanted to be like them," he said wistfully, gesturing towards a little group of people I hadn't noticed.

They were huddling together, some with chairs and some standing. In their hands were instruments. I watched as they settled into a semicircle and poised themselves in a long pause. A man with a violin lifted his bow and pulled it across the instrument's string, letting out a wavering sorrowful note. He played a few measures of music before the rest of his group joined in, weaving together the beginnings of a sad melody.

"You wanted to be a musician?" I asked as I stared at them.

When I didn't get a reply, I looked up at Theseus to see that he too was watching the players. The easy smile that he had kept throughout dinner had fallen into a frown, his eyes mirroring the sorrowful tunes that the musicians played.

INTO THE SEAS EMBRACE

He looked back at me as I continued to study him. "I wanted to be a musician. But that was before my accident."

I bit the inside of my cheek, trying not to let the tears come to my eyes. "But there are plenty of deaf musicians, aren't there? I mean, Beethoven was deaf, and he was probably one of the world's greatest composers and musicians."

"I guess I just don't have that kind of resilience," he said, bitterness spitting out with every word.

I pulled away from him, feeling a little stung by the self-loathing and hatred in his eyes. I knew it wasn't directed at me, but I couldn't help it.

He noticed this, and that spark of hatred dissipated immediately, leaving behind only self-loathing. He turned his face away from me, effectively cutting me off.

I bit the inside of my cheek harder and the remnants of warmth from our dinner began to fade. This date had been going so well. Neither of us had actually called it a date, but it had felt like one.

I ran my hand up and down along my opposite arm, feeling my mind sinking back into the darkness of my thoughts.

'You always ruin things'

'Why do you bother trying?'

'Look how upset you made him.'

I felt a warm hand lay on top of mine which was still running up and down my arm. It pulled me from my thoughts.

I looked up at Theseus. He was still looking over at the musicians, but the self-loathing and sadness that I had seen were no longer there. Instead, reflected in his gray blue gaze was something akin to determination.

I stopped rubbing my arm and clasped his hand in mine. I realized that this was the hand of someone who understood pain; someone who had the same demons lurking behind those smiles. In that moment, I felt a kinsmanship.

With a gentle tug, I pulled him away from the musicians and turned us back in the opposite direction towards his car.

The walk wasn't uncomfortable as we made our way back along the street, but it was silent. I pondered what it must be like for him. While there was silence between us, there was not silence around us. I could still hear the musicians in the distance along with the children's laughter. People were conversing with each other as we passed and there was the light sound of our footsteps, almost buried by the whipping of the wind. Yet I knew that to him, none of it existed. What was most likely only the memory of sounds were seen through his eyes. That was the world he lived in.

I wanted to know what instrument he played, but I knew asking right then would not be a good idea. I did not want to rub salt into what was already an open wound.

But I could not stop myself from asking the less important question.

I tapped him on the shoulder to get his attention. He looked down at me and I said. "How did you lose your hearing?"

He did as most do when posed with the question of their past. He looked up to the sky, thinking about it for a moment before he replied.

"It was an accident," he said, his voice distant as memories that I could not see flashed across his mind. "It certainly wasn't on purpose. There was a fight and I got into the middle of it. I knew I shouldn't have, but I was prone to heroics back then. I was badly injured and by the time help came, it was already too late. Parts of my inner ear were completely damaged. My left one worse than my right and I could hear out of it for a while, but eventually that faded too."

"What happened to the people that did it? The ones who hurt you, I mean?" I asked.

"Well," he sighed. "The ones that started the fight were punished."

I noticed how he only mentioned the ones that started the fight and not the ones who actually hurt him. I wasn't going to go digging any further. If he wanted to tell me more, he would.

I gripped his hand tighter in mine and for some reason brought his hand up to kiss the side of his palm.

"I do really well, though, for being crippled! I mean, look how long it took you to realize that I was deaf. If I was more careful, I could've kept it going whole week, if not a whole two weeks." He laughed, even though it didn't really seem to reach his eyes. I just smiled at him now and let him have it.

"Yeah you're pretty sneaky." I wiggled my finger in front of him. "But don't underestimate my powers of observation!"

"Your powers of observation, huh?" he challenged before placing his hand up to my eyes and blocking my vision.

I could feel his hot breath fresh against my ear. "Tell me how many red cars there are on the street."

"I said that I had powers of observation, not the powers of a psychic!" I squealed, unable to suppress my giggle fit.

Theseus snorted. "Shawn Spencer isn't a psychic. But with his amazing abilities of observation, he can fool most people into believing he is."

"Who's Shawn Spencer? Is he some Marvel character?" I asked.

"Oh, I'm sure he would love to be. Now, hush and tell me how many red cars are on the street."

Even with his hands covering my eyes, I felt the need to close them as I pictured the street behind us, trying to remember how many cars I saw and how many of them were red.

"Umm, 6?" I guessed.

He made a harsh buzzer sound. "Not even close. You're not very good at this. What happened to those powers of observation?"

I laughed and pulled his hand from my eyes. "I guess my powers are better used towards reading people and not counting how many red cars there are on the street. It's not like that's very useful information anyway."

"My dear little psychic. Knowing that kind of information could save your life one day."

I met his eyes and realized that he was standing mere inches from me. His eyes were sparkling with humor. His smile was beautiful, and it made my breath hitch. He noticed my response, his eyes widening and his mouth opening ever so slightly. Those gray-blue orbs flickered between my own eyes and my mouth.

I wanted him to kiss me. To pull me close like Percy had done and ravage my mouth. But he stayed a mere three inches from my face. Unmoving.

Then I remembered. He was waiting for the 'perfect moment'. I felt that we would be waiting forever if he was constantly always looking for that perfect second in time. So, I seized this moment now and leaned in the rest of the way to claim his mouth. If it wasn't perfect now, then when?

The moment my lips touched his, I expected him to hesitate, but he didn't. He pulled me close like I wanted and kissed me so hard I was sure that my lips would bruise. His hands came up to cup my cheeks. My hands gripped his jacket, holding on for fear that my knees would give out from under me with the power of that kiss.

The inferno that had finally tamped down during dinner shot up, making me moan into his mouth. This encouraged him, and he tilted my head slightly to the side, teasing my lips open with his tongue. He may have tasted like the garlic bread we had for dinner, but I didn't care. I bet that I was no better, having had three rolls myself.

I wanted him closer, his hands touching all the parts of me that ached, but I also wanted us to not be in a public place.

Someone cat-called us, pulling my mind back to where we were: near the middle of the town square in plain view of everyone. I pulled away from him with a gasp. He looked at me confused for a moment before I twirled my finger around, reminding him where we were.

His eyes flicked to the side and he chuckled. "I suppose we better actually get a room this time. Or at least go somewhere more private."

I nodded, unable to say anything, my lips tingling.

He took my hand and we ran, giddy in our lust.

Hopping into his car, we shared several more passionate kisses, not wanting to break away but also having to constantly remind ourselves that we were still in the public's eye.

We headed back towards my house. At first, I thought we were done, and he was being the chivalrous knight and taking me home, but halfway there we pulled off to the side of the road under one of the few street lamps around for miles. Without hesitation, I crawled out of my seat and into his lap.

My hands buried in his hair as I went back to kissing him. At first, it was a little uncomfortable with the steering wheel poking into my back. As if he read my mind, one of Theseus' hands grabbed my ass and the other reached out in front of him, pulling a lever, sending the seat jerking backwards and giving us much more room.

As he continued to fondle my ass, I couldn't help but grind against the hardness between his thighs, making us both groan into each other's mouths.

The hand that had jerked us backwards slowly ran up and cupped my breast over my shirt.

He pulled away, breaking our kiss. "Is this okay?"

"Yes," I nodded and then added, "but the clothes need to stay on."

I looked at him, making sure that he was watching me when I said it. He was certainly staring at my lips intensely enough.

"As you wish," he breathed before pulling me back to his mouth.

God, his lips were soft. I wanted him closer, I wanted to feel his bare skin beneath my fingers.

Reaching down, I pulled on the lever that controlled the back of the seat, sending us falling flat. It was much better. I could feel his whole body pressed against me.

My breasts were rubbing up and down against his chest. My hard nipples were screaming for him to touch them, with his hands or with his mouth - it didn't matter.

My hands went back up to his neck only to run down the length of his jacket, pulling down the zipper along the way. Underneath he was wearing what I assumed to be a T-shirt, the soft cotton-like fabric taut against the lean muscles of his chest. My hands trailed further until I met the seam of his shirt. I hesitated for a moment before I slid my fingers underneath to feel his extremely warm smooth skin.

He took that as encouragement, the hand which had been on my ass sliding up under my own jacket to lightly caress down my spine before delving right into my pants to cup my ass again, and now we were skin to skin.

I continued to grind against him, breaking our kiss to mimic what Jason had done to me not a few days before. I licked and nipped the side of Theseus' neck. He tasted heavily of salt. I wondered if he had been at the gym earlier that day and had yet to take a shower.

He groaned, his other hand sliding beneath my pants to cup my other ass cheek, encouraging the rocking of my hips back and forth along his clothed cock.

"Theseus, touch me," I said, with no reply from him.

A moment later I mentally slapped myself and then pulled away from his neck. His eyes were closed, lips parted. I ran my fingertips above his brow, making him snap his eyelids back open, those gray-blue orbs dark like a fierce storm.

'Touch me,' I mouthed, not bothering with my own voice.

His brows scrunched for a second in confusion before I ran my hand along his arm and pulled one of his palms away from my ass and towards my center.

"Oh, baby, you're so wet for me right now. Do you want me to put my fingers inside this sweet pussy?"

I bit my lip and then nodded.

He took his sweet ass time, running his fingers up and down the lips, teasing my clit with light touches. Just as I was about to let out a growl of frustration, he plunged a finger inside of me.

Now I wasn't completely inexperienced with men, or even a virgin for that matter. In fact, my virginity at one point meant so little to me that I honestly couldn't tell you the guy's name who took it. It was during the dark time in my life, and I had honestly just wanted to see if I could feel something.

One night when I was 14, Cal and I snuck off to a party. One of those ragers where drugs and alcohol were in easy abundance and people were openly making out and grinding on each other all over the place. I thought the guy was cute and he seemed sweet as we spent what few hours we had together laughing. When he asked me if I wanted to go up to one of the more private rooms, I was jumping to say yes.

It had been an awkward affair. I believe he was a senior in high school, but the self-proclaimed ladies' man didn't last longer than two minutes. By the end of it, I laid on those sheets, in all sorts of fluids including my own virginal blood, with the guy practically passed out next to me. Feeling like the biggest piece of used garbage there ever was.

From there, my downward spiral had only gotten worse until the government had to step in. Since then, I had had a few trysts with the guys from other high schools but nothing ever too serious.

This didn't just feel like a tryst though, this felt special. Intimate. Raw. Hungry. Full of passion.

Emotion. It felt like a ball of emotion just building up inside of me.

No, wait, I think that was just the orgasm.

Theseus added a second finger, curling them in and touching against a spot inside me that set the inferno in my stomach exploding.

I groaned loudly as he continued to finger me, his palm rubbing perfectly against my clit.

I felt frantic as I kissed his lips, his neck, running my hands up into his hair as he built me up higher.

His free hand came up and pulled my hair, tilting my head to the side so he could mimic me by nipping right under my ear before running his tongue down to the crook of my shoulder.

"Theseus," I moaned as I rocked back and forth against his hand.

He began to hum against my throat as he kissed and sucked. His voice made my head go all fuzzy.

"Cum for me, Atalanta," He demanded, curling his fingers, rubbing them right against that sweet spot.

It was like my body had no choice but to heed to his to his demands. I came crashing over that crest. Everything in me tightened up as my orgasm flashed hot.

"Yeah, baby, that's it," he whispered.

I ground against his hand desperately, riding out my orgasm till I collapsed on top of him, breathing hard. I felt him moving around and heard the sound of a click, his fingers slipping out of me, his hand coming to my ass.

"I want to taste you," Theseus growled.

The next thing I knew, I was tumbling over the armrest onto my back in the passenger seat. Theseus loomed over me, lust still burning in his eyes. A shiver of pleasure ran up my sides which morphed into a shiver of horror as he began to fumble with my pants.

I panicked. "Theseus, don't!"

But it was too late, and it wasn't like he could hear me anyway. He pulled my pants down around my knees, revealing the iridescent scar tissue that littered my thighs.

He halted with a gasp, which he held as his eyes stared down at the grotesque remains of my legs. On my left leg was a large indented scar which I knew ran from the top of my hip down to right above my knee. A good four inches thick, the old scar gleamed in the white light of the street lamps, given to me by my torturers and the doctors who tried desperately to save my life. Next to it were several dozen thin lines crossing this way and that, the ones I had given myself. All different lengths, yet the consistent width of a razor blade. My right leg mirrored it.

I was as still as a statue, a ball the size of an apple sitting in the pit of my stomach as I stared up at him.

I watched as his eyes began to turn red as they misted over with tears. His lips wobbled as he lightly ran his fingers over the thin self-inflicted scars.

His eyes flicked to mine and he asked, "Do you still do this to yourself?"

There wasn't any judgement in his voice but its croaky tone, full of love and sorrow broke me a little. My insides cracked as tears began to come forth.

"I haven't in a couple years," I replied, gulping down the frog in my throat.

"That's good," he ran his hands lightly over the scars, moving towards the larger one. "And this one?"

I couldn't meet his eyes this time. "An accident."

He leaned back, his eyes wide. He ran a hand through his hair and sighed heavily in a way that people do when presented with a large problem or a harsh reality.

I pulled my pants up and brought my legs close to my chest, curling up in a tight ball. I'd like to think that no one had seen my scars before, but I knew they had. I knew that the large one had a photo sitting in an evidence lockup, much newer looking, the box it was in gathering dust. I knew that plenty of psychiatrists and nurses had seen the self-inflicted ones while I had sat in my protective little room, much like a cell, for several weeks before they no longer considered me a risk to myself and handed me back to good old Sam. And eventually back to my broken father and now sober sister.

His hand came up to brush my cheek. "I'm not going to pressure you for answers, Atalanta. I do hope you'll give them to me freely one day."

I glanced up at him. He looked uncomfortable, physically at least—scrunched awkwardly with me in the passenger seat— but his eyes were warm, and he wore a soft smile.

I nodded before going back to looking at my knees. I felt him lean over and his lips touch the top of my brow. Carefully, he climbed back over to the driver's seat and readjusted it.

Without a word, he shifted the car back into drive and took me home.

Chapter Eighteen

Hip

I pulled up into the dirt driveway of my home, my legs tingling as the motorcycle's engine rumbled beneath me. I could hear barking in the distance, the sound racing closer and closer to me with each second before the pack of dogs were upon me.

I smiled. "Hey, you little rascals."

I climbed off my bike and braced myself as the large furry bodies bombarded me with love, wet tongues, and long claws. Two border collies, an Irish wolfhound, and the ballsiest little shih-tzu you'd ever seen hopped around me as I tried to make my way to the front door.

I laughed. "Alright, alright. Let's get you guys fed before you decide to eat me."

I opened the front door, its creaky hinges reminding me that I needed to fix them. I was assaulted by the drool-worthy smell of my Abuela's Gambas al Ajillo.

After breathing it in deeply, I called, "I'm home!"

"Don't track in any mud or I'll skin you alive!" came the high shrill of the woman who raised me.

"I love you too!" I yelled back.

Tugging off my boots, I walked into the kitchen, dropping my backpack on the table. By the stove stood an old woman no taller than four and a half feet. Her hips swayed back and forth as she listened to Julio

Iglesias serenade her on the radio. I walked over and kissed her on the cheek before heading over to the dogs' food bin and scooping up three buckets of dry food and a small can of wet food for the shih-tzu.

After feeding the dogs, I came back in. "Is there anything that I can help with?"

"Harold clogged the toilet again-" she began before being interrupted by another voice coming from the living room.

"I did not! It was you, you old bat!"

She rolled her eyes. "Regardless, we can't fix it. Can you take a look at it?"

I nodded. "Sure."

Heading out of the kitchen, I caught a glimpse of my grandfather lounging in his recliner, reading the farmer's almanac. Both he and my Abuela bickered back and forth with each other about whose fault it was the toilet was clogged again. I knew it was probably hers, as she tended to flush things that had no business being flushed.

"You're insane!" she bitched.

"And you're just as beautiful as the day I married you!" he said, leaning back in his recliner to give me a wink.

I shook my head. I asked him once why he married my Abuela all those years ago. She was a kind woman but could be a bit of a spitfire and had no qualms about hitting you with her slipper when you pissed her off. He told me that he just had a thing for Hispanic women, and the moment he saw her he knew they were meant to be together.

Opening the bathroom door, I looked at the toilet, which was in fact overflowing with water. I sighed and took off my socks to tiptoe over the dirty water on the floor. I picked up the top of the water tank to check if everything inside was okay. It was, so I did the stupid thing and attempted to flush the toilet. Unfortunately, this didn't work, and the water that came rushing into the toilet only ended up on the floor. The damage was already done. I grabbed the plunger and attempted to fix it that way as well. Nothing happened.

I blew out a breath and held up my hand to the toilet. "If the human method ain't gonna work..."

Concentrating, I held up my hand and mentally commanded the water to push past the clog, forcing God knows what to break apart and down the pipes like it should have. All the water which had been in the bowl drained away. With a sigh of relief, I flushed the toilet; the water flowed steadily.

"There we go," I muttered and then grimaced when I realized that I was still standing in brown water. Yuck.

Closing my eyes, I concentrated again, willing all the water off the ground and into the toilet. Brown puddles and droplets collected into a steady stream which arced off the ground and into the bowl. When the floor was 'clean', I flushed away all the dirty water. I would have to mop later.

INTO THE SEAS EMBRACE

I had debated about using my powers to do it in the first place, but it took a lot of energy out of me to just do this simple task.

"Thank you, sweetheart," my Abuela said behind me.

I chuckled and turned to her. "That's what almighty power over an element is for. Unclogging the toilet."

"And watering the garden," she added.

I chuckled. "And the garden. I'm going to go take a shower and do some homework, okay?"

"Dinner will be ready in half an hour," she replied before going back to the kitchen.

I nodded and made my way up the stairs to my room.

I wouldn't say I was a homebody, but I loved my room and would happily curl up in the warm brown sheets of my king bed all day, listening to music as I stared mindlessly up at the ceiling where my *The Adicts* poster was.

Pulling off my clothes, I was mindful about making sure to toss them in the basket. I knew if my room was even a bit messy, I would be meeting the wrong end of a slipper.

Strolling proudly naked into my own personal bathroom, another benefit of having my room, I stepped into the shower. Not even bothering to wait for warm water, I turned the knobs and let the icy cold wash over me.

My scales rippled over my body, their silver color combining with the water to make the light dance across the walls. I smiled and leaned my head back into the spray. I knew it was happening because I was tired and unable to really sustain my human form with the water washing over me, but the light show was always beautiful to watch.

Speaking of beautiful to watch, my mind flashed back to the girl I had a hardcore crush on. She just looked breathtaking today as she read that book, her cheeks flushed and mouth parted, pupils blown up with arousal. I wanted to be the one to stoke that fire. And I was so concentrated on doing that, that I hadn't even realized I had tag teamed with Ajax.

My heart sunk as I thought about what Percy said.

There were others.

While it hurt a little, I was determined. I may not be the only one she was interested in, but I would definitely be one of the ones she chose, if not the only one.

Percy said that it was normal for our kind to mate in harems as there weren't many females. But Atalanta was human, raised with different ideas, especially in America where a relationship was almost always one plus one equals two.

Well.

I wasn't much different.

Unlike Percy and the others in this town, I was raised as a human just like Atalanta.

INTO THE SEAS EMBRACE

Adopted as a baby, I wasn't actually related to my grandparents at all. Just an old couple with empty nest syndrome and a lot of love to give. My three older siblings were human and had left home many years ago. I saw my sister Anita far more often than my brothers, who I only saw once or twice a year around the holidays. They all had their own families now.

I loved my family. They treated me no differently despite knowing I wasn't human. But being raised by humans did come at a disadvantage. I really didn't know much, if anything, about my culture and absolutely nothing about my heritage.

At least a few of the older of my kind in town were kind enough to teach me a bit about my powers. Though, I believe that was only because they didn't want an untrained idiot making a mess of things. Once they were done teaching me the basics, they had, so to speak, tossed me up the creek without a paddle.

In any case, I think my unique situation awarded me an advantage. I could relate to Atalanta more than the others. I knew how scary and confusing it was to be seeing this town as an outsider, for people to be keeping secrets from you. Always steering the conversation away from the truth.

I never intended to lie to her, but I knew how important this secret was, so I was only waiting for her to ask me. Just like I knew she had asked Percy and Jason.

Okay, fine. Maybe I was making it a little hard on her.

Today, she had tried to ask me several times, but I avoided it, easily dodging her attempts at finding answers. If she wanted answers, she at least had to work harder for it.

Was that cruel of me?

Probably.

Yet, she could have asked me while we were at the library. We had ample amount of time alone together, but she only sat there and read her book. A book with lustrous— even if inaccurate— sex scenes.

I had noticed she was off work today. I thought she had a fever or was injured as she shifted and twitched, uncomfortable all through lunch with red cheeks. When I saw her reading that book, it came crashing down on me that she was horny. Oh, did I ever want to pull her into my lap and light a fire under her and ignite that passion.

Run my hands over her body, play with those tits. Licking and biting till I had her moaning my name.

Before I realized it, my hand was wrapped around my hard cock, stroking myself as I thought about Atalanta splayed beneath me, her breasts bouncing as I rammed into her over and over again.

Quickly, my fantasy shifted. Her mouth wrapped around my cock, taking me deep inside her throat, tongue running slowly along the tip.

I bit my lip, stroking faster, rubbing the head, giving it attention as I imagined she would with her mouth.

INTO THE SEAS EMBRACE

I hissed. "Atalanta."

My hands ran into her short curly hair, demanding more from her. Her hand coming up to cup my balls. My hand mirrored the image.

I was close, but the water was distracting. Hitting the knob, I shut off the water. Grabbing the bar of soap, I used it combined with the humidity in the air to work my hand up and down my hard length. Images of her continued to flash across my mind until I felt my balls draw tight in a familiar sensation as I came, painting the wall in front of me white.

I panted, legs shaking as my orgasm rocked through me.

I heaved in a breath and sprayed down the side of the shower, cleaning myself before stepping out into the steamy bathroom air.

I stared at my reflection in the mirror and tried to convince myself that I didn't have it as bad as I thought, but it wasn't working. That was the fourth or fifth time this week I came with fantasies of her.

Who was I trying to fool? I had just been thinking about how I would be the one to win her over. I was falling for her like a feather weighted down by a bowling ball.

Drying off, I walked back into my room and threw open the window. I inhaled the smell of apples and sea breeze, grimacing when I felt a burning sensation in my gut. Pulling on some shorts and a shirt I practically ran back down the stairs, skipping steps on the way down.

"Hey bud, where's the fire?" Grandpa asked as my footsteps stomped down.

"I gotta go swimming," I panted.

"Oh, um, be sure to tell Marisol."

I nodded and slipped into the kitchen.

"Abuelita, I have to go."

She spun around and slapped her shoulder towel against the kitchen table. "¡Aye que no! You're not going to eat my food?! Ungrateful boy, breaking an old woman's heart! Maldito sea! After I slaved all day at this stove!"

"I wouldn't dare miss your delicious dinner," I said, hoping to placate her. "But I need to go take a swim."

"I don't care if you're the king of the ocean! You will sit down to dinner with your familia!" she shouted and snapped her fingers to my seat.

My insides were crawling at the moment, but I sighed heavily and said okay. Walking over to the cabinet I pulled out a large cup, grabbed sea salt off the counter, and made myself some impromptu sea water. Chugging it down, I felt a little better.

Dinner was delicious and as always, my parents were hilarious entertainment as they bickered back and forth over the salad. After I helped clean up the dishes, I left, slipping on my sandals and jogging the mile or so to the beach.

Any normal human would have been crazy to be out in this weather in such little clothing but below the

INTO THE SEAS EMBRACE

surface of the water could be much colder than this, so I hardly felt it.

Reaching the cliff, I looked down. Four hundred or so feet below me the waves were crashing. Without hesitation, I tore off my clothes, my naked ass free and bare to the world. With a smile, I backed up before running forward, and with the form of a professional diver I sprung off the edge of the cliff.

Chapter Nineteen

Atalanta

"I finally saved up enough for that boat and am going to buy it today," Dad announced to us over the breakfast table.

"That's great!" Cal exclaimed.

She had an excited look on her face, but I could see the dread in her eyes. She may love the ocean, but she hated boats. She got sea sick easily and hated fishing. She would oblige us with fishing on the dock, but she would avoid any boat fishing like her life depended on it. I was curious to see if she would turn him down when he inevitably asked us to go on the maiden voyage with him to do a little fishing trip.

"I was thinking you and your sister would come out with me after you get out of school, Atalanta, for her maiden voyage? Maybe do some fishing?"

Yep, there it was. And there was Cal's look of disgust, which she quickly morphed into a tight, pleasant smile. Now, how would she respond?

"That sounds like a great idea!" Cal said, her voice a high-pitched chirp.

My eyebrows rose, a little shocked and proud of her for giving Dad this. I was excited to see what I could catch going further out into the water, but then I remembered what day it was.

"I have work, but I should be getting off around five or six. Can we do it then?" I asked.

He nodded. "That's alright. We don't have to be out super long. Besides, I can see how easy she is to handle in the dark this way."

I smiled and turned my eyes to Cal, who looked positively green. Well, as green as someone with our skin tone could. "Sounds like a plan."

When Cal dropped me off at school, Hip and Jason were waiting out front. Their combined hotness was almost too much for my fluttery heart. I couldn't forget my plans to spy on them later at their swim practice.

I skipped up to them. "Guess whose father got a boat and gets to go out on it later today after work?"

"You're chipper this morning," Jason commented while Hip replied, "George Clooney?"

"I had a good day yesterday, and actually woke up on the right side of the bed this morning. My father's announcement about the boat was icing on the cake." I grinned.

I wasn't lying. Despite the crashing disaster that was Theseus' discovery of my scars, he still gave me a kiss goodbye and promises for more in the future. Later that night, I slept pretty soundly with thoughts of him and the other guys floating through my mind. Taking in the news about the boat and my impending discovery behind the weird shit going on in this town, I was downright Santa Claus level jolly.

Jason smiled. "I'm glad. It does the heart good to smile."

Hip rolled his eyes. "You're so cheesy."

"So? People love cheese."

Hip pointed at him. "You don't, though."

Jason's eyes widened. "How did you-?"

"Know you hated cheese? I have eyes, Monroe." Hip replied, his usual grin absent.

The bell rang, signaling for us to start heading to class. Hip took my hand and gave my palm a slow kiss before taking off without a word. As I watched him leave, I realized that Hip seemed a bit off today. Not bad, per se, but there was something different. I wondered if it had anything to do with what happened yesterday.

I turned to look at Jason. He was watching Hip as well, his eyebrows furrowed, face set into a full frown. I was confused, then I realized that was the first time Hip had done something that intimate to me in public and it was in front of Jason. As far as I was aware, he had no idea about the others and might think that he and I were exclusive now.

"Jason…"

His eyes snapped to me. "Yes?"

I opened my mouth, but no sound came out. I didn't know what to say! It wasn't like I could outright say, 'Hey, you're not the only guy I'm interested in or is interested in me.'

I never felt like more of a whore in that moment.

I couldn't look at him. Instead I shut my mouth and stared down at my shoes like they were the most interesting things in the world.

"I talked to Percy the other day," Jason began. I saw him shifting around out of the corner of my eye, messing with the old satchel at his side. "He told me about...he told me he had feelings for you."

My heart stopped for a moment and my gaze left my shoes to look up at him, my eyes wide.

"He also said he wasn't the only one," he added.

Oh my God, I wasn't ready for this. He knew. I couldn't do this. What did he think of me? Why did I care? I shouldn't care what he or any one of the other guys thought of me, but I did.

Not really knowing what to do, I bolted. Like a coward, I tried to justify my running with the fact that class was about to start, and I didn't want to be late. I didn't get far.

Jason shouted my name and took my hand, jerking me backwards. I looked at him, anxiety quickly morphing into panic.

I said the only thing I could think of. "Jason, please believe me that I'm not trying to take Percy from you. I swear, when he kissed me I—"

"He kissed you?" he interrupted.

"Yes," I squeaked.

"He didn't tell me that. When did he kiss you?"

I couldn't look him in the eyes, so I stared down at my shoes again. "The day that he took me home."

He growled. "That fucker...Well at least it was before."

I glanced back up at him. "Before what?"

"Before I told him how I felt about you."

"Jason, I'm sorry," I said, knowing that my apology meant nothing.

"When he kissed you, did you stop him because you wanted to or because you were afraid to hurt me?"

"I didn't want to hurt you," I replied, surprised by his question.

"But not really because we were literally going on a date the next day, or because I was interested in you. But because I told you of my feelings for him," he pointed out.

He wasn't wrong. That day, while I had felt somewhat bad about kissing Percy when I had a date with Jason, I had honestly been more worried about hurting Jason's feelings over kissing his longtime crush.

I bit my lip and nodded in confirmation.

His face scrunched up and he leaned forward and ran his hands through his hair. "Ugh! I don't know what I'm supposed to do."

"Jason, I'm—"

"No," he held his hand up. "Please don't apologize again. I don't hold a monopoly on who Percy likes, and your feelings are your own. If you have feelings for Percy...or even Hip, that's none of my business. I asked you on a date, not to be a nun."

"But—"

He shook his head, halting me again. "Just tell me one thing. Do I stand a chance? Because I could handle this a lot better if I wasn't fooling myself into trying to think that I actually stood a chance being with you."

What the fuck do you say to something like that? When someone begs you to consider them. Of course, I thought about Jason. And yes, I could admit that I liked him. But to basically be asking someone to be okay with being one of several, vying for my attention?

It wasn't right, and I should just lie and tell him I felt nothing for him. Break his heart so he could go find someone else.

I certainly should, and I would, and—OMG, WHY WAS I KISSING HIM?!

My lips were currently locked onto his, my hands up into his hair keeping him close to me like my life depended on it. His own hands hesitated for a moment before sweeping right under my butt and pulling. My legs were heaved up and wrapped around him. He held me up, devouring my mouth.

I felt us moving until there was a wall at my back. He pressed into me about as close as he possibly could be, grinding himself against me.

In the back of my mind I knew that we were outside the school, and there were probably stragglers who were seeing a show, but I didn't care. All I cared about right then was having Jason and keeping his lips on mine.

"Atalanta," he murmured against my lips between kisses.

I hummed in question. I tugged lightly at his hair, enticing a hiss from him. I was rewarded with him grinding just a bit harder against me.

He broke away with a gasp. "We should probably stop."

I growled and used my hold on his hair to pull him back towards me. I wanted to finish what he had started the other day. This time with no broken table to get in our way.

Of course, I didn't consider teachers being worse than coffee tables.

I heard a throat being cleared once, twice, three times, and didn't even consider what the sound meant until someone said, "Oh, for fuck's sake. Will you break it up before I have to give you both detention for indecent behavior?"

I pulled my mouth away to see Mr. K standing next to us, his arms crossed and his eyebrow quirked.

The flare of embarrassment nearly doused the warmth of my arousal as I hopped out of Jason's arms.

Mr. K smirked. "Get to class, Ms. North."

He moved aside and gestured towards the front door. I looked back at Jason. His eyes were crazed as he breathed heavily and stared at me like a man starved and I was a huge steak.

As I walked away, I could have sworn I saw Jason begin to follow me, but Mr. K stopped him.

My head down, I made my way to get a tardy slip from the front office and then head to class. I made some excuse about having woman problems and the thirty something year old male history professor clamped right up about my tardiness.

A few of the students stared at me curiously, but none with the look that said, 'I know what you've been doing'.

That didn't last long, as by second period I was getting those looks, and whispers were flying around the classroom. By third period, I got my first question.

"Did you really get caught giving Jason Monroe a blowjob?" a girl with huge glasses and braces asked me.

I scrunched my nose at her. "What? No."

"Oh, okay," she said, but it didn't really look like she believed me.

After that, I noticed as I walked the halls that people were staring and murmuring under their breath.

I wouldn't have cared about the rumors, but so many eyes on me at once made me nervous and for some reason Jason didn't meet me in between classes like he normally did, so I suffered through the discomfort alone.

By the time lunch had rolled around I had been asked twice about giving Jason a blow job, three times about being caught just fucking in front of the school, and one time a guy asked me if it was true that I let Jason do me in the ass. The rumor mill was a funny thing. The truth hardly ever stayed the same color.

Jason wasn't at the door to my classroom when the bell rang, and he wasn't outside sitting with Davie and Margo either. As they weren't technically my friends, I was nervous to approach them without Jason.

"Come on, Atalanta, there's nothing to be afraid of. They like you even without him around," a voice whispered next to me. It was warm like honey and soothed my nerves.

Looking over my shoulder, I saw Hip standing there, gazing down at me. His face was set into an encouraging smile. Confidence radiated off of him, seeping into me like a warm summer's day.

I nodded and the two of us made our way out to the bench to sit down with Davie and Margo.

"Hey, guys," Margo beamed up at us. "Where's Jason?"

I shrugged. "I was hoping you knew. I haven't seen him since this morning."

"You mean since you two had kinky sex out on the school's lawn?" Davie asked, holding back laughter as he shoveled pasta into his mouth.

Hip choked on his juice, snorting and coughing till some of it came out of his nose. I stared at him for a second before breaking out into laughter, a full belly laughter that had me rocking back on the bench seat and almost falling over, which only made me laugh more.

"That's not funny! Did you really have sex with Jason on the front lawn?" Hip asked, looking really perturbed.

I frowned, my laughter dying out. "I didn't. They are all simply rumors."

"Have you not heard them today, Hip? Everyone's talking about it," Margo asked.

He shook his head. "I've honestly been preoccupied all morning."

It was odd for him not to have noticed something. He was usually so observant.

I gently put my hand on his shoulder.

"Are you okay?" I whispered.

He didn't look at me. "I'm alright. Just eat your lunch."

He slipped an apple off his tray and put it in front of me. I picked it up and stared at it before looking up at Margo and Davie across from me. They were glancing between Hip and I, curious looks on their faces.

Davie, the ever tactful, suddenly blurted out, "Which one are you dating?"

Margo jabbed her elbow into his side before saying, "What he means is, we are curious. Are you and Hip dating, or are you with Jason?"

This day was just full of awkward questions, wasn't it?

I cleared my throat. "I'm not dating either of them. Please excuse me."

Honestly done with people and their questions for the moment, I stood up from the table, planning on hiding out the rest of lunch in the bathroom. I started to walk away when I heard Margo call my name, and felt small, feminine hands grab my arm. I yelped and tugged my arm out of Margo's grasp, clutching it close to my chest.

Margo looked hurt and confused. I felt terrible for reacting like that. It wasn't her fault I was so weird.

"I'm sorry," I said before I turned and left.

A dark mood settled over my shoulders as I stormed inside the school building and into the women's bathroom. As I locked myself in the large handicap stall and slumped down next to the toilet, I realized that this feeling had been following me all day. This little dark weight in the center of my chest had been growing steadily since the encounter with Jason this morning.

I shouldn't have kissed him. I should have just simply told him I wasn't interested and walked away.

All the mixed-up emotions that had been building in the past few weeks burst forth. The guilt, the confusion, the anger, the elation, the lust, and the happiness.

INTO THE SEAS EMBRACE

Everything that this town, these men had brought out in me. Suddenly, everything that had been going on these past few weeks flashed to the forefront of my mind.

Meeting the guys, being attacked by those girls, the odd looks I got around town, the lies.

There was just too much. Too much going on, and it needed to stop.

I couldn't handle it.

I clutched my head and curled up into a ball, my breaths coming out uneven and quick, my face wet with tears.

I wanted it to stop. All these emotions, I wanted them to stop.

I needed a blade, I needed something sharp.

Pain.

Pain would stop this flood of emotion and confusion.

I clutched my wrist and my chest wracked with quiet sobs. *Try to remember what the doctors said.*

Count backwards from ten.

Breathe slowly.

Remember, it's only temporary.

It wasn't working.

I bit my lip, but the pain wasn't enough. Taking the palm of my hand into my mouth, I bit down on it.

Hard. The twinges of pain calmed me down a fraction and made me focus just a bit more.

Hurting yourself won't help.

But it would. It does. But I knew it was wrong.

I felt a weight rest on my shoulder. Jumping, I saw Hip. Somehow, he had slipped into the stall without me noticing and sat down next to me, his head resting on my shoulder.

Shame washed over me, and I immediately tore my hand out my mouth.

"H-Hip?"

"I'm here. You're safe," he said, his voice full of warmth.

I sucked in a ragged breath, my eyes wide.

"Just breathe," he whispered.

He wasn't looking at me directly. He just stared ahead, the weight of his head on my shoulder a reassurance and an anchor.

But my shame wouldn't be abated now, adding to the ugly pile of emotions that stormed inside of me. I hugged my knees and sobbed some more.

I felt a little ridiculous. This wasn't my first panic attack and I knew it wouldn't be my last, but it didn't stop me from feeling stupid.

"You're not weak or stupid you know."

I hiccupped. "Are you some freaky mind reader or something?"

INTO THE SEAS EMBRACE

He was way too good at knowing what I was thinking half the time.

"No, I'm just good at reading people," He replied.

We didn't say anything else for a few minutes. I was grateful that no one else came into the bathroom during that time. I honestly don't think I could have handled someone else getting all up in my business and failing to calm me down. Especially if that someone was a girl.

Hip was good, though. He didn't try to brush me off or tell me to calm down. He just sat next to me, patiently waiting for it to pass, his head resting on my shoulder.

I still felt ashamed that he had caught me biting myself. I had just told Theseus yesterday that I had stopped doing it years ago. Yet here I was craving the feel of the cold blade against my skin and the sharp sting it left behind.

My hand, the one I had bitten, came down and rested into Hip's, seeking out his comfort. His acceptance.

He squeezed my hand, assuring me, "It's okay. I'm right here."

Eventually, I heard the bell ring, signaling the end of lunch.

"Do you think you're okay with going to class?" He asked.

I shook my head. I wasn't ready to face the other students with more of their questions and judgmental stares.

"Okay."

Soon, the bell for the high school students to start class rang. It also signaled for the middle school kids to come down from the second floor and begin their lunch. A few girls came barging through the bathroom door, yammering about some gossip. A couple of them tried to get through the stall door but once I yelped that someone was already in here, they left it alone.

"Did you hear a couple of the high school kids were caught fucking in front of the school this morning?"

I internally groaned and banged my head against my knees. Damn it for small towns and their gossip!

Hip squeezed my hand and scooted closer to me, his presence making it just a little better.

"Like literally in front of the school?!" a second girl asked incredulously.

"Yeah! Right near the front door, apparently."

"Do you know who?"

"No, but I do know it was that hot teacher, Dr. Kline, that found them."

A third girl piped up. "He is just too good looking. I can't wait till next year and I get him for English. The perfect amount of eye candy to get me through the day."

"Yeah, seeing as some of the hottest guys in school are leaving this year."

"Do you think that senior, that really hot blonde one with the motorcycle, would ever consider going out with an underclassman?" Girl Two asked wistfully.

I chuckled softly and stared up at Hip who was looking at me. He smiled and rolled his eyes.

"I don't know, Rache. I heard he was raised by humans." Girl Three said, her tone harsh and full of judgement.

My eyebrows scrunched. Humans? They were saying it like they weren't, and neither was Hip. I was still staring up at him, but his smile had turned into a scowl and he averted his gaze.

I had my suspicions, but that just confirmed it.

The girl I assumed was Rache gasped. "Really?"

"Yeah. My mom said he's got that dirty blood," Three replied, her tone haughty.

"But how? He's not a half, right?" Girl One hopped in, apparently curious now too.

"That's the thing. No one knows. I heard my grandpa say he was just washed up on shore. They think some human just abandoned him."

"Oh, but that just makes his mischievous bad boy thing so much hotter. He's got a mysterious past."

The girls finally left the bathroom, taking their conversation and knowledge right along with them.

I sighed and leaned heavily into him. "So, you want to tell me what they meant when they said you were raised by humans?"

He hummed. "I'll tell you, but it won't be on the bathroom floor. Or at school for that matter."

I was taken aback. He didn't try to lie or deny what we just heard. I wanted to demand answers from him now, but I was afraid he would clam up like the rest if I pushed too hard.

"Okay, but where's a good place to tell me?" I pushed.

He was silent for a moment before asking. "You're working today, right?"

"Yeah, and you have practice." I pointed out.

"I'll tell you after practice if you've got the time."

I tilted my head, thinking about how I promised Dad I would go out on the boat with him, but this was my chance to get some answers. He would forgive me if I was a little late.

"I'll make the time."

Chapter Twenty

Atalanta

We eventually left the bathroom, waiting for the next bell to ring so we could blend in with the other students. My legs were stiff and my ass was cold, feeling bruised from sitting on the hard ground for so long.

Before Hip and I separated, he slowly brought me in for a hug, giving me ample time to pull away if I wanted, but I didn't. As his arms wrapped around me, I didn't feel sympathy or judgement. Just the warmth of friendship.

That warmth carried me through the rest of the day with people's stares and annoying questions.

Jason never showed up to any of the classes.

I gave into the urge once the bell for the end of the school day rang and pulled out my phone.

Jason? Are you okay?

When I didn't get a reply immediately, I slipped the phone back onto my pocket.

"You look worried," Hip asked as he suddenly appeared next to me.

I jumped a little. "You have a habit of doing that."

"Of being amazingly sneaky?" He shrugged. "It's less of a habit and more of a talent."

I sighed. "I haven't seen or heard anything from Jason."

"I'm sure he's fine. Mr. Perfect was probably called away to become the next President of the United States."

I snorted. "I could believe that."

He tilted his head towards the parking lot. "Give you a ride to the center?"

I nodded, and we made our way over to his bike.

When we reached the community center, the parking lot had several more cars than usual. Students piled out of a few of them and made their way to the center. The swim team, I guessed. There were more people than I would have expected.

Going through the entrance, I noticed Theseus at the counter talking to Lidia. A little flicker of jealousy sparked in me as I saw how Lidia looked at him. Her eyes constantly running down his torso and back up to his mouth, licking her lips seductively. When she reached across the counter to stroke his hand, I couldn't help but growl.

"Down, girl," Hip said with a chuckle. "Lidia isn't much of a threat to you."

"She looks like she wants to have him for dinner," I grumbled.

"She looks at almost all guys like that, but most of us wouldn't touch her with a ten-foot pole."

It was then that I realized that I was being openly territorial right in front of one of the guys.

"Shit, Hip. I'm sorry, I probably just hurt your feelings."

He shook his head. "You didn't. Well, perhaps a little, but it's something that we're gonna talk about later. For now, know that it's okay."

I smoothed down the sleeves of my jacket. "Okay."

"I'm going to head to practice. You have a good day at work," he said, before kissing my forehead and sauntering down the hall which I knew lead to the pool.

I took a deep breath before walking up and behind the counter to put my things in the office and grabbing my work clothes out of my bag.

I felt familiar hands slide along my hips and down to the tops of my thighs before sliding back up again.

"You didn't say hi," Theseus whispered in my ear.

I turned so that I was facing him, his hands still at my hips. "I didn't want to interrupt your conversation."

I tried to keep the jealous expression off my face, and I knew I succeeded when Theseus did not look concerned.

He nuzzled my nose with his. "I'll happily take an interruption from you any time."

I giggled, and with a little surge of courage, got up on my tip toes and gave him a peck on the lips. I saw behind Theseus that Lidia was glaring at us, which made me reach back up on my toes to kiss him again, this time less chaste and with more claim to it.

Mine.

When I pulled away, his lips tried to follow mine, his eyes closed.

I tapped on his chest. "I'm gonna go get changed and we can get started, okay?"

He nodded, the look in his eyes telling me he wasn't just staring at my lips to read what I was saying.

With a bit of a skip in my step, I went to the bathroom and quickly swapped out my...somewhat nice jacket and jeans with sweat pants and an old long sleeve that had holes in a couple of places.

Today we worked front to back, going from room to room to tidy up and swap out the trash bags people had filled up since yesterday. My mind was constantly wandering to where I knew the swim team was practicing and hoping I would get a chance to slip away to watch them before they finished. I was also thinking about Jason and why I hadn't heard back from him personally.

Not long after my shift started, I got a text message from Hip—I don't know how he got my phone and put his contact info in under 'Usain Bolt'— with a photo of Jason in a speedo, the caption reading:

"It seems Mr. Perfect has lost the election and decided to return."

INTO THE SEAS EMBRACE

I was glad Jason was okay, but I wish he would have texted me himself. In fact, I wondered how I had even missed his arrival.

I stood up and bent backwards, my spine cracking as I had been crouched over these toilets for a while. Those porcelain thrones were shining and fit for a king. Proud of my work, I picked up my bucket with a smile.

This was my chance to sneak a peek at the swim team.

Bucket in hand, I walked down the hall towards the doors to the pool. It was noisy, the sounds of bodies splashing through the water as their coach shouted random things from the sidelines. I don't know how he expected the swimmers to hear him when they were under the water half the time.

Peeking in, I saw a group of people standing off to the side. Girls in tight one-piece dark blue swim suits and guys in dark blue speedos. They were chatting as they watched the six or so people slice through the water. The coach, a rather large man I had seen a few times, was running up and down the sides of the pool, following the swimmers with a whistle in his hands. I was waiting for him to fall at any moment.

He didn't though, and when I guess the swimmers completed the exercise, he blew on his whistle, signaling for all the swimmers to a halt. They did and with a fluid efficiency they pulled themselves out of the water.

"Monroe! Good job! I noticed a little hesitancy on your turn, don't be afraid of the pool wall, it's not gonna reach out and bite you! McNab! Sloppy! I want you running extra laps with Clark! His form is better than Monroe's. Good work!"

My eyes focused on the people who had just come out of the pool when I heard my guys' names. And fuck, shit, damn, my jaw was on the ground. Those two in nothing but tight speedos and caps? My-oh-my, I was about fanning myself.

Both of them were well muscled and glistening from the water dripping down their bodies. This was the first time I had seen either of them without a t-shirt and I had to say, I wasn't disappointed. My eyes skimmed each one of them up and down, the little pervert in me taking notes on their junk. Though, it wasn't like either of them were hard at the moment, so I couldn't really judge.

I noticed how much paler Jason was compared to Hip, who had a nice, even, golden tan. However, Jason was a lot bulkier in his frame compared to Hip, and noticeably taller as well. It reminded me that Hip was actually the shortest of the guys, the tallest I think being Theseus, and then Ajax.

I shook my head, reminding myself I wasn't there to ogle the guys. I was there to…um, well, watch them intensely until they slipped up and revealed something? Wow, ogling them sounded a lot better in my head than just basically stalking them. Nevertheless, I watched them as I moved into the room under the pretense of tidying up. Straightening chairs, picking up nonexistent trash, picking up actual pool toys. You know. Janitor stuff.

Unfortunately, I didn't notice anything odd beyond how fast in the water both of them were, but it wasn't supernatural fast, just fast. The two of them were clearly the best on the team and it was obvious by the way all of the girls— and a couple of guys— watched them that they were desired and envied.

I did make a note that neither of them seemed to interact with each other. Between turns lapping in the pool, the two of them would break off into separate groups as if not noticing each other's existence. I knew that both of them shared a couple of classes together, combined with being on the swim team and having both grown up in Argos, I was surprised they weren't friends before I met them. Though, they weren't really friends now either. Jason seemed to tolerate Hip's presence at the lunch table and Hip liked to antagonize Jason, so I don't think there was much budding bromance coming from him either.

Was I the only reason they even spoke?

After a half hour of covert sleuthing, I came to the frustrating conclusion that I wasn't going to get anything juicy today. I consoled myself with the idea that Hip was going to tell me everything once I got off of work. Hopefully.

Heading back into the hallway, I met up with Theseus and helped him take out the trash he had collected. Together, the two of us worked to clean the rest of the rooms. We finished up around five o'clock, long after the swim team had ended their practice and not long before the nightly people would come for their classes and mess up the whole place again for us to reclean the next day.

Hip had texted that he was waiting in the library for me to get off of work. I blushed, thinking about how he and Percy might be talking about me right that moment, but I tried to reassure myself that they were probably doing their own things. Hip listening to music and Percy staring at his computer, bored.

I texted him that I would be done in a couple of minutes, I just had to get the trash from the pool's locker rooms and take it out to the bin.

Theseus and I double teamed; he would get the men's while I got the women's. The locker rooms were right near the entrance of the pool and when you entered it was easy to have your back turned to the pool most of the time, only really seeing it in your peripherals.

Which is probably why I didn't see the body when I first entered.

Heavy trash bag in hand, I waddled out of the women's locker rooms facing the pool's blue surface. But it wasn't completely blue, there was an odd reflection of something under the surface, like a tan blob. Thinking that someone had just been an asshole and tossed clothes into the pool or something, I got closer to get a better look.

And dropped the bag of trash right on my foot, my face contorted in horror.

INTO THE SEAS EMBRACE

I screamed.

There, resting at the bottom of the pool, was Jason.

"JASON, NO!!"

Without a thought, I acted, running forward and diving into the pool. The water was warm and the resistance frustrating as I frantically swam down. It was a deep pool, at least 10 feet at its deepest end, and Jason was all the way down there. I also wasn't that great of a swimmer. But I didn't care.

I had to get to him.

I had to save him.

My lungs were already burning by the time I got to him but thanks to the adrenaline, I hardly noticed as I reached the bottom, wrapped my arms around him and shoved off the pools' floor. Swimming back towards the surface was much harder, but it went fast.

There was one moment where Jason began to thrash in my arms and all I could think was 'Oh thank fuck he's still alive! I could still save him!'.

I breached the surface, taking in huge lungfuls of air before I screamed. "Help! Help me please!"

As I thrashed to the side trying to get out of the water, I could see Theseus at the edge of the pool, looking frantic. Then Ajax came running through the door, his expression matching Theseus'. I would stop to wonder why Ajax was there later. Just then, all I could think about was getting Jason out of the pool and performing CPR or something ASAP!

"What the fuck are you doing!?" someone shouted in my ear.

My head whipped around to see my cargo, the cargo I thought was dead or dying staring right at me, his eyes wide and angry.

I screamed again, more out of shock than fear this time, letting go of Jason in surprise.

I felt hands wrap underneath my armpits, and with great strength hauled me out of the water and deposited my soaking wet body on the floor's rough surface. I looked up to see Percy staring down at me, his eyes behind his glasses full of concern. Next to him was Hip, who's face showed about the same level of concern as Percy's.

My eyes shot back to the completely fine and alive Jason who was taking Theseus' hand and heaving himself out of the pool.

"Y-you're okay!" I said, my voice cracking from shock. Hot tears began to pour down my cheeks.

"Of course I'm fucking okay. What were you thinking?" he shouted, his dark green eyes burning with rage. His jaw was tight, fists clenched at his side.

My head snapped back as if I had been punched. "I was thinking I was saving your life!"

"You could have killed yourself trying to save me!"

"I THOUGHT YOU WERE DEAD!" I shouted back.

I tried to stand up, to be on his level at least a little as he stared me down in fury, but my legs wouldn't support my weight. I slumped down on my ass like a newborn baby who didn't know how to walk. I was shaking horribly. I was now aware how cold I was as my bones seemed to rattle and bounce off each other with my shaking.

Someone gathered me into their arms, putting my wet body in their lap. Ajax. His huge body gave off so much warmth and soothing comfort as he rocked me back and forth, murmuring that it was okay, and that I was safe now. I didn't want to be held like a crying child!

I shoved him away until I sprawled out of his lap, looking up at Jason and shouting. "How are you okay!?"

His whole body clenched that much tighter and he looked away.

"Atalanta," Theseus said, his palms out like he was approaching an injured animal. "Let's calm down for a moment."

When he said it, I felt that cotton brain feeling wash over me. NO! I shook my head furiously, trying and succeeding to burn away the cotton.

"No! I will not calm down!"

I stood, finally finding my legs and pointing my finger at him. "And don't you try to use your freaky mind control thing on me! I want answers and I want them now!"

"What the fuck, Jason," I heard Hip whisper behind me.

"I must have dozed off," Jason whispered back in reply.

They were terrible whisperers.

I whipped around to face them. "Dozed off? DOZED OFF!!? YOU FELL ASLEEP AT THE BOTTOM OF THE FUCKING POOL?"

We stood there, Jason and I glaring daggers at one another. He wasn't budging on answers, so I turned to Hip.

"I want the truth."

"You already know the truth, Atalanta." This came from Percy, who said my name for the first time, and I didn't even get a chance to enjoy it.

"What?" I threw my hands up in the air. "That you all are some mythical fairytale creatures?! *Or* that you're in some sort of weird cult? Because those are my best guesses!"

"A cult?" Hip snorted.

I snarled at him like a rabid dog.

His chuckling halted immediately.

"I'm tired of you fuckers dancing around the truth."

"Why should we give you the truth, huh? It's not like you've been very forthcoming with us!" Jason snapped.

My stomach dropped, but I was too angry right that moment to start worrying. "What are you talking about?"

"You lie all the time," Jason said, stalking closer to me. "You lie about your family, you lie about your past, you lie about yourself."

"No, I don't," I tried to say firmly, but my mask was cracking.

Jason was right in my face.

His tone was venomous when he spoke, like a viper striking right at my heart. "Who are you, Atalanta North? Because all I know is that you're just some slut who's playing all of us."

Chapter Twenty-One

Jason

I regretted the words the moment I said them. I also knew I deserved the bitch slap she gave me right across the face before she stormed off without another word, tears streaming down her face.

I moved to follow her but was stopped when Ajax stepped in front of me, his hulking frame blocking the doorway while three sets of hands gripped me tightly.

"You're not going anywhere near her until you calm down," Percy said.

"He shouldn't go anywhere near her, period!" Hip growled.

"I'm honestly missing something. What's going on? What did you say to her?" Poor Theseus and his fucking busted hearing. He probably missed half of what was being said. All he knew was that Atalanta was upset and I was the culprit.

I felt Percy let go and out of the corner of my eye I saw his hands moving rapidly. I didn't know he knew sign language. Neither did Theseus, judging by the shock on his face, which quickly morphed into rage.

Suddenly the man who I always thought was a bit docile was punching me square in the jaw, causing me to fall backwards onto my ass. I clutched my face, which now hurt like a bitch, and stared up at the seething Theseus. I was lucky for my dense bones and weak attacker or else I would be sporting a broken jaw right then.

"You don't fucking know anything do you, you little brat?!" Theseus shouted, probably much louder than he had meant too.

"What the hell does that mean?" I shot back defensively.

Theseus pointed in the direction which Atalanta fled. "It doesn't take an idiot to see that that girl's been through something and she doesn't deserve your judgement."

I looked down, ashamed, but my pride told me that I needed to defend myself. "Well, I mean, she is lying to us."

"And we're lying to her, Jason," Hip said, poking me in the chest. "We've all got our secrets and our pasts. Regardless, we didn't need you throwing what's going on in her face. She feels guilty enough."

All the anger finally leaked out of me, leaving me feeling like the hollow asshole I knew I really was. When I had woken up to Atalanta frantically pulling me towards the surface of the water, I didn't know what to think. At first the flood of fear and self-loathing came, fear for her and the danger I just put her in, and self-loathing for fucking up and basically handing her proof of everything she had been suspecting.

I touched the three thin slits at the side of my neck. The gills which I sported on each side of my neck were flush against the skin now and would only really be seen if someone looked rather closely. Unlike our scales and other attributes, which could be hidden, our gills were always present.

"She's talked to you about it?" I said, my voice a hoarse whisper.

He huffed. "Not in so many words."

I looked around slowly at all the men around me. "Have *we* decided what's going on? Are all of you even aware of it?"

"I believe young Theseus is the only one I haven't spoken to about it," Percy replied.

"I'm deaf, not blind. I was probably aware of it before even you were, Percival." Theseus hissed.

Ajax spoke, his low voice which I so rarely heard startling me. "We should stop dancing around the subject like it's taboo. We all have feelings for Atalanta."

"And she doesn't seem to prefer one of us over the other." Percy added.

The group fell into an awkward silence. Hip and Theseus were glaring daggers at me while Percy studied us as he always did, gauging our reactions so he could pick his best course of action. And, well, I had never been very good at reading Ajax. From what I knew of him, he was old. Older than most of the people in the town, but you wouldn't guess it by his appearance. Though, that was common for our kind, as aging was more of a choice than a fact of time.

I was the first to speak. "What do we do?"

"You shouldn't be doing anything," Hip growled, pointing at me. "Fuck, Jason. You shouldn't even be in the conversation. Not after what you just said to her."

He was right, I shouldn't.

"Whether you like it or not, Mr. Clark, he's involved in this." Percy said, crossing his arms. "But I do think we need to talk about what just happened. Why wouldn't you just tell her, Jason?"

"Because she's lying about something. Because maybe she's not who she says she is," I replied, knowing that it was only half of the truth.

Percy nodded. "Perhaps. But I think it goes a lot deeper than that. Does it have something to do with your family?"

I glared at him. "Can we please not go poking into my issues when we have other things to worry about?"

"Yes, please," Hip groaned. "I'm done with this idiot."

I narrowed my eyes at him. Until Atalanta came to town, Hip and I had hardly ever spoken. I always thought he was too cocky for his own good, but I never really treated him like some of the others in town did. Yet, ever since we were children, he held a level of hostility towards me. It was easier for us to avoid each other and for years I hardly gave him a thought. But now he was always around and constantly poking in all the wrong places. Anger built back up in the pit of my stomach and without thinking I shot up and tackled Hip into the pool.

Water surged around us as I grabbed at his shirt and tried to land a good hit on him. Our scales rippled over our skin as we tumbled through the water, cursing and kicking at each other. For the first time in my life it was almost if the water was working against me. My movements were slow whereas his were quick. He landed a punch to my shoulder and face while I had only managed to hit him once.

Suddenly I was being pushed away, a strong current pulling me from Hip and out of the pool.

Confused, I slipped and slid as I tried to scramble to a standing position. Without effort, Hip jumped out of the water and charged right at me, the pool water almost following behind him. I had heard rumors that Hip was a water elemental, but I didn't think they were true. If he had full use of his power, I was totally outmatched. I wouldn't just lay on my back and take it though. Slowly, I got to my feet and readied to strike first.

Before I could make another move, I felt a large hand wrapping around the back of my neck.

"That is enough!" Percy shouted, his hand on my neck tightening, demanding for me to stay still.

Far too quickly, the murderous rage on Hip's face calmed, his fangs receding and his eyes returning to normal.

"He started it!" Hip shouted, pointing in my direction.

INTO THE SEAS EMBRACE

"And I'm ending it," Percy snarled. "I will not have you two fighting like toddlers. There are bigger matters we must discuss.

It was rare to see the calm and collected librarian show anything more than mild annoyance when upset. Seeing him show genuine anger and dominance was a bit of a turn on. He was right though, we had other problems right now.

I nodded, and Percy released me. The water, which had been building up like a wall behind Hip, dropped and splashed back into the pool, spraying all of us. Hip looked behind him, eyes wide as if he himself had no idea what he'd just done.

I glanced around and saw Theseus and Ajax standing by the doors, Theseus looking worried while Ajax looking as stoic as ever.

"We should leave," Ajax said.

Confused, I heard the commotion coming from behind the door. Shouts of confusion and banging on the door's metal surface clued me in that we had drawn quite the audience. Theseus and Ajax must have been keeping anyone else from coming in.

Percy, whose demeanor sank back to calm, tilted his head towards the emergency exit at the back of the room. "Let's go then."

The five of us were on the move, exiting the building and running into the woods behind the center. The tension was palpable as we settled amongst the trees, none of us looking at each other.

Thinking back to the matter at hand, I felt conflicted. Atalanta was her own person, and if she wanted to be with all of us, who were we to stop her? Jealousy raged in my mind, demanding to keep her to myself and have a normal monogamous relationship like the humans do. But if I did that, told her to choose, who was to say she would choose me?

It was actually Ajax who spoke up first. "We should establish rules."

"Rules? You don't suggest we go along with this? Share Atalanta?" Hip asked, voicing what we were all thinking.

"If it's what she wants." He shrugged.

Theseus and Percy — who stood as far as they could from each other in the small clearing — just nodded, not looking conflicted at all.

"And it doesn't bother you?" I hopped in. "The three of you seem so okay with this."

"Simple cultural differences," Percy began. "Monogamy is uncommon for our kind. There are too few females, so it's rare that you find one who doesn't have multiple mates. It's understandable for you two to shy away from the idea, having grown up around humans."

"Whoa, whoa, whoa, who said anything about mating?" Hip sputtered, looking panicked.

"Is there another girl you're interested in, Hip?" Theseus asked an eyebrow cocked at the blond mer.

He shook his head. "No. It's just...aren't we all a little young to be thinking about mating? I mean, it's like marriage, right?"

Theseus shrugged. "Some of us are a lot older than you think."

I had always assumed Theseus wasn't much older than me, but perhaps I was wrong. And while I knew Percy's actual age, I could only guess about Ajax, who I kind of assumed was the same as Percy.

Hip's brows furrowed. "I don't understand."

The elders hadn't even told him this much? I felt bad for him in that moment, being so far out of the loop when it came to his kind.

"Merfolk are immortal," Ajax said.

"It is a lot more complex than that, Ajax," Percy said before looking at Hip. "but yes, we are a particularly long-lived species. Therefore, our age does not necessarily match our outward appearance."

Hip's jaw fell open, his eyes darting between the four of us before settling on me, his eyes full of accusation.

"Don't look at me. You and I are the same age." I said, shaking my head. I wasn't sure about jumping on the mate bandwagon like the other three either, and I didn't think we should be discussing it right then. "I don't think we should be making such a decision without Atalanta here." I looked down and muttered, "I also need apologize to her."

Hip jumped on this. "Yeah, we should wait. Especially since this is just as big, if not a bigger decision for her."

Ajax and Theseus agreed. Percy, however, looked upset. Until then he had been resting calmly against a tree. Now he was standing straight, his foot tapping against the ground as he shifted around restlessly.

"Percy?" I asked, worried that he was angry with our decision.

At the sound of my voice, his eyes snapped to mine.

"Mm? Oh, yes. Fine." He waved as if dismissing us, clearly distracted.

I was about to push for him to talk to me when I felt a tingling sensation that was all too familiar at the back of skull, and a knowing feeling washed over me.

I looked up to the sky, which was cloudy but calm. "It's going to storm tonight. And it's gonna be a pretty bad one."

"Can you tell where it's coming from?" Percy asked, surging towards me, his expression intense.

"From the west. It's on the ocean right now, picking up speed. Why?"

Hip jumped in, his eyes full of panic. "Didn't Atalanta say that she was going out with her dad? To test out his new boat?"

I shook my head, staring at Percy. "You don't think…"

Percy swore. "I knew it. I suspected this might happen with my developing feelings for her. We need to leave."

Without any more information, Percy took off running into the woods towards the beach. The four of us stood there looking at each other, confused and afraid, before taking off after him.

"What might happen? What's going on?" Hip asked, looking back and forth at all of us, trying to keep up.

I felt my body tense up, my heart pounding as I look directly at Hip. "Percy is a Guardian."

Chapter Twenty-Two

Atalanta

I called Cal the moment I pulled my stuff out of the office and ran outside. I tried to hold back the sniffles and clear the croakiness in my voice as I asked her for a ride. She definitely suspected something as she agreed slowly, her tone full of curiosity.

I kept looking behind my shoulder, expecting one of the guys to come running out to me, but no one came. I was alone.

I wiped the tears off my cheeks and slumped to the cold steps of the center.

The snow fell lightly, slowly covering the parking lot. It was quiet and peaceful, but that only made the despair I felt inside all the more prominent. I'd been called many different things over the years, but slut was a new one and fuck did it sting.

Is he wrong? I mean, five guys.

I shoved away that little voice in my head which had surfaced recently after a few blissful years of... well, not a *total* lack of self-deprecation, but I had been on a much better track before all this shit happened.

I was so done with this town. Tonight, I would tell Dad that we needed to leave. If not for the betterment of my mental state, then because some of the people suspected something.

Maybe we would go further south, stay near the coast so Dad could keep his new shiny boat. But maybe someplace warmer, like California.

I tried not to think of the guys and the pain I felt at never being able to see them again, but fuck it. I hardly knew them! I would not let myself pine over them. Besides, they were part of the reason the little voice came back.

When Cal pulled up, I gave her a big, if slightly watery, smile. When I hopped in the car and she gave me that expectant look that I knew was coming, I simply said that it had been a rough day, not giving her anything else. She shrugged, probably deciding she would squeeze it out of me later when I was in a better mood out on the boat.

When we got home, the redness in my eyes had cleared up and Dad was none the wiser. He was so excited when he switched places with Cal and drove us down to the docks.

I hadn't been there yet, though they looked just like any of the other docks I'd seen over the years. There was a long, stretching boardwalk that ran along the water, branching out to a bunch of mini docks that housed a couple hundred boats, bobbing up and down as the waves rolled in beneath them. Large, hulking seamen with ocean rough skin and scruffy beards shuffled around each other, several of them shouting orders.

The three of us walked through the little pockets of the crowd, fishing gear in hand. I remembered Dad's comments regarding the odd behavior of the workers. There were a few odd stares, but nothing abnormal, at least nothing I thought roused suspicion. But Dad was even better than me at reading others, so he probably saw something I didn't.

He led us down one of the small docking bays before standing in front of a boat, his hands on his hips, chest puffed out proudly.

"Behold!" He swept out his hands towards the boat. "The Flying Sea Scallop!"

It was a decent sized boat, with a boxed in wheelhouse and two seats welded in the back, made for someone to sit in with their fishing rods.

"The Flying Sea Scallop?" Cal asked with a snicker.

He scowled. "I wasn't the one who picked the name."

"It sounds like the name of a little dingy," I said.

Cal clapped her hands together and tilted her head like she was looking at something cuddily. "It's a cute little dingy."

"This is not a dingy! It is a man's boat!" he boasted, hitting his chest like a freaking gorilla.

"If you say so, Dad," Cal and I said together, giggling as we climbed aboard the boat.

It wasn't in horrible shape. Most of the problems looked cosmetic: some grime on the inside of the walls, the pleather seats were torn and the color bleached.

INTO THE SEAS EMBRACE

Our dad wouldn't have bought it if there were any mechanical problems, so that was reassuring.

"If you say so, Dad," he said his voice high pitch and full of annoyance, which only made Cal and me laugh harder.

After about twenty minutes of showing us around the basic controls, we shoved off, slowly floating out into the harbor before revving the engine and speeding out into deeper water. The boat glided smoothly across the ocean. The speed and the wind whipping across my face was exhilarating, clearing away some of the shadow in my heart.

Reaching a good spot, Dad slowed us down, the boat rocking peacefully. Poor Cal was sprawled across a bench seat next to the fishing chairs.

"Why did I come along?" she groaned.

As I was prepared for this scenario, I pulled a little box out of my jacket pocket and shook it at her. "Because you love us."

Her eyes went wide as she caught sight of the box of sea sickness patches in my hand. "You bitch! Why are you only telling me you had some now! Why not when I was throwing up?"

"Because I wanted to see if you overcame your sea sickness," I grinned wickedly. "Mind over matter, Calz."

"Atalanta, just give your sister the medicine," Dad said, his voice and face deadpan as he worked to set up our poles.

I tossed Cal the box and went to help Dad.

Cal decided to stay on the bench seat while Dad and I strapped into the seats. The fishing chairs were pretty cool. They had buckles to strap a person down in case the seas were a little rough, along with little metal foot rests and a long tube for us to stick our fishing rods into.

Like the other day, we sat quietly as we fished, comfortable with sparse conversation over the next hour. What little we did say was mostly about how our days were today. There was subtle prodding from Cal for me to say more than 'my day was good'. I knew I would, but in time. I had to work up the courage to suggest to Dad that we should leave.

"Those clouds don't look so good," Cal commented.

Swiveling the chair around, I squinted in the direction she was staring. In the distance of the darkening sky were clouds as black as pitch. Shadowing below them indicated heavy rain.

Dad, who sat in the chair to my left, turned and looked at the clouds as well. "That looks a long way off. We should be okay for a bit but should start heading back home soon."

Home. Back to the cabin, to Argos. Back to the guys.

"We need to move." I blurted.

Dad and Cal whipped around to face me, their eyes wide.

"Why? Did you get another call?"

I shook my head, knowing that he was referring to the time I had received a call from my living nightmare. His voice, filled with malice and excitement as he told me that he was close. That once he got his hands on me, he would enjoy making me suffer.

We had packed up our bags in the hour. Our aliases burned. Phones tossed and moving on to the next location.

"No, nothing like that. I..." I fidgeted with the ends of my sleeves. "I'm not doing well. I had an attack earlier."

My dad's brows furrowed, his voice full of hurt. "Hun, why didn't you tell me it was getting that bad?"

"I didn't realize it was," I said, hugging my middle.

"Is this about those boys?" Cal asked.

Dad looked between the two of us, confused. "Boys? What boys? There's more than just that one guy? Jason?"

I shot a glare at Cal. "There are some other guys. Friends I've met. And no. This isn't their fault. Just something about this town."

I wasn't completely lying. This town, while nice, put me on edge with its mysteries. For some reason, I didn't want to smear the guys' names. While they were the cause of my distress, it wasn't actually their fault and I didn't want my dad to blame them.

"But that still doesn't explain why you didn't tell me, Atalanta." Dad sighed. "I thought we were past this."

"I was trying to handle it on my own! Despite what that ID says, I am a grown woman." I said defensively.

He rubbed his face in frustration. "This isn't about you being a grown woman. This is about talking to me when things are going wrong."

"We've been a bit busy! Fuck, Dad. I've hardly seen you in the last month." I said throwing my hands up.

He pointed at me. "Don't you use that against me. I've been trying to provide for this family!"

"So have I!" I shot back.

"Guys!" Cal shouted but we ignored her.

"I know it hasn't been easy, Atalanta, but it won't last forever," he growled.

"It's been eight years, Dad!" I shook my head. "Eight years of hiding all because of me. I'm tired of it."

His face fell, the fight beginning to drain from him. "Atalanta…"

But anger burned in my chest and I wasn't done. "For fuck's sake, don't call me that! It's not my name!"

"GUYS!" Cal shrieked, her voice bordering on terror.

Our heads snapped to Cal. "WHAT?"

She wasn't looking at us. She was staring up at the sky, her eyes wide with fear.

INTO THE SEAS EMBRACE

"Oh, no." I gasped.

In all our fighting, we didn't realize the wind had picked up and the boat subtly rocked more and more as the waves became progressively more violent.

The storm was upon us.

Black clouds, huge and menacing, were baring down on us. In a matter of seconds, a heavy pouring rain swamped us before Dad and I even had the chance to get out of our seats. The boat rocked as the waves churned. Dad finally managed to undo his buckle, shouting for me to stay strapped down and for Cal to get into his chair.

He scurried across the deck and grabbed ahold of the steering wheel, turning the key over and over, shouting and banging at the boat's dashboard. My heart sank, terrified that the boat wouldn't start, but with one well aimed kick I felt the propellers revving to life beneath me. He pushed on the throttle, trying to navigate the boat through the choppy waves as quickly as possible.

Nearby, Cal slipped and slid trying to get into the seat next to me as the boat continued to thrash this way and that. Everything was soaked as the rain continued to pour down on us in buckets.

I leaned as far as the straps would let me, holding out my hand for Cal to grab onto. She did and with all of my strength I pulled her towards me, closer to the other chair. She dragged herself into the chair and desperately tried to grab onto the straps and buckle herself in.

I heard Dad shouting from inside the wheelhouse, but I couldn't hear him over the rain and screaming wind.

He was probably trying to warn us about the wave.

The giant wave crashed over us and swept across the deck of the boat with a vengeance. Sea water slammed into me and would have probably torn me right out of the chair if I hadn't been strapped in. Salt water filled my mouth and I spluttered and gasped for breath when the water receded.

I looked back at Dad, who was fine within the boxed in wheelhouse, but when I turned to look at Cal in the chair next to me it was empty. Cal wasn't in the seat, its straps swinging wildly in the wind.

I looked around frantically. She wasn't on the boat.

SHE WASN'T ON THE BOAT!

"CAL!" I screamed.

I saw her, way too far from us, out in the water. Her small form thrashing around in the waves.

I screamed for her again, tearing at the buckles on the chair. It took too fucking long to get them off but when I did, I was running to the side of the boat where I saw her. Scanning the water, I saw her for only a split second, at least I thought. The water was like black oil, dangerous and unforgiving. In that split second, I saw her, and she looked so much further than before.

I screamed for Cal, screamed for my father.

INTO THE SEAS EMBRACE

I quickly looked back over to him through the windows of the wheelhouse. His eyes were wide, so wide with terror as he realized what was happening that I hardly saw anything but the white of his eyes.

I grabbed the life preserver next to me, and with one last glance at my father, dove off the boat into the water.

Ice. It was like diving into a pool full of ice.

Immediately, my body seized up with the shock of it, my brain screaming:

WARNING! DANGER! DANGER!

But I had to save my sister.

With all the strength I had, I swam in the direction I last saw her. The waves were merciless, beating against me constantly, pushing me back.

I tried to keep calm, tried to keep pushing myself forward, but the sheer panic of what was going on clouded my mind.

Everything was screaming.

My mind was screaming for me to save my sister, my body was screaming from the pain of the cold water and waved bashing into me like brick walls, my lungs were screaming for the air I wasn't getting.

They say your life flashes before your eyes when you're about to die. But as a particularly powerful wave sent me backwards, slamming my head into something, and my body sank beneath the surface of the water like a stone, I didn't see anything like that.

THE NAMELESS SYREN SERIES BOOK 1

The only thing I saw as my lungs burned and my vision hazed over was a strange blue glow in the dark water.

Chapter Twenty-Three

Percy

As the five of us sped through the water, our powerful tails eating up the distance, a small drumming in my chest beat wildly and it wasn't my heart.

A Guardian.

Something I hadn't been called in a long time, but Jason hadn't been wrong. Those of my pod had always been Guardians. The abilities we had from birth made us well suited for protecting others. Our enhanced strength and ability to forge bonds with people without having to mate with them were indispensable qualities.

Those bonds would allow a Guardian to always know when their bonded was in danger, acting as a literal GPS.

I had suspected I'd unintentionally bonded to Atalanta the day that I had kissed her, but seeing as I had never been bonded to a charge, I was stupid and didn't recognize the signs when my instincts had told me to find her.

"Do you know where we're going!?" Hip shouted, his voice carrying through the water much more clearly than that of a human's.

"I do not have an exact location, but I know she's in this direction," I called back.

I was leading the five us as we torpedoed through the water in a tight V formation. The luminescent streaks that ran down the spines along my back and at the sides of my tail acted as beacons in the dark water. Not that I needed it. My light sensitive eyes made the water in front of me as easy to see through as if it were streaming with daylight.

"So that's your ability?"

I looked back at the blond youngling. I heard that he was raised by humans, and the elders in the town were tight lipped about what they told him. Considering how confused he had been earlier, it seemed the rumor was true. Old jackasses.

"He's deep sea." Ajax said.

"Deep sea? Is that why he looks so much different?" There wasn't judgement in his voice, but I still felt a twinge in my chest.

Yes, beyond their color differences, the other four looked very much alike in their true forms. Their spines, which ran along their lower backs down their tails and on their forearms were on the short, wispy side, whereas mine were large, sprouting from my back like spikes. My dorsal fins, while smaller, were a similar shape.

The differences did not stop with just the tails and spines, as my skin was sickly pale, if a little blue, my fangs and tail longer. Overall, much more menacing looking than the men at my sides.

"Can we talk about this later?" Jason asked, panic evident in his voice.

The tension was high, and my protective instincts called for me to do something about it, but there wasn't an antagonistic villain to fight at the moment, only our own worry for the woman we had quickly come to care about. For the time being, I had to keep calm and follow the bond which drew me to her.

The thrum in my chest sped up, prompting me to push harder.

Chapter Twenty-Four

Ajax

I watched the deep-sea Mer as we tore through the water. I could tell he was extremely worried underneath that calm exterior. The others were just as bad, their fear crashing in on me like a two-ton anvil, and it took everything in me not to reach out and pull the emotion from them. The fear they felt was good. It was what pushed them to move faster and kept them alert.

One benefit was that their emotions were enough to distract me from my own panic. I had tried not to let myself care so much about this girl I had only just met, but she warmed my heart. I constantly found myself thinking of ways to make her happy and feel the little fire of her warmth race across my senses.

Suddenly in the back of my mind I felt another wave, but this time it wasn't fear. This emotion was coming from the one called Jason. It was like I had just swallowed a gallon of rotten milk. A sickly churning in my lower stomach. It was guilt.

Jason should rightfully feel guilty after what he had said to Atalanta, but he had been scared when Atalanta pulled him up from the pool. Scared for her or himself I couldn't completely tell, but I knew how that could cause people to say things they didn't mean. It didn't stop my own feelings of resentment towards him, but it was a little satisfying that he at least felt bad about what happened.

This emotion I should remove, at least temporarily. We needed him to focus. Swimming closer, I brushed my arm against his, pulling that guilt into me. I almost tripped over my own fins, if that was possible, as the sickening feeling I had sensed from him doubled as it settled under my skin.

Jason's head whipped around to look at me directly. "What did you just do? I feel so much lighter."

"It's part of my ability." I said.

His brow furrowed. "I thought you were just an empath. I wasn't aware you could actually affect our emotions."

I looked away from his scrutinizing gaze. "I don't broadcast it for a reason."

The few people who knew about that aspect of my power in the past either wanted me to use it to their advantage or outright mistrusted me. After a good fifty years, I learned to just keep my mouth shut about it.

He nodded. "Makes sense."

I blinked, surprised I didn't feel any resentment or mistrust from him. Jason seemed to be the one amongst us with the most to work through emotionally. Well, besides... my eyes automatically shot to Theseus, who emanated a slew of dark emotions. Whenever I was near him, it was hard to not want to take away all of it or simply run from him altogether. I didn't believe he was a bad guy per se—in fact, he was a genuinely nice person—but he certainly had his own mess of issues to work through.

On the outside of my radius I sensed someone else, yet every time I looked no one was there. As they didn't have any malcontent and simply seemed curious, I brushed it off. I had heard of a few with the ability of camouflage but didn't think I knew anyone personally who had it. At least if they did, they never divulged it. Such an ability would be about as useful as mine.

"We're getting close!" Percy called back to us.

I looked up. We might have been deep enough underneath the surface to not feel the violent churning of the waves as intensely, but lightning was flashing across the sky, giving enough light to see the giant shadows of waves as they crested. I shivered with the knowledge that waves like that could easily destroy a small fishing vessel.

Taking a deep breath in through my gills, I focused to expand the radius of my ability. I felt it extend beyond its usual sixty feet, and I knew the moment I reached Atalanta and her family because soul-gouging fear slammed into me.

I curled in on myself, trying to breath heavily through it. Theseus, who had been slimly behind me on my left, halted with me but I shook my head and doubled my previous speed. My larger tail allowed for me to perhaps be the fastest of the five of us.

I shot past Percy and shouted, "This way!"

INTO THE SEAS EMBRACE

Damn if I wasn't panicking more than they were.

Ahead, I saw the boat as another bit of lightning streaked across the sky, a dark grey form amidst the blackness of the water surrounding us. I saw as a wave particularly large wave slam into the boat, pushing it further away from our group.

"Hip! Can you try and calm down these waves?" Jason shouted as we got closer to the surface the currents pushing us around and making it harder to get to the boat.

"I don't know how!" Hip yelled back as a current swept us off course again.

"You were able to control the pool water!" Jason shot back.

"I didn't do that on purpose!"

"Well, try!" Percy and Jason shouted at the same time.

He held up his hand, concentration straining his features. I felt the water around us grow still, but only for a moment as Hip gasped and held his hand.

"It's too much!"

My eyes snapped away from the struggling Hip when I felt stomach dropping terror coming from the three humans. I watched helplessly as a wave crashed into the boat nearly capsizing it. Pain was added to the mix of terror and panic.

I thought I saw something fall overboard. My heart dropped, thinking it was Atalanta, but I still felt her on

337

the boat. Focusing, I felt someone else, but only for a second as they quickly swept far out of my range.

I looked over to Hip. "I think her sister fell off!"

I pointed in the direction I felt the other person. He nodded and shot off in the direction I pointed. Looking back at the boat, my heart plummeted as I saw a second, more familiar form fall into the water.

"Fuck!" Percy swore.

We were too far. The water was pushing us around as much as the boat.

My own muscles burned as I fought the current, trying to get closer to the form that I knew was Atalanta. Each strike of lighting made her silhouette clearer to me. Her small body was being tossed around like a rag doll.

I watched, powerless as her body slammed into the side of the boat before going completely limp, another wave pulling her beneath the water's surface.

Desperation tore through me, pushing my body to its limits, trying to work against the current to get to her.

Somehow, Jason was able to reach her first, scooping up her body and dragging her to the surface for air. Moments later, we reached them.

The surface was chaos incarnate, rain pouring down on our heads almost as hard as hail, lightning flashing and thunder crashing as if it was trying to outdo the

INTO THE SEAS EMBRACE

powerful sound of the ocean as the waves crashed and collided over and over.

I could hardly hear Jason as he clutched Atalanta's unconscious form against his chest.

"She's not w-ing -p!"

"What!?" I shouted and cupped my ears to try and hear him better.

"She's not waking up!"

I came closer and touched her cheek. I wasn't gauging much from her, but that wasn't unusual from someone who was knocked out. I moved my hand over her mouth.

"She's not breathing!" I shouted.

"What?!"

I cursed to myself and pulled Jason—still clutching Atalanta—beneath the surface. Away from all the rain and the chaotic sounds.

"Ajax, what are you doing?" Jason yelled, pulling against me as we dove.

"She's not breathing, Jason. And we can't help her if we can't hear each other," I reasoned.

"We need to pull the water from her lungs." Jason said.

Percy's head swirled around. "Where's Hip? He might be able to do it."

Guilt crept in with the panic and I said, "I sent him after her sister."

"We're wasting time," Jason blurted before pulling her back to the surface.

I followed, my ears hurting from the deafening sounds. Above, Jason had his mouth over Atalanta's. Instead of breathing into her lungs, he appeared to be sucking in, his cheeks hollow. I watched as his gills opened wide and I think I saw water pour out of them. It was hard to tell in all of the rain. Percy and Theseus were on either side of them, trying to keep them steady and above the surface as the waves thrashed.

Jason removed his mouth from Atalanta's after switching from pulling water to breathing in air. He patted her cheek, but she wasn't moving. I held my arms out and gently took her. Putting my head up to her chest, I could hear her heart beating but only faintly with all of the other noise. Her pulse only confirmed what I heard, and that was not good.

I looked to the other three. "If we don't get her help—and soon—she's not going to make it."

"We are miles out from land, there's not going to be any help!"

This came from Theseus, who had been quiet the whole time, his disability making him pretty useless in situations like this where visibility was low.

A few moments later, the blond head that was Hip came tearing through the water, halting in front of us.

"I wasn't able to find her sister. Are you sure she fell? What's wrong? Is she okay?" He asked, his voice frantic.

INTO THE SEAS EMBRACE

Jason and Percy ignored him and shared a look.

Percy shook his head and I hardly heard when he said, "She might not survive, Jason."

"She's probably not got to survive anyway!" he shouted, the desperation on his face mirroring everyone else's emotions including my own.

"This is your decision. I can't subject her to—" his voice cracked.

Jason nodded, and his desperation morphed to determination. Gripping Atalanta tightly, he dove back under the water, the four of us following after him. He dragged her body far below where the current stopped churning.

Hip was almost in a rage as he tried to get to Atalanta, not understanding what was going on. Percy, with his Guardian strength, held the young man back. After whispering something in his ear, Hip settled.

I was worried. I had an inkling of what was happening, and I didn't know if I should let it happen or stop it.

My fears were confirmed the moment Jason pulled down her pants to just below her hips.

I raced forward. "Are you sure?"

He nodded. "If it will save her."

"You'll be sentencing her to a hard life."

"I'll make that life worth living," he murmured, stroking his thumb against her face.

Slowly he reached down, his hand running down along his tail.

With a sharp tug, he pulled out one of the thick blueish-purple iridescent scales.

Holding up the scale, he looked each one of us in the eye before saying, "Embrace the sea and become one with it."

He shoved the scale into her flesh just at her hip.

After a few moments, nothing happened. The space around us was silent, the only noise coming from the storm above.

But then it happened.

Atalanta's eyes flew open wide. Her once beautiful brown eyes were now mismatched like mine. One, her original brown, while the other, a brilliant green.

She opened her mouth, inhaling water into her lungs.

We all let out a collective breath.

And then she let out a horrid scream.

Chapter Twenty-Five

Jason

As soon as she opened those beautiful eyes, one of them now matching mine, a spark of hope flickered in my chest. But when a moment later she let out a dreadful cry, I couldn't help but cringe and grip her tighter.

"We need to get her on land," Ajax said, the urgency in his voice confusing me.

"But won't the transition go smoother if we keep her in the water?" I asked.

He shook his head. "Not in that condition. Her body won't be able to handle it. We need to get her warm."

I stared at Ajax's own multi colored eyes and conceded. He would understand what she was about to go through more than any of us here.

I looked back at the woman in my arms. Her eyes were rolled back into her head and she was beginning to shake violently as if she were having a seizure. She was breathing, though, and that's what mattered.

I clutched her close to my chest and turned towards the shore. "Let's get going!"

We sped through the water, with myself in the lead this time. My tail kicked furiously and every few moments I looked down at Atalanta. Her eyelids had fallen shut and scrunched tightly. I longed for her to be conscious, to be looking at me with that little smile she got when she thought I was acting too 'perfect'. I knew I wasn't perfect. I had one hell of a temper and the insecurities of a thirteen-year-old girl but for some reason she thought I was this Disney movie near flawless person.

Most of the school thought I was like that, but at least Atalanta wasn't afraid to call me on my shit.

It took way too long to finally reach land.

Atalanta had gone from shivering to full-on writhing in my arms as the scale did its work, the magic rushing through her, altering her very DNA. She was still freezing and in danger of hypothermia while she remained partially human.

My little spark of hope was burning away in the terror I felt.

The five of us rushed up the shore and practically flew up the cliff to her home. We had to get her out of this cold! Pulling the door open, Ajax and Percy made quick work of starting a fire while Thesis whispered to her, singing softly, his siren voice coaxing her, keeping her as calm as possible. Hip rushed through the small cabin. I could hear him smashing around before coming back out with arms full of blankets.

Gingerly, I laid her down. "Sweetheart, we need to remove your clothes. Do you understand?"

For a moment I didn't believe she heard me, until her hand came up and gripped my arm with the force of a python. Her eyes wide, she shook her head

INTO THE SEAS EMBRACE

vigorously, begging me. I apologized profusely, but I needed to take these clothes off of her.

As quickly and as gently as we could, Hip, Percy, and I made quick work of taking off her clothing, while Thesis crouched by her head, singing even louder to her. Her pain and confusion were almost too powerful to hear him.

A few times she jerked, her mouth opening, shrieking like a banshee. The first time it happened I heard Ajax fall to the floor, his abilities forcing him to experience most of the agony along with her.

It wasn't until we removed the last of her clothing that I realized why she had been so adamant.

Her body was covered in scars. Several large ones graced her torso, a bullet wound, slashes from a...knife. Her forearms had dozens of small nicks, no doubt caused by self-harm. There was a surgical scar that ran down her right thigh, not too far from where my scale sat, forever embedded in her skin.

I couldn't take it, and neither could the others as I heard several swear words and something being smashed to pieces. It was Theseus who broke away and wrapped her up in a blanket. His eyes were as red and full of tears as mine, his hands shaking as he made quick work of wrapping Atalanta up.

Unable to stand her being out of my reach for a moment, I scooped her back into my arms, rocking her back and forth. The others huddled around me, rubbing her blanketed body, stroking her hair, hoping to give her as much warmth as possible.

345

I begged. I begged whatever gods or god that she made it through the change. She had a 30% chance of survival, perhaps even lower because of the circumstances. If she didn't survive, I knew I would be haunted by last thing I said to her for the rest of my unnaturally long life. Because I knew that if it wasn't for me, she wouldn't have been out on that boat. I would have warned her in time. She would have believed me.

"Someone needs to go get her father." Percy whispered, his tone urgent but soft, yet no one moved an inch to do so.

As if my stomach could sink any further. I hadn't even thought of her dad, too worried about the flickering life in my hands. He would be a goner as well if we left him in this storm. If the boat hadn't already capsized, it would soon.

Atalanta let out another agonized scream, her body arching upwards, eyes wide and skin as pale as its natural mocha color could be. Ajax slumped again, hand clutching his chest, tears streamed down his cheeks. He focused his multi-colored eyes hard on her face.

I reached out to touch his shoulder. "Ajax, maybe you should."

"No. Please. I can't." He shook his head.

Percy spoke up, trying to back me up. "She'll be in even more pain when she comes out of it and finds out her father is gone too. So please. You know she wouldn't want you to go through this with her."

He looked at Percy, looked at all of us desperately.

Hip was the brave one, though. He stood up and tugged at Ajax's arm. "Come on, big guy. We'll be more useful to her if we go and save her father."

At a hurried pace, Hip pulled Ajax out of the cabin, rushing back into the storm to go rescue Atalanta's father.

We sat in semi-silence, the three of us huddled closely to Atalanta as she infrequently spasmed from the pain of the change. Thesis continuing to hum to her, keeping her calm. But she was incoherent; I doubted she consciously heard his song.

"Did I do the right thing? Do you think I could have saved her any other way?"

Percy looked up from Atalanta to meet my eyes, his expression somber. "I don't know."

Chapter Twenty-Six

Theseus

The room was quiet. Well, it was always quiet to me, but I didn't see anyone speaking as we all huddled close to Jason as he held Atalanta. For the moment, her writhing had calmed down as she seemed to have fallen into a deep sleep. I continued to hum anyway, pushing energy into the tune with the hope that it would keep her calm.

It was odd. I knew I often hummed to myself as I worked, but it was moments like this, when it was on purpose and I could feel the vibration in my throat, not hearing the sound, that it felt weird.

I stroked the top of her head and then paused. Holding the strands between my fingers, I couldn't help but notice that the once coarse strands were becoming softer, the tight curls almost turning to loose loops before my very eyes.

I didn't know that the physical changes from Jason's scale would go that far. I couldn't help but think that I was a little upset about it; the changes seeing it fit to make everything more attractive to lure in prey more easily.

Merfolk hadn't been the cold-blooded creatures that hunted humans in generations, and I liked her hair the way it had been.

INTO THE SEAS EMBRACE

We sat there inside the rundown cabin, Jason, Percy and I close together, not speaking to each other. Every once in a while, she would wake up, her eyes wide, mouth open in a scream I could not hear. Although I could not hear them physically, I felt those shrieks go right to my heart.

When it happened, my hums would turn into full-on song as I used my gift to try and soothe her back to sleep.

Eventually, perhaps hours later, Hip returned. He told us how he and Ajax found the father alive. The boat hadn't capsized, but her father was in rough shape. Evidently, he had hit his head pretty hard while the boat was tossed about.

The two of them navigated the boat back to the dock and got some of the dock workers, some of our people, to help Hip and Ajax take him to the nearest hospital.

Ajax was with them now.

Hip came closer after telling us everything, crouching down where the three of us sat. He gently stroked her cheek with the back of his hand.

'How is she?'

'She's,' Jason began, but his lips stayed open not forming words for a few moments, 'she's past the worst of it, I think. I don't know too much about the transition outside of what my parents told me.'

Hips brows shot up. 'Is that what's happening? She's becoming one of us? I didn't know we could do that.'

349

'She will be a little different from born Mer, but yes,' Percy said.

'It's not something we often do. Normally only to those we hope to have as prospective mates. My father was turned by my mother.' Jason added.

I watched as Jason snuggled Atalanta close to him and kissed the top of her head. There was a small part of me that was jealous, seeing his open affection for her. This jealousy wasn't born from insecurities, but more from my own need to be that close to her. To have her in my arms. I settled for reaching out and entangling my fingers in her limp ones.

'Why not more often?' Hip asked. 'From what I've heard, our numbers are down.'

Percy nodded. 'Our female to male ratio is 1 to 6. The elders believe that turning people willy-nilly could expose us.'

"What Percival is neglecting to mention is that the survival rate is extremely low. Even more so for women. Most don't want to needlessly kill innocent people just to increase our numbers," I snorted.

The three of them looked at me. Hip looked a bit scared while Jason and Percy twinned a deadpanned annoyed look.

"Not helping, Theseus." Percy signed.

I shrugged. "It's true."

It was still a bit of a shock that he knew sign language. In the years since my accident, he had never once spoken to me this way. It was almost insulting that he was doing it now.

I ignored him and looked directly at Hip. "She's doing really well. So, unless she takes a turn for the worse, I think she'll be one of the ones to make it through."

Looking relieved, Hip nodded. Instead of sitting down with us he moved throughout the cabin. He was as curious as the rest of us. I hadn't seen past the little living space of the cabin, but what I saw was bare and run down.

I watched as Hip went back and forth between the back rooms and where we sat, checking in on Atalanta before going back to snooping. The others had gone back to being eerily quiet, their mouths in perpetual frowns.

There was this terrifying moment when Atalanta went into a horrible fit. Her eyes snapped open, and she released a scream I couldn't hear, thrashing around so much she pushed her way out of the cocoon of the blanket I had wrapped her in.

Jason, being unable to hold her in her fit, moved back as she tumbled to the floor. Hip came running back in, and when I looked up at him, I saw him saying, 'What's going on?'

I looked down at her. This was a particularly violent fit. Her now naked body thrashed about. Her hands were shifted, nails long and very sharp, a thin webbing between each finger. Scales rippled along her skin. These were the ubiquitous signs of a Mer in distress as our true forms fought to the surface to defend us, but the question was, what was wrong with her?

Percy grabbed her flailing arms and easily held them down to her chest with one hand as he looked at us.

'I think she needs to be in the water.'

'It's too dangerous for her to be in the cold water right now,' Hip said.

I looked over at Hip. "Does she have a tub? We could fill that up with warm water and pour salt into it."

He nodded, 'There's a large tub in the master bathroom.'

With that, Hip rushed off to, I assume, fill said tub. Carefully, Percy lifted Atalanta, being sure to restrain her as she bucked and screamed.

Jason and I stayed close, useless, as we didn't have the ability to restrain her or calm her down. I tried singing, my desperation filling the song, but it was no use. She couldn't hear me and if anything, it was making it worse as the others could only stave off my power's effects for so long. Percy, who was closest to me, stumbled and almost dropped her. When he shot a look at me, I shut my mouth, realizing he had almost fallen into sleepy land.

I followed him into the first room. Like the rest of the cabin, the room was very bare, with only a blowup mattress and a few boxes stacked up in one of the corners.

Opposite from the entrance was another door. Percy carried Atalanta into it. Peeking my head in, I saw that it was a small bathroom. Hip stood by the tub, his hand out, face scrunched in concentration. The water was gushing out of the faucet with the power of a waterfall, much more powerful than any faucet I'd ever seen.

I'd met a few elementals over the years, but it was always amazing to watch their abilities in action. They were rare and coveted in the city. Especially the fire wielders. Lighting fires deep underwater was a feat that showed the wondrous magic of our species. It had come as a surprise that the rumors had been true about Hip's abilities.

With Hip's help, the tub filled up in mere moments. Behind me, I felt the vibrating thud of heavy footsteps on the floor. Looking back, I saw that Jason had run off somewhere, probably to the kitchen. A few moments later he came back and in his outstretched hand was a bottle of sea salt. I took it from him and carefully maneuvered into the cramped room, Percy with Atalanta in his arms pressed up against the wall and Hip wedged between the toilet and tub.

I tore open the bottle and dumped most of it into the water. Even though it no longer poured out of the faucet, the water churned, stirring the sea salt until it all dissolved. I looked over at Hip, whose hand was still up.

Quickly I moved back, switching places with Percy. Gently, he lowered the thrashing girl into the tub, submerging her under the water. She continued to thrash for a while. It was weird to watch as she flailed around underneath Percy's hands. The water in the tub sloshed with her but never left the tub; any water that should have escaped somehow sprung back. Almost as if it had turned to loose gelatin.

After a few moments, Atalanta's fit ceased, her movements in the water around her calming. Looking over Percy's shoulder, I could see that she wasn't technically unconscious. Her eyes were open, but their heterochromic colors were unseeing, just wide, staring up at the ceiling.

I rushed forward and pushed Percy aside. Shoving my hands into the water, I checked her pulse.

It wasn't there.

Immediately, I hauled her body out of the water, bringing her to the floor and beginning chest compressions.

It was chaos around me. I could feel the other three moving, probably shouting at me or each other, I didn't know. All I knew was that I had to get her heart beating again.

28...

29...

30...

I put my mouth over hers and breathed into her lungs. She couldn't have drowned because her gills were fully formed. Which meant that the change was too much, and it had stopped her heart.

Well fuck, if I wasn't gonna—

Suddenly, Percy was beside me, a blue box in his hand. Curious, but not wanting to stop, I continued to

INTO THE SEAS EMBRACE

perform my second round of CPR while Percy began wipe down her skin with a towel and put patches in place that had long wires attached to the box.

During chest compressions, Percy hit my shoulder to get my attention. I looked up at him while continuing to mentally count.

15...

16...

'It's going to search for a pulse and tell us when to shock her. Keep going and step back when I hit you.'

I nodded. He said it so quickly I was worried I hadn't caught all of it but when a few moments when he tapped my shoulder, I stopped the compressions and leaned back away from her.

Her body jerked upward slightly. Glancing at the blue box that Percy had brought, I saw that it read DEFIBRILLATOR. Where the fuck did they find that?

When Atalanta's body slumped back to the ground, a red light on the box flashed for a few moments before turning green. Percy sat back, relief flooding his features. I quickly moved back to Atalanta to check her pulse. Sure enough, there was a small *bump-bump*, *bump-bump* beneath my fingertips.

I let out a shaking sob and tucked her body close to mine.

That had been far too close.

After a few moments, I looked up and studied the room. Jason was on his hands and knees right next to me, his eyes filled with tears, pleading for me to let him hold her. I conceded and as gently as I could, I moved her into Jason's arms.

He rocked back and forth with her, his head buried in the crook of her shoulder.

I saw Hip standing just inside the door. He was shaking and breathing heavily. His arms were wrapped around himself like a lifeline.

I looked back over to Percy who looked equally shaken. "Where did you find the defibrillator?"

His response was to point back at Hip. I looked back at him and watched as his lips formed the words:

'I saw it when I was snooping through the sister's room earlier. She practically had a whole emergency room tucked in there. Bandages, packages of IV kits, antibiotics.'

I was curious as to why they would have such an excessive amount of first aid supplies.

'Where did you learn CPR?' Hip asked.

I shrugged. "I used to teach classes at the center before some of the people thought it was unethical for a deaf person to train in first aid."

His lip raised in disgust, 'That's stupid.'

I nodded but didn't say anything else about it.

I looked back at Atalanta. With her heart beating again, I could see that the changes were underway. Her naked body was covered in small scales: over the back of her hands, at her hips, and running the flat of her

INTO THE SEAS EMBRACE

stomach up all the way to cover her breasts. Below her hips, the scales got larger and crept down the sides of her thighs, tapering off at the knees.

They were a beautiful mix of blue and purple, the same color as Jason's. There was something I noticed, though. Her scars, which were still there, were covered in electric blue scales, making them stand out against the darker hue of the other ones.

I touched the light blotch of scales which covered the large scar on her hip. The thin self-harm scars were also a light blue and a stark reminder that this girl had been through way too much in her short life.

Her face was—to my relief—no longer scrunched in pain, but relaxed, as if she were sleeping. There was also a thin wave of scales stretching from her hairline to the crest of each cheek. She looked beautiful.

Her mouth opened as if in a half yawn before closing again. At the gesture, Jason, whose head was still in the crook of her neck began shaking, as if he was laughing. I looked at Hip and then Percy who were both laughing as well.

Percy, who noticed my confusion, signed between chuckles. "She just snored."

I shook my head, my mouth cracking into a smile. I shoved down my disappointment at not being able to hear what an adorable snore she probably had with the reminder that, for now, she was alive.

Chapter Twenty-Seven

Hip

I was still shaking, the leftover adrenaline from the day coursing through my body. I honestly wanted to just slump to the floor and curl up with Atalanta like Jason was doing, but I knew this wasn't over, and I couldn't rest until it was. There was also that other thing.

"Hey, guys," I said hoarsely.

Percy and Jason looked over to me, Theseus following when he noticed their heads turned.

I pointed to the living room. "There's something I need to show you."

Carefully, Jason stood up with his precious bundle and followed me out back into the empty living room.

Just as we were coming out, Ajax practically burst through the door. He looked at us, looked at the beautifully scaly girl in Jason's arms, and sighed in relief.

"She's still alive," he said. Not a question, but a statement.

"It was touch and go for a bit there, but yeah," I said, putting my hand on his shoulder.

"How's her father doing?" Percy asked, coming to stand by us near the front door.

INTO THE SEAS EMBRACE

"The doctor has him in a medically-induced coma while they wait for the brain swelling to go down."

Percy looked down, his face showing the guilt that I had felt since the moment I realized Atalanta's sister was lost.

I had searched all over for a good two miles before the need to go back to everyone was too great. She was nowhere to be seen. Between the storm and her being human, there probably wasn't a good chance we would find her, let alone find her alive. I'd keep searching, though. Even if she weren't alive, I would at least be able to give Atalanta and her father some peace.

"We should have left someone behind to help him," Percy whispered.

"We should have, but we made that mistake, and now we must lay with it." Ajax replied.

I studied him. He looked as disheveled as the rest of us. Though, unlike the rest of us, he was in clothes. I blushed at this realization and looked around the room. Yep, lots of dicks hanging free, including my own. We had been so preoccupied that the thought of decency wasn't at the top of our list.

Most certainly sensing my sudden discomfort, Ajax looked at me and then looked at the others, his eyebrows shooting up as he came to the same conclusion I had.

"I brought clothes." He stated before walking outside and coming back a few moments later with the clothes we had all discarded on the shore.

Awkwardly, we all got dressed, Ajax taking a still naked Atalanta into his arms while Jason pulled up his pants.

Seeing the two of them together I wanted to slap myself for not noticing the connection before. "You're a made Mer, aren't you? It's why you have different colored eyes."

Ajax stared at me, his brows furrowed. "You didn't know?"

"I only just found out we could even do that. Make more of us, I mean." I said, annoyed at my level of ignorance.

"The elders really kept you in the dark," Jason said as he threw on his shirt.

I snorted. "I probably know about as much as our girl over here."

Jason looked a little uncomfortable when I said the words 'our girl,' but I ignored it, remembering the reason I brought them out here.

I walked down the hall to the blue folders which I had discarded on the floor the moment I heard Atalanta's screams.

Picking them up, I waved them in front of everyone. "You're not going to believe what I found."

I opened the first file. Inside was a photo of Atalanta's sister with the caption of CALILOPE NORTH. Flipping to the second page, I began reading aloud.

"Calilope North, Age: 25, Birthday: May 18th, 1992, Place of birth: Flint, Michigan, Favorite color: Purple," and on I went, listing things like her favorite movies, where she went to school, what she majored in college.

The second file was one for their father, Titus North, mainly listing the same information, birthday, where he was born, etc. It was the last file that got me. It had a photo of Atalanta.

"Atalanta North, Age: 18, Birthday: November 9th, Place of birth: Flint, Michigan. She likes horses, and her favorite color is blue. She's afraid of spiders," I flipped the page, this section showing family history. "Says here her mother was a professional figure skater and died of cancer when Atalanta was three. There's a note here next to the father: 'worked as a fisherman whole life. Moved around a lot?' I don't know if she was trying to remember something or—"

"I've heard enough," Jason growled. He was pacing now, something I noticed he tended to do when he was frustrated.

"What does this mean? Why would they have profiles on themselves?" Theseus asked.

Percy, whose brows were furrowed in concentration, said, "They aren't profiles on themselves."

"They are fake identities," Ajax hopped in.

Percy nodded. "Those of us who are older have to get them every so often when we continue to live on the surface. New names, new social securities, new everything."

"Why would they have something like that? Are they illegal immigrants or something?" Jason asked, his pacing only increasing. It was beginning to annoy me. Just stand still, damn it.

"I was worried something like this might be going on. With how the girls behaved and, well..." Percy's eyes ran along her body, focusing on the light patches of scales which now covered her extensive scar tissue. "I thought it might be some form of abuse."

My stomach churned just thinking about seeing all the scars on her body and how much pain she must have been in when she got them.

"You knew about her scars?" Jason asked, his tone full of disbelief.

"Not exactly. I had a guess that she might have a few self-harm scars with the way she behaved when I first met her." Percy replied.

Hurt clouded Jason's eyes. "I can't believe this. You knew and didn't tell me."

I knew Jason had feelings for the man, yet whenever I had seen the two of them interact it, seemed that Percy, despite also having feelings for Jason—whether he realized it or not—acted more like a mentor to him. I couldn't help but see how Jason might feel a little betrayed right now.

Theseus raised his hand, drawing our attention. "I knew."

"You knew what?" Jason growled.

Theseus took a deep breath in before saying, "I knew about the scars beforehand. I saw them one night when we... I just didn't know how bad they were."

"I knew, too," I said, throwing myself under the bus that was Jason's growing anger.

But he didn't look angry, for once. He just looked...sad.

"Did everybody know but me?" he asked, his voice small.

I cleared my throat. "I only knew because I paid attention, Jason. It may be winter, but we've never once seen her without long sleeves on. Even during gym class, she wears that stupid 'under armor'. Whenever she's nervous, she plays with her sleeves, tugging them down. And yesterday, I found her in the bathroom biting her hand to calm down from a panic attack. It wasn't a far stretch to think she might have scars like that."

Jason looked over at Theseus. "And why didn't you tell us?"

"Because I had no reason to," he shrugged. "Look, we may have known each other for years, but we don't actually know each other. We aren't friends, we are barely even colleagues. Hell, before Atalanta came to town, I hardly recall ever having a conversation with most of you. So when I saw those scars, I thought it best to keep it to myself. Scars like those... they each have their own story. And those stories aren't mine to tell."

I was worried Jason would blow up again, but he continued to look broken. He took a deep breath and held it before letting it out. "You're right. I'm sorry."

I watched as he walked over to where Ajax held Atalanta in his arms. "Whatever the truth is, we'll figure it out once this is all over."

With a little reluctance on his face, Ajax handed Atalanta back over to Jason and said, "Stay close to her."

"Why?"

"It will help keep her alive," he replied.

Jason looked down at the sleeping girl in his arms and with resolve, nodded.

From there, we all kind of slinked off to different rooms of the cabin. It had to be around four in the morning. I honestly couldn't tell because there were no clocks in the house and none of us had our phones.

Dead on my feet, I joined Jason who was in what I assumed to be the father's room. He laid down on the air mattress with the still naked and sleeping Atalanta curled up next to him, his arms wrapped around her possessively.

I shrugged and crawled onto the mattress next to them.

Jason grumbled. "Get your own bed."

I yawned. "This one is big enough for the three of us."

INTO THE SEAS EMBRACE

"So?"

"So, I wanna get some cuddle action too. Don't be selfish."

"Is this really the right time for this?" he hissed.

I chuckled. "Why? Because she's naked? 'Cause we were all just as exposed earlier."

Jason sat up a little, his green eyes trying to sear a hole into my skull. "Because she's unconscious!"

"Well, if we go by that logic then neither of us should be in bed with her," I said, grinning from ear to ear. Not backing down.

"Will you two shut up and go to sleep?" Percy called from what I believe was the sister's room.

Jason scowled and flopped back down again.

I smirked and made a point to snuggle closer to Atalanta, my hand resting on her hip right near Jason's arm. He seemed to have conceded because he didn't try to move my hand. It was either that, or he was now as dead to the world as she was.

I closed my eyes, a lot more comfortable than I would have thought. My mind slowly drifted off to sleep.

At some point during the night, I was pulled from my sleep just long enough to hear the others one by one tip-toeing into the room and settling down near the mattress, until eventually all of us were surrounding the sleeping beauty.

Chapter Twenty-Eight

Atalanta

Why did I feel like my body had been put through a wood chipper and then stuffed into a sack? With my eyes closed, I took mental stock. Everything ached, just as it had the day I woke up in the hospital over eight years ago. My chest, head, and legs pounded with each *thump* of my heart.

For a moment I panicked, thinking I had somehow ended up back in the hospital. But no, while I was curled up in probably the hardest bed I'd ever been in, I was pleasantly warm all over. And no hospital was ever this warm or familiar feeling. They were always cold and scary.

My restarting brain tried to recall the last thing I remembered before going to bed that night.

Nothing.

At first, I thought my sluggish brain was the reason I couldn't remember even going to bed last night, let alone what I had been doing beforehand. But no, pushing harder, I found that there was just a space in my memory. The last thing I recalled was Dad telling Cal and me about going out on the boat this morning and then nothing. I didn't remember going back to bed or even going to school.

I inhaled nice and deep, the way you normally do when you first wake up. Something weird happened. It felt strange, all wrong. Everything was wrong.

My eyes snapped open. All I could see was white. Reaching my hand out, I felt a smooth white wall underneath my fingertips. It was almost like porcelain.

What was wrong with my hand?

I brought my hand close to my face, but it was blurry, the way everything looked when you were swimming in a pool without goggles.

I froze as I realized why that warm feeling was familiar, why the bed I was in was white and hard as stone.

I sat up in the tub, water streaming down my body as I surfaced. I tried to inhale sweet, sweet oxygen but my lungs were preoccupied as water came pouring out of my mouth. I could literally feel the water being pushed from my lungs. *I had been breathing underwater.* I HAD BEEN BREATHING UNDERWATER AND NOW THAT WATER WAS BEING PUSHED FROM MY BODY.

As soon as all of the water evacuated my lungs, I took deep, ragged breaths. I didn't feel starved for oxygen like I should have. I had been sleeping under the water, for fuck's sake.

I felt something wet sticking to the side of my cheek. Pulling at it, I saw that it was hair. My hair. Hair that was attached to my head. When did my hair get so long??

I shrieked.

My hand! Oh my God, my hand!!

It looked like something out of the Black Lagoon! Thin webbing between my fingers, scales covering the back of my hand, and *holy fucking shit,* I had claws!

I brought up my other hand to see it was the same. Tiny blue and purple scales ran along the back of my hands and up my arms.

"You're awake."

My eyes snapped to my right and there sitting on the toilet with a book in his lap was Jason.

"Jason?"

He slid off the toilet and crouched down to be eye level to me. Damn. He looked, well, to be frank, not good. His hair, which was usually nicely combed, was sticking up at odd ends, dark shadows graced the area under his eyes, and his cheeks looked a little hollowed, like he had missed several meals. I think he had been asleep on that toilet.

"Jason, what's going on?" I asked with a shaky voice.

He gave a wobbly smile. "I'm so sorry, Atalanta. It was all my fault. This was the only way I could think to save you."

"Save me from what?"

He was really freaking me the fuck out. And that was saying something, because my freaked-out meter was already at a ten.

He held out his hand. "Come on, I'll explain everything. Can you stand?"

I shook my head and backed away from him as far as I could.

A small voice in me whispered to trust him. Fuck that voice, freaked-out logic was in charge at the moment and there was no way in hell I was leaving the safety of this tub.

"I told you he'd scare her. Would scare me too, looking like an undead zombie spouting cryptic crap."

Behind Jason, Hip and Percy stood in the doorway.

"I just need some sleep," Jason shot back, looking over his shoulder.

"Uh-huh. And when are you gonna actually let yourself have any?" Hip made his way into the room and nudged Jason aside. "Hey, Speedy. Welcome back to the land of the living."

My brows scrunched up as I stared at the two men. "Are either of you going to tell me why my arms look like a lizard had sex with a rainbow? And why I just woke up in the bathtub!?"

"We will. Though, don't you think you might want to get out of the tub first?" Percy asked, his voice warmer than usual.

I looked down and tried to use my legs, but they wouldn't budge.

I looked back up at Hip.

"Need help?" he chuckled.

I nodded. Hip reached over and without much effort scooped me up out of the tub and carefully placed me on my feet. He and Jason support me as I tried to walk.

Getting a good look at my body, I noticed that I was in a super large shirt that went down to my knees. Said T-shirt was also soaking wet and clinging to my body like an ugly skintight dress. I'm pretty sure I wasn't wearing any underwear underneath the shirt either.

"Please tell me I was always in the shirt and none of you changed my clothes," I said looking back and forth between my two glorified walking staffs.

Jason blushed, bringing some much-needed color back into his cheeks. "Unfortunately, we can't tell you that."

I groaned. "Oh, great."

As the two of them half carried me out of the bathroom, I caught my reflection in the mirror and gasped.

Do you ever have those moments, where you look at your reflection and the person staring back didn't feel like you?

Well, the person staring back at me was definitely not me.

INTO THE SEAS EMBRACE

This person was beautiful, with long hair that—despite being wet—curled gently down to the shoulders. She had brilliant multicolored eyes, one a deep green, and the other a more familiar hazel brown that looked back at me. But this gorgeous reflection was also not human, as scales like the ones on my arms graced the tops of my cheeks and in my mouth were *fangs*. I had fangs!

I gulped. "Oh my God, I'm a mutant."

"No, you're not." Jason said, his tone comforting.

"Well, I mean, technically she is."

Jason growled. "Not the time, Hip."

They pulled me away from the mirrored horror of my reflection into a somewhat large and recognizable room.

"We're in the cabin? Where's my father?"

"One thing at a time, Atalanta," Percy said as he held out a towel for me to dry off with.

It was useless while I still wore the shirt, but at least I could feel some semblance of dryness. Gently, Jason and Hip guided me over to the air mattress. I couldn't help but notice that there were a bunch of pillows and blankets covering it and the floor around it.

Wait, did Percy just call me by my first name?

Now settled down on the mattress, my attention switched between staring down at my arms in near horror and back up at the guys in utter confusion.

"I don't even know where to start."

Percy crouched down in front of me. "Let's start with asking, what is the last thing you remember?"

I studied my hands. The webbing between my fingers had little veins that ran through them.

"I remember talking to my dad about going out on his boat." I replied.

"And nothing else?"

I shook my head as I continued to marvel at the shimmering scales. "No."

I felt a finger come up under my chin and lift my head to look directly at Percy. "That was two weeks ago."

"T-two weeks?" I squeaked.

He nodded and began to explain to me about going out on the boat with my dad, how there was a storm, how I hit my head after jumping overboard to save my sister, and the five of them coming to the rescue. Ajax and Hip saved my father, who was in the hospital. And Cal...was missing.

He left out a considerable chunk, specifically the chunk where I been in a two-week long coma and somehow turned into some sort of mutant. What he did say, I could hardly believe, precisely because I didn't remember any of it. Our father would have never gone out during a storm.

It was a lie. It had to be.

INTO THE SEAS EMBRACE

This was some weird hoax made to scare me. My hands were just covered in clever makeup.

Finding my strength, I stood up and stumbled out of the room. "Cal! Dad!"

I called for them as I walked through the cabin, slowly at first, until I was running through the rooms over and over again to be sure that I wasn't crazy. They weren't there. Judging by the layer of dust that had settled onto the boxes in Cal's room, they hadn't been there for a while.

I tore into my room and began to rifle through my things.

"Where is it?" I shouted.

"Where's what?" one of the guys said behind me.

"My fucking phone! We never leave the house without our phones!"

"Oh," Hip walked out of the room and came back a minute later as I continued to destroy my room. "It was on you when you went out to the boat. It was pretty wrecked by the water."

He held out my phone. I snatched it from him and tried to get it started but the stupid thing was dead. I threw it to the ground in frustration, breaking it apart in the process.

"Oh, no." I groaned, slumping to the floor, and tried to pick up the pieces of the phone.

Jason, who I hadn't even realized was in the room, got on his knees next to me.

"They aren't going to answer, Atty," he said gently, holding out his own phone.

I flinched at his use of Cal's nickname for me and snatched the phone from him. The date that was in big white letters on his screen confirmed that it had been a good two weeks from the date I knew it to be.

"No! Because if what you said wasn't a lie that means that…" My voice cracked. "that means that my sister is dead! And I can't believe that."

"The likelihood that a human could survive that long out in open water…they aren't good odds," Percy said from the doorway.

"She's not dead!" I unlocked Jason's phone, having to maneuver around the long claw-like nails at the end of my fingers, and dialed her number.

It went right to voicemail. It never went to voicemail. We always made sure our phones were charged.

I redialed it with the same result. I then called my father's phone. It was the same.

I took a deep breath in. I would not lose it. I would stay calm.

Stay calm.

I felt for the wall beside me and leaned up against it. It would help me breathe.

Yep, everything was fine. There was a reasonable explanation for all of this. The phone lines were just down. Yeah, satellites fell out of the sky and messed up

INTO THE SEAS EMBRACE

all our phones. Two weeks hadn't passed, I wasn't some mutant swamp monster, my family was okay.

My freaking arms felt so uncomfortable that even rubbing them wasn't making them feel better.

But I was fine.

Everything was okay.

"Someone get Ajax," I heard someone whisper.

Ajax was here too? That was good. He would be upfront with me about everything, because obviously these three were lying.

I felt the heavy footfalls coming towards me, but I couldn't see him because the world had begun to go dark around the edges. That was normal, though. It was supposed to happen.

I was *fine*.

A warm hand caressed my cheek and the world went back into focus, the blackness clearing from my vision and the chaos that was my mind halting.

I looked up to see my bear staring down at me with a soft smile. "Welcome back."

"I left?" I asked, my body shaking like a leaf.

He gave me a small smile. "For a little bit."

"Ajax. Is it true? Is Cal really gone?" I asked, desperate and clutching his arm like a lifeline.

He nodded. "I'm sorry."

The growing dread in the pit of my stomach ceased up for a moment before pouring out and into my heart as I felt the warmth of tears streak down my cheeks.

"And," I began to hyperventilate. "And am I really a swamp monster?"

"You're not a swamp monster."

"But I'm covered in scales! And I have webbed hands!" I exclaimed, holding them out for him to see.

"Let's get you some food and we'll explain." His voice was so soft and comforting.

Ajax took my hand and gently urged me to my feet. I looked around and noticed all the guys were standing in my room, including Theseus, though I didn't remember when he got there.

With Ajax's hand on my lower back, I shuffled passed the guys and out of my room, back to my father's room. On the way, we moved in front of Cal's open door and I just couldn't take it. I broke down.

Bending over in stomach-wrenching sobs, I screamed.

I begged and screamed and begged some more. I didn't want it to be true, I wanted one of them to be lying. Screw being scaly, I wanted my sister.

Someone, I assume Ajax based on the woodsy smell, picked up my curled form and cuddled me to his chest, rocking me back and forth like a child as we made our way down the hall.

INTO THE SEAS EMBRACE

We eventually made it into my father's room and with me still in his arms, Ajax sat down on the air mattress. It bounced beneath us causing me to bite my tongue between my sobs, which only made me cry harder.

It felt like hours later that my tears dried up and my already aching body ached that much more.

I wasn't okay, but I was alright enough to hear them out.

I sat up from Ajax's tear-soaked shirt and looked around at all the others who had stuck close by through this whole thing.

"Okay," I sniffed and wiped at my eyes. "Someone start from the beginning."

It was Jason who went first. "You were right about us. All along."

"That you're some cult who worships the ocean or something?"

There was a round of chuckles before he replied, "No. We are Merfolk. Or, more specifically, Mermen."

"That was my other theory," I grumbled.

And so, they told me. As I sat in Ajax's lap in the old cabin, they told me about being Merfolk, a fact which I had suspected but never thought was actually true. They showed me their own scaly arms as proof. Watching the multi-colored scales surface on their skin was fascinating to watch.

They also told me the details Percy had omitted about the accident. How Jason had figured out that I was in danger and in their Mer forms, they all came after me, reaching me just after I had jumped in the water. How, knowing I was on the cusp of death, Jason made the decision to give me one of his scales.

"Wait," I interrupted. "What does that mean? Gave me one of his scales?"

Ajax was the one who replied. "You're not human anymore."

"I gathered that."

"No," His hand came up and brushed across the scales on my left cheek. "I mean you are not human anymore Atalanta. You are not the same girl who came to Argos. You're…more."

His voice was full of so much pain and empathy. Like he understood what it meant to be in my very position. Looking up into his blue and brown eyes and remembering my reflection in the mirror, I thought that perhaps he did understand. Better than anyone else.

"Jason's scale kind of acted as a parasite. It tore through your system and altered your very DNA. You aren't some human-Mer hybrid. You are just a Mermaid now," Theseus said from his position by the door.

I looked down at my hands. "Oh…"

"It saved your life," Jason's voice came from somewhere around me.

I sought him out in the room. He was sitting on the floor in the furthest corner from all of us.

Ajax leaned in close and whispered, "He's been by your side through the whole transition. I don't know how much he's slept."

I nodded and got up from his lap and walked over to Jason.

Crouching down in front of him, I took his hands. "Thank you."

He didn't look at me when he spoke. "It was my fault you were out there in the first place."

"I was planning on going out on that boat," I shot back.

"No...I said some things that day. Things you don't remember. And if I hadn't said them, you probably wouldn't have gone, and your father wouldn't be in the hospital and your sister—" His voice cracked, tears welling up in his eyes, making him unable to finish his sentence.

I sighed. "I may not be able to remember everything that happened, but whatever you said, it was still my decision to get out on that boat."

"Yeah. But—"

"But nothing. You saved my life, Jason. So, thank you."

He stared up at me, his green eyes glistening like emeralds from the tears, full of shame and relief. His mouth opened and then closed a couple of times, as if he were trying to figure out something to say. Finally, he settled into a careful smile, his hand reaching up to brush my now long hair behind my ear.

Epilogue

Atalanta

To say that I was an emotional wreck over the next two days was an understatement. As if I were a pregnant woman with out-of-whack hormones, my mood swung from hysterical laughter at something one of the guys said to sobbing in a matter of seconds.

The guys were troopers, though. One of them was with me at all times while I recovered and had my mood swings, bringing me food and clean clothes when I needed it. Apparently having your very DNA altered was very tiring on the body, as I constantly felt in need of a nap or some kind of food.

The first time I changed out of the enormous T-shirt I woke up in was quite the shock. The scales that covered my arms didn't stop there. They ran down the whole front and back of my body all the way to my knees. While it was weird, I'm not gonna lie when I say that I looked beautiful, in a sort of exotic, alien way.

I also discovered that I had gills on either side of my neck. Upon inspection, I found out that the guys had them too.

"Why am I covered in scales and you're not?" I asked on the third day.

Percy and Ajax were in my father's room with me while the others were out. I think Jason finally went to go talk to his parents, same as Hip. Theseus was at the community center.

Percy glanced at me from where he sat on the edge of my father's mattress, a book in his hands. "You're a little different from us."

I began to panic. "Does that mean I'll always have scales? How am I supposed to go out in public looking like a sparkly fish!?"

Percy chuckled. "You'll learn to hide most of your scales. Though, I believe made Mer can't hide all of them."

He looked over to Ajax, who nodded and raised the hem of his shirt. Turning, he revealed a patch of scales that ran across the tops of his shoulders. His scales were black with a rainbow of colors that ran through them. It reminded me of oil slick.

"Does that mean I won't be able to wear bathing suits ever again?" I asked.

Percy cocked an eyebrow at me. "That's what you're worried about?"

"I'm worried about a lot of things right now. But it is nice to distract myself with simple problems rather than the big ones."

"Way to keep yourself sane." Ajax said.

I giggled and went back to the book that I had been reading. Tomorrow, the guys were going to see about sneaking me over to the hospital to see my father. I was

INTO THE SEAS EMBRACE

excited and raring to right at that moment, but they insisted that I was still too unwell to travel that far.

I guess they had a point, as even sitting here with a book in my hand was exhausting.

I was just drifting off for another nap when a loud banging jolted me awake. Someone was knocking on the door.

I shared a look with the other two. None of the guys had knocked so far since I had woken up, which meant this wasn't one of them.

As quiet as a mouse and as sneaky as a ninja, Percy slid off the bed and navigated his way out of the room. He came back a few minutes later, his look of concern morphing into one of confusion.

"It seems there is a federal agent at your door."

My heart sank, and my eyes widened. With a little help from Percy and Ajax, I got myself out of bed and to the front of the cabin.

I stood on my tiptoes and peeked through the peephole. Sure enough, standing on the porch was a man in a sleek tailored suit and perfectly styled hair. The good news was this man wasn't a stranger. The bad news was this man was not a stranger.

"It's Clint," I hissed.

"Who's Clint?" Ajax asked.

I gulped.

Clint was my family's handler.

THE NAMELESS SYREN SERIES BOOK 1

To Be Continued…

Acknowledgments

I would like to first and foremost to again thank my two best friends who not only helped me come up with these wonderful characters but then helped with the truly difficult part of writing a book, the editing *insert dramatic music and thunder claps here*. I honestly couldn't afford to hire an editor this time around, so Emilee And Amber took time away from their lives to help me try and perfect this book

That being said, no one catches everything. So if you kind reader notice something I would be very grateful if you contacted me through one of the links on the next page. After a couple months, I'll compile all the edits fans have noticed and update the book. Thank you in advance.

I would also like to thank my family and friends for your kind words and constant encouragement.

Most of all I would like to thank you fellow readers. Without you, authors like me would have to find other passions to make a living from, and at least for me, weaving stories and building worlds is one of the greatest gifts I was given.

About The Author

Avery Thorn is the Pseudonym for the Young Adult author Jennifer Natoli and it's a pretty cool fake name if I do say so myself. An artist from South Florida I've dabbled in all sorts of mediums, such as: paint, wood, clay, glass, and the classic pen and pencil. Not just visual arts either, as for many years I performed music with Tuba, the violin, and my own vocal cords. Writing and reading have always been my real passion though, and I love that I have the opportunity to get my stories in the hands of readers around the world.

You can find out more information about my other work and connect with me and other readers such as yourself through these links below:

FB: https://www.facebook.com/AverysThorns

Website: https://www.jennifernatoli.com

Email: natolibooks@hotmail.com

Thank you.